TUI T. SUTHERLAND

WINGS OF FIRE

THE ĐARK SECRET

MSCHOLASTIC

Scholastic Children's Books
An imprint of Scholastic Ltd
Euston House, 24 Eversholt Street
London, NW1 1DB, UK
Registered office: Westfield Road, Southam, Warwickshire, CV47 0RA
SCHOLASTIC and associated logos are trademarks and/or registered trademarks of
Scholastic Inc.

First published in the US by Scholastic Inc, 2013
First published in the UK by Scholastic Ltd, 2014

Text copyright © 2013 by Tui T. Sutherland
Map design © 2012 by Mike Schley
Dragon illustrations © 2012 by Joy Ang
Cover illustration © 2014 Angelo Rinaldi

The right of Tui T. Sutherland to be identified as the author
of this work has been asserted by her.

ISBN 978 1407 14782 6

British Library Cataloguing-in-Publication Data.
A CIP catalogue record for this book is available from the British Library.

Printed and bound by CPI Group (UK) Ltd, Croydon, CR0 4YY
Papers used by Scholastic Children's Books are made from wood grown in
sustainable forests.

1 3 5 7 9 10 8 6 4 2

www.scholastic.co.uk

For Jonah and Elliot's first tribe:
Willamina and Wyatt, Ashwin and Syrus,
Leo and Maya, Amelie, Charlie, Adam, Stella,
Rady and Lyla, Sylvie and Penelope, Calvin,
Evie and Joshua, and Noah and Grace

A NIGHTWING GUIDE TO
THE DRAGONS OF PYRRHIA

MUDWINGS

DESCRIPTION: thick, armoured brown scales, sometimes with amber and gold underscales; large, flat heads with nostrils on top of the snout

ABILITIES: can breathe fire (if warm enough), hold their breath for up to an hour, blend into large mud puddles; usually very strong

QUEEN: Queen Moorhen

ALLIANCES: currently allied with Burn and the SkyWings in the great war

SANDWINGS

DESCRIPTION: pale gold or white scales the colour of desert sand; poisonous barbed tail; forked black tongues

ABILITIES: can survive a long time without water, poison enemies with the tips of their tails like scorpions, bury themselves for camouflage in the desert sand, breathe fire

QUEEN: Since the death of Queen Oasis, the tribe is split between three rivals for the throne: sisters Burn, Blister, and Blaze.

ALLIANCES: Burn fights alongside SkyWings and MudWings; Blister is allied with the SeaWings; and Blaze has the support of most SandWings as well as an alliance with the IceWings.

SKYWINGS

DESCRIPTION: red-gold or orange scales; enormous wings

ABILITIES: powerful fighters and fliers, can breathe fire

QUEEN: Queen Scarlet

ALLIANCES: currently allied with Burn and the MudWings in the great war

SEAWINGS

DESCRIPTION: blue or green or aquamarine scales; webs between their claws; gills on their necks; glow-in-the-dark stripes on their tails/snouts/underbellies

ABILITIES: can breathe underwater, see in the dark, create huge waves with one splash of their powerful tails; excellent swimmers

QUEEN: Queen Coral

ALLIANCES: currently allied with Blister in the great war

RAINWINGS

DESCRIPTION: scales constantly shift colours, usually bright like birds of paradise; prehensile tails

ABILITIES: can camouflage their scales to blend into their surroundings, use their prehensile tails for climbing; no known natural weapons

QUEEN: Queen Dazzling

ALLIANCES: not involved in the great war

ICEWINGS

DESCRIPTION: silvery scales like the moon or pale blue like ice; ridged claws to grip the ice; forked blue tongues; tails narrow to a whip-thin end

ABILITIES: can withstand subzero temperatures and bright light, exhale a deadly freezing breath

QUEEN: Queen Glacier

ALLIANCES: currently allied with Blaze and most of the SandWings in the great war

NIGHTWINGS

DESCRIPTION: purplish-black scales and scattered silver scales on the underside of their wings, like a night sky full of stars; forked black tongues

ABILITIES: can breathe fire, disappear into dark shadows, read minds, foretell the future

QUEEN: a closely guarded secret

ALLIANCES: too mysterious and powerful to be part of the war

THE DRAGONET PROPHECY

When the war has lasted twenty years. . .
the dragonets will come.
When the land is soaked in blood and tears. . .
the dragonets will come.

Find the SeaWing egg of deepest blue.
Wings of night shall come to you.
The largest egg in mountain high
will give to you the wings of sky.
For wings of earth, search through the mud
for an egg the colour of dragon blood.
And hidden alone from the rival queens,
the SandWing egg awaits unseen.

Of three queens who blister and blaze and burn,
two shall die and one shall learn
if she bows to a fate that is stronger and higher,
she'll have the power of wings of fire.

Five eggs to hatch on brightest night,
five dragons born to end the fight.
Darkness will rise to bring the light.
The dragonets are coming. . .

PROLOGUE

The ice dragons came out of nowhere.

It should have been a quiet night; they shouldn't have seen anyone but SkyWings and other MudWings on their patrol along the mountainous border between their kingdoms. There hadn't been a battle near their village since the one where they lost Crane, sixteen days ago.

Reed still couldn't think about that battle without feeling a huge pit open inside his chest. Sometimes he wanted to close his eyes and fall into that pit and never come out. But he couldn't: he had four other brothers and sisters who depended on him. He was their leader, their bigwings – even though he knew now that he wasn't supposed to be. It should have been their brother Clay, whose egg was stolen before they all hatched.

"Did you hear that?" Umber whispered, darting up to fly beside him. The smallest dragon in their MudWing troop of siblings, Umber was also the most observant. Reed knew by now that it was always worth listening to him.

"What?" Reed whispered back, tilting his head and straining his ears. His wings caught the air currents as they both soared higher, and he studied the dark, jagged shapes of the Claws of the Clouds Mountains. He couldn't see any movement or hear any wingbeats.

Still, he twisted around to check on his brothers and sisters, calling them closer with a flick of his tail. In a moment, Pheasant, Sora and Marsh were flying in a close formation behind him.

"I thought I heard hissing," Umber said. "Somewhere close by."

Reed glanced down uneasily at the shadowy trees that covered the mountain slope below them. Anything could be hiding in there.

But the only sound he heard was the SandWing general up ahead, calling at top volume as if "stealth patrol" were only a funny name for what they were doing.

"Move it, MudWings!" bellowed the sand dragon. His squadron of seven SandWings, all fiercely loyal to Queen Burn, hovered behind him, grunting. "I want to wrap up this patrol and get some sleep tonight!"

"It was probably nothing," Umber said to Reed.

And that was when the nine ice dragons suddenly shot out of the forest and attacked the SandWings.

It was so fast, so calculated and swift and sudden, that two SandWings were sent spiralling towards the ground with shredded wings and blood pouring from their throats before Reed could even process that this was a real attack.

Marsh shrieked with terror and grabbed Reed, nearly

tumbling the bigwings out of the sky. Marsh had never really recovered from their first battle, where he'd seen their sister Crane die in front of him. *I need to do something about that,* Reed thought, *but not right now.*

"Marsh, keep it together!" he shouted, pulling his wing free. "Come on, quick, we have to help!"

He saw the hesitation on all their faces and caught himself wondering – *again* – what Clay would have done in this situation, and whether the others would have been happier and safer following him . . . and also wondering whether *they* were wondering that, too.

But no one said what they must be thinking – *it's a suicide mission; what help can we be; I don't want to lose another sibling.* Instead they formed up behind him and dived towards the writhing dragons.

Reed hated fighting IceWings. Their serrated claws seemed ten times sharper than normal claws, and their whip-thin tails left stinging marks across his snout and wings. Worst of all, they could just *breathe* on you and kill you.

He shot a burst of fire at the biggest IceWing, who was grappling with the SandWing general. Her teeth snapped shut and she hissed at him, but she was too busy with the SandWing to come after Reed. He spun in the air, lashing out at silvery white scales as another IceWing attacked his flank. They clutched each other with fierce talons for a moment, the wind buffeting their wings.

3

Finally Reed managed to cough out another bolt of flames and the IceWing jerked away, narrowly avoiding a singed nose.

Reed spotted an IceWing diving towards Umber and leaped to knock his brother aside, catching the brunt of the white dragon's momentum against his chest. As he staggered back, he saw another IceWing wrap her dangerous claws around Sora's neck, and he roared with fury. Pheasant was there in an instant, throwing the IceWing off Sora, but the ice dragon came back at them with her mouth open to shoot her frostbreath.

I can't lose anyone else, Reed thought. *It'll kill me.* He smashed into the IceWing's side and sliced his claws across her throat while she was twisting to breathe on him. Her eyes went wide and she made an agonized, gargling noise as blood bubbled from the wounds. When he let go of her, the IceWing soldier fell towards the dark forest, her wings twitching feebly like a dying grasshopper.

"Retreat!" a voice suddenly howled. Reed's heart jumped hopefully, thinking the IceWings were giving up – but then he realized it was the SandWing general. "Retreat!" the sand dragon yelled again.

Reed thought they might defeat the IceWings if they kept fighting, but it wasn't worth the risk. Every moment was another opportunity for an IceWing to kill one of his brothers or sisters. Retreating meant keeping them alive.

"Retreat," he echoed the general, grabbing Umber and pulling him back. "Fall back! Pheasant, you too!" He scanned the struggling shapes in the moonlight and picked out his troop: all still alive, for now.

His sister sank her teeth into her opponent's forearm and he released her with a shriek of pain. In a flash she was at Reed's side, and they soared up into the sky with Marsh, Sora, and Umber right beside them.

Reed saw the SandWings take off towards the mountains. Most of the IceWings shot after them; only two turned to pursue him and his siblings.

"This way!" he cried, diving for the forest. If IceWings could hide in there, so could his dragons. He wasn't obligated to follow the SandWings – they'd probably make a run for the Sky Palace anyway. And he didn't want to lead the IceWings back to his village.

Pine branches whipped against his face as he hit the trees. His brothers and sisters had practised a formation like this, zipping through an overgrown forest while staying together. He had to trust that they'd remember and be close behind him.

He heard the sound of thrashing wings further back and risked a glance over his shoulder. Even in the shadows, he recognized the shape of how his brothers and sisters flew; they were all there. It must be the IceWings who'd got caught in the upper branches.

Reed took a chance and landed. The others dropped to the ground with him, and they all immediately flattened themselves with wings outstretched, becoming puddles of shadow on the dark forest floor.

Silence fell. No one breathed. The branches creaked overhead, and small night animals skittered through the bushes around them. Reed felt a squirrel dart over his foot, but he didn't move a muscle.

After a long while, they heard a faraway whistle and the sound of wings in the distance, as if the IceWings had reassembled to fly away.

Reed still didn't move. He waited for almost an hour, until he couldn't hold his breath any longer, until any and all dragon noises had faded long ago.

Then, very carefully and quietly, he inhaled. He heard the others do the same.

"Is anyone hurt?" Reed asked softly.

"That was awful," Marsh whispered. "I thought we were all going to die."

"I'm fine," Pheasant said. "Nothing that won't heal soon."

"I'm all right, too," Sora said hoarsely.

"Umber?" Reed said when the smallest dragonet didn't respond.

"I hate this war," Umber burst out. "I don't understand what we're even fighting for. Who cares who the SandWing queen is? I've never met Burn and I don't want to. Why am

I fighting an IceWing over a throne that has nothing to do with either of us?"

"Because our queen says we have to," Pheasant said, with a little more sarcasm than Reed thought was safe, even if there was no one to overhear.

"Queen Moorhen must have a good reason for allying with Burn and the SkyWings," Reed said. "We shouldn't doubt her."

"Besides, the war will be over soon," Sora said unexpectedly. She hardly ever spoke, and she'd spoken even less since Crane's death. Reed turned and saw her eyes reflecting the glow of the moonlight. "Clay is going to end it."

There was something about the way she said Clay's name that made Reed want to sink into a mud puddle and stay there for a month. She sounded as if she believed in him so much – a dragon they'd barely met. They followed Reed and they loved him, he knew that. But surely they must wonder what could have been . . . and whether Crane might still be alive if Clay were their bigwings all along.

"That's true," Umber said, lifting his head. "Clay and his friends – they're going to save us soon."

"How soon?" Marsh asked. "I thought the prophecy said twenty years – doesn't that mean two more years before they end the war?"

"Actually," Pheasant said, "some dragons think it

depends on when you start counting. If you count from the first battle, then it's only been eighteen years. But if you go back to the death of Queen Oasis, which is really when this whole thing started, then it's been almost twenty." She caught the tilt of Reed's head and shrugged. "I've been reading about the prophecy since we realized Clay is in it."

There was a pause as they all had their own thoughts about Clay, the war and the prophecy.

"If you're all unhappy," Reed said tentatively, "we could – I mean, we could try to find the Talons of Peace."

Pheasant let out a shocked *hiss*. "I may not like this war, but that doesn't mean we should leave our tribe and our home. We're MudWings. We belong in our village."

"Unless *you* think we should leave," Marsh said, leaning against Reed's side. "I'll do whatever you decide."

"We all will," Umber said.

Reed knew they would. But should they? He had no idea what to do – betray his tribe, or keep risking his siblings' lives?

"You don't have to decide tonight," Pheasant said, more gently. "We just had a narrow escape. Let's go home and sleep. We'll all feel better in the morning."

Reed nodded, and they gathered themselves, stretching their cramped wings as best they could under the trees. Showers of pine needles slid across their scales, smelling of winter fires.

"What were those IceWings doing here anyway?" Marsh asked, stamping his feet.

"I have no idea," Reed said. "It seemed as though they were lying in wait for us, but it's not like we're an important patrol. Perhaps they were here for something else and we were unlucky enough to attract their attention."

"Maybe they were here for the scavenger den," Umber said.

"What scavenger den?" Reed glanced at him, surprised.

"Can't you smell it?" Umber asked. "We flew over part of it, too – it's pretty well hidden in the forest."

"How do you *notice* something like that in the middle of a frantic escape?" Pheasant demanded.

Umber shrugged.

"Why would the IceWings care about a scavenger den?" Sora asked softly.

They all thought for a moment, then looked at Reed.

"I don't know," he said helplessly. It felt like he was saying that all the time these days.

"Well," Pheasant said, spreading her wings, "it doesn't matter. What matters is we survived another battle, thanks to Reed."

I wonder if they really feel that way, he thought. *I certainly don't.*

"I hope we survive the next one," Marsh said gloomily.

"I hope we don't have to," Umber said. "I hope Clay

fulfils the prophecy and ends the war and saves the world really soon, before we have to do any more fighting. Don't you think? Maybe he will?"

"Maybe," Pheasant said. "I hope so."

"I do, too," Reed said. He looked up at the stars. *Before the war takes anyone else I care about. Before our village is destroyed; before I have to choose between loyalty to my tribe and the safety of my brothers and sisters. Before we have to kill anyone else.* "I hope so, too."

PART ONE
THE SECRET PLAN

CHAPTER 1

Where is she?

Starflight suspected that he might be dead, except that everything hurt so much. Darkness pressed against his eyes whenever he tried to open them. His nose and throat ached in a fierce, raw way, as if they'd been scraped out with a crocodile tail.

Is she all right?

He couldn't remember what he'd dreamed and what was real.

Perhaps he was still under the mountain. Perhaps his friends had never tried to escape their guardians. Maybe this was one long nightmare that had started with the threat of Morrowseer's visit.

But Starflight was sure he could remember the large NightWing taking him aside. There was a lecture about how "NightWings have a reputation to uphold" and "NightWings are natural leaders" and "you must make the others respect you, fear you, and follow you, or you'll be the greatest disappointment our tribe has ever produced" . . . Starflight couldn't have conjured that from his own brain. That was all real.

He curled on to his side and felt jagged rocks press into his scales.

Was the SkyWing palace real? The dragonets captured before even tasting sunlight. The prison on the tower of rock. The baking-hot arena sands that smelled of blood and terror. Queen Scarlet's delight at capturing him, a real NightWing out in the world, and her plans to make him fight, and her excitement about the prospect of watching him die.

No, that had to be real, because Starflight remembered being "rescued" by the NightWings. He remembered watching his friends turn into small dots below him, blue and brown and bright, and he knew it was real because it felt so much like *this* felt: as if he were a scroll ripped in half down the middle so none of the words made any sense any more.

Will I ever see her again?

I hope she's not here. I hope she's safe somewhere.

"I think there's something wrong with him."

Was that a voice?

He tried to listen, but his dreams dragged him back down.

There had been another stern lecture from Morrowseer. It was essential for Starflight to be the leader of the dragonets; *everything depended on him*. And a new order: he must convince the others to choose Blister as the next SandWing queen.

"Maybe they killed him by accident. That'd be all right. Maybe I'll get to be in the prophecy instead."

"I don't think that's how it works, Fierceteeth."

And then there was the Kingdom of the Sea. No one would listen to him. He couldn't lead anyone. His friends practically laughed at him when he tried to support Blister.

Another prison; another escape where Starflight did just about nothing to help. And then the rainforest and the strange unnatural tunnels: one to the Kingdom of Sand and one, apparently, to the secret home of the NightWings.

That Starflight remembered.

He remembered staring up at it – the dark hole in the tree that led to a home he'd never seen.

"I bet he'd wake up if I bit him."

"*I* bet Morrowseer would throw you in the volcano if he found tooth marks on his prophecy pet."

"I bet my mom would have him for lunch if he tried!"

He was definitely hearing voices – unfamiliar voices, very close by.

The memory of the rainforest was blurring. Starflight tried to fix his mind on it – on those last moments, guarding the tunnel so the NightWings wouldn't come through and attack the RainWings. What had happened?

"Well, he'd better wake up and be interesting soon, or Morrowseer will take him away again before we get to ask him anything."

"Ooh, I have an idea."

Claws scrabbled on rock, and then there was quiet.

Starflight's eyelids felt too heavy to open, as if extra scales were piled on top of them. He let the darkness drift up over him again.

Right – guarding the hole. With Clay. Morning sunbeams flickering through the green leaves, octopus-blue flowers turning their heads up to the light. Sunny was back in the village, with Tsunami, watching Glory try to become queen of the RainWings, of all things.

Sunny had brought them food the night before, her golden scales brushing against his dark wings as she passed him strange little purple fruits.

I love you, he would never say. *Don't hate me because of what the other NightWings have done. Don't think I'm like my tribe. Don't listen to Glory's description of my kingdom, the smoke and the fire and the smell and the death and the trapped, tortured RainWings and the cruel black dragons. Don't look at me like I'm one of them, like I could ever do what they've done, please.*

And then she'd glanced up at him and smiled, and in Sunny's eyes he could see himself as Starflight, just fine the way he was.

Her friend.

Which made everything better and worse all at the same time.

"Careful! I'm not going back for more if you spill it, idiot."

"Get your great honking wings out of my way then, fathead."

The voices again. Starflight caught at the memories, trying to remember the last thing that had happened before everything went dark.

He'd been staring at the hole, wondering what the other NightWings were really like. Wondering if they were all as scary as Morrowseer. Wondering if he went through and talked to them, whether they would listen. What if he could stop the NightWings and RainWings from fighting? What if his tribe understood him and believed in him; what if they thought it was better to be smart than brave? What if they didn't care that he had no special NightWing powers?

What would Sunny think of me then?

She'd probably think: who are you, and what have you done with Starflight? Because there was no way he'd ever be brave enough to go through that tunnel on his own.

And then Clay had yelped, "Did you see that? I think it was a boar! I'll be right back!" And poor ever-hungry Clay had charged off into the trees, leaving Starflight to watch the hole alone. . .

In a heartbeat, dark wings had boiled out of the hole; dark claws had circled his snout; a dark voice had hissed in

17

his ear, "Silence if you want your friend to live." Another dark voice: "Better safe than sorry," although he hadn't made a sound, and he'd known it would hurt right before the blow struck his head and pain blazed through him, and that was the last thing he—

SPLASH!

Starflight jolted up with a yell. His eyes popped open. Freezing salt water cascaded over his snout and snaked down his neck, seeping into his scales. The muddled heavy feeling vanished in an instant.

"It worked!" cheered one of the unfamiliar voices.

"Drat," said another. "I really thought he was dead."

Starflight shook his head and the pain ricocheted around inside. He rubbed at his snout, trying to clear the ocean water from his stinging eyes.

Six or seven or maybe eight dark blurry shapes surrounded him. Beyond them, glowing red light pulsed in lines along the walls. The freezing water had cleared his nose for a moment, but heavy, smoky air was already pressing back in.

"Who are you?" Starflight gasped, or tried to.

"Huh. I thought he might attack us," said a third voice. "That's what I would do."

"He doesn't look very dangerous," said another voice sceptically. "They should have picked someone bigger. Don't you think? Bigger and scarier and fiercer."

"Like me," said the voice who had hoped Starflight was dead.

"You all have tiny RainWing brains," said yet another voice. Starflight was losing count. "He was still inside his egg when they took him. They didn't know if he'd be big or scary or even if he'd be male or female. Otherwise, of course, they would have picked a girl, obviously."

"Like *me*."

"Hello," Starflight coughed. "Hello?"

One of the shapes came close enough for him to make out the features of a disgruntled-looking dragonet a year or two older than himself. She poked at his mouth and peered at his teeth, jabbed at his chest so he coughed again, inspected his claws, and sighed huffily.

"Weak," she declared. "I'd have sent him back, too."

"You're just saying that because you're hoping they'll pick you instead," said another dragonet, pushing forward. He patted Starflight's head in an almost friendly way. "But prophecies don't work like that."

"We'll see," she muttered.

"That's Fierceteeth," said the friendlier dragonet to Starflight. "Don't mind her. Older sisters always think they can do whatever you're doing better than you can. I know, I've got one, too. I'm Mightyclaws, by the way."

"Older sister?" Starflight echoed, blinking at Fierceteeth.

"Yes, this is the touching family reunion part," she said. "Same mother, different fathers, we assume. How do you feel?" She eyed him from horns to tail. "Ill? Very ill? Dying, perhaps?"

"What part of *brightest night* are you having trouble with?" said another dragonet behind Fierceteeth. "Haven't you been listening in class? Events have to match the prophecies. Hi, strange dragon. I'm Mindreader. But don't worry, I promise I'll stay out of your head."

The older dragonets in the room laughed uproariously, as if this was the most hilarious joke in Pyrrhia history. The three dragonets who looked younger than Starflight rolled their eyes, like they were used to hearing jokes that made no sense from that group.

Starflight rubbed his wet scales, confused.

Now that his sight was clearing, he could see that he was in a long, narrow cave lined with indentations in the rock at regular intervals, all the right size for dragonet beds. He was curled on one of these, not far from a large archway that seemed to be the only exit from the room. Next to him on the floor was a large hollow stone, which was apparently what the dragonets had used to collect the seawater they'd just poured all over him.

It didn't look like a prison. It looked like a dormitory.

Hot coals smouldered in alcoves in the walls, lending a red glow to the room. A skylight at each end of the cave allowed a bit of dim grey light to filter in.

There were at least fifty sleeping spots that Starflight could see, but only about eleven of them looked slept in. Several had rough blankets heaped on them in messy piles, while others were scattered with objects that looked like seashells and twisted bits of rock. A few of the blanket-covered beds had a scroll lying next to them, which made Starflight's claws itch with longing. But most of the beds were completely bare.

Places for dragonets, but no dragonets to fill them.

Starflight remembered something Morrowseer had said offhandedly, shortly after rescuing Starflight from the SkyWings. He'd said, "We can't afford to lose any NightWings, even peculiar little ones."

Maybe there is something wrong with my tribe, Starflight thought. *Maybe they're losing dragonets somehow – or not having enough of them in the first place.*

Everything smelled like sulphur and decaying animals. As Fierceteeth leaned over and jabbed his stomach again, Starflight realized that a lot of the decaying smell came from the dragonets. They all had horrendously bad breath. Morrowseer's breath had never been wonderful either, but this was much worse. It took all of Starflight's willpower not to recoil when they spoke to him.

They were also shockingly thin, every one of them, with narrow chests, bloodshot eyes and hacking coughs. *Even the dragonets who survive are in pretty bad shape,* Starflight thought.

He stretched gingerly, eyeing the door. It didn't seem to be barricaded in any way; as far as Starflight could tell, he could walk right out into the caves beyond. *There's probably a guard,* he thought. *Or LOTS of guards. Or maybe something really creepy, like Queen Coral's electric eels. Or a lava river like the one that keeps the RainWings trapped in their prison caves.*

A shiver of fear ran down his spine.

"Why am I here?" he blurted.

The little crowd of dragonets exchanged glances.

"Because you failed," Fierceteeth offered. "I assume."

"We don't know that," Mightyclaws interjected. "A couple of the big dragons dropped you here a few hours ago and you've been muttering and thrashing around ever since."

"Yeah, lots of worrying about Sunny. Who's Sunny?" one of the other dragonets demanded.

Starflight considered throwing himself into the volcano. "Another dragonet," he mumbled. *I hope she's safe.*

"I want to hear about the mainland," Mindreader said eagerly. "Tell us everything. We've heard there are trees taller than dragons and that in some places the sky is blue. True? False? What's the coolest thing you've seen? What's the best thing you've eaten?"

"You've never been to the mainland?" Starflight said.

"Dragonets aren't allowed to leave the island until

we're ten years old," Mightyclaws said. "Apparently we can't be trusted to keep all the NightWing secrets until then."

Almost in unison, all the dragonets snorted impatiently.

"You're the only exception," Fierceteeth said in a voice dripping with scorn.

"Him and the other one," Mindreader said. "I heard my mom say there was another."

"I don't know any NightWing secrets," Starflight said.

"Oh," said Mightyclaws. "I guess that's one way to make sure you keep them!"

The scrabble of claws in the hall outside heralded the appearance of a dragonet smaller than the others, perhaps three years old. She raced into the room and gasped, "He's coming!"

Immediately the dragonets scattered to their sleeping spots. Half of them dived into their blankets and pretended to be asleep. A few of them grabbed their scrolls and looked studious; others fussed busily with the objects around their beds. Fierceteeth sat down on her bed, folded her wings, and glared at the doorway.

Starflight wished he was unconscious again as he heard heavy footsteps tramping towards the room. He glanced up at the skylight, wondering if he could fit through it but knowing perfectly well he was too terrified to try.

With a scraping, hissing sound, Morrowseer slithered into the room. He frowned at Fierceteeth, then looked coldly down his long nose at Starflight.

"Up," he snarled. "The queen of the NightWings wants to see you."

CHAPTER 2

Starflight's experience with dragon queens thus far had not been exactly wonderful.

"M-me?" he stammered. "Now? You mean, right now? Shouldn't I – I mean, I'm not really prepared to, or, I – I don't really look – to see a queen, I mean – maybe—"

"Stop blithering and follow me." Morrowseer swept out of the cave with a growl.

"Go, go, go," Mightyclaws hissed, flapping his wings as Starflight hesitated.

Starflight's claws caught on small holes in the rocky floor and he stumbled as he chased after the giant NightWing. *Volcanic rock,* he thought, peering at the walls around him. *I wonder when it last erupted.* From the rumbling under his talons and the heat rising through the floor, it didn't seem like the most dormant volcano.

Morrowseer led the way up a winding tunnel without looking back.

"My friends—" Starflight started to say. "Sunny and the others – are they—"

The large black dragon didn't turn around.

Starflight kept walking for a few minutes, then took a deep breath and tried again. "When can I go back?"

His only answer was a snort of disgust. Starflight swallowed his questions and nervously tucked his wings in. The walls felt like they were getting closer.

He didn't see any guards or rivers of lava. He didn't see any other NightWings at all.

But as they moved along the tunnel, Starflight heard something up ahead – a hissing, murmuring sound that grew louder as they approached.

Dragon voices, jumbled and arguing.

Dread prickled through every scale on Starflight's body. If he hadn't been more terrified of what Morrowseer would do to him, he would have turned and bolted back down the tunnel.

Finally Morrowseer and Starflight stepped through an archway into a cave full of dragons. The walls were packed with dragon wings, with NightWings hanging from crags and rocks and the ceiling like bats. One by one, dark-scaled dragon heads turned towards them. The gathered NightWings fell silent.

A last voice cried, "We should attack *now*. We should have attacked *yester*—!" before cutting off abruptly as the speaker noticed Starflight.

Starflight wondered again if he was dreaming, because this was his biggest nightmare come to life: a room full of angry NightWings, all of them glaring at him.

"Watch it," Morrowseer growled as Starflight stumbled

into him, and then Starflight saw what lay ahead of their talons.

A few steps into the cave, the rocky path abruptly fell away on either side, leaving only a thin strip of stone to stand on. Below him was a bubbling lake of glowing orange lava. He could feel the heat crackling along his scales.

Morrowseer stepped back to the safety of the doorway and prodded Starflight forward, so the dragonet was left alone on the spur of rock, surrounded by lava.

Lava and NightWings.

And they're all reading my mind, he thought with another jolt of terror. *They can see all my thoughts. They know I'm terrified and weak and useless and that I don't think Blister should be the next SandWing queen and that I think this is a horrible place to live and—*

Stop thinking about all the things I don't want them to see in my head!

With a massive effort, Starflight focused on the details of the room around him. *Think about what you see. Don't think about anything else.*

First, there weren't actually hundreds of dragons staring at him. He did a quick estimate, hiding his other thoughts inside mountains of numbers. Maybe forty. About forty black dragons filled the cave, most of them as large as Morrowseer, which meant they must be quite old. They were all as thin as the dragonets in the dormitory, and many of

27

them had worn patches on their scales, sores on their snouts and wings, and traces of blood around their nostrils. These dragons looked like the tribal opposite of the colourful, healthy, well-fed RainWings.

There was a clear spot on the cave walls right across from him. It looked like a circle had been carved into the rock, as wide across as Starflight's wingspan, and then jabbed full of small holes, none of them bigger than a dragon's eye.

The other dragons kept glancing at this circle as if waiting for it to do something.

On a ledge beside the circle perched a dragon with a scar rippling down her chest. Her wings drooped in an odd way, as if they were weighted down with rocks, and she wore a cluster of diamonds around her neck. Another chain of smaller teardrop diamonds was wound around the horns on her head.

But that can't be the queen, Starflight thought. She didn't have authority in her bones. She didn't radiate power all the way through her wingtips, like the other queens he'd met.

It took him only a moment of puzzling this out before he realized that there must be a dragon *behind* the screen, staring through those holes at him. A chill sliced through his scales. Nobody could see her, but her presence filled the cave like heavy smoke.

The queen of the NightWings.

The scrolls always referred to her as mysterious and unknown, but Starflight hadn't imagined that she would keep herself hidden even from her own tribe.

Why?

Because it's extra-terrifying, he answered himself.

"*This* is him?" barked one of the dragons.

"Yes," Morrowseer growled. "We snatched him from the rainforest this morning."

Wings rustled uneasily all around the cave.

"Has he told us anything?" asked another dragon. "What do they know? What are they planning?"

"How soon will they attack?" growled another.

"And how did that RainWing escape?" another one shouted as several dragons began to speak at once. "We've heard reports that there was a MudWing with her. A MudWing! How did he get here? Why didn't we kill them before they got away?"

They're talking about Glory and Clay, Starflight thought with a shudder.

"That's the RainWing I warned you about," Morrowseer snarled. "The one the Talons of Peace got to replace the SkyWing they lost." He spat into the lava. "This is exactly why I told them to kill her."

"A RainWing, of all things," said the dragon with the diamonds. "What an unfortunate mistake."

"We had her," said a dragon with twisted horns. "*Here*. In our talons. *And nobody killed her?*"

"Who knows what she saw?" cried another dragon. "If she warns the RainWings what we're planning—"

"She can't possibly know that," Morrowseer said.

"She knows about the tunnel between our kingdoms," challenged a dragon from the far wall. "And that little one escaped with her. She'll have told her everything she saw in the fortress. What if they figure it out?"

A clamour of voices filled the cave.

Figure what out? Starflight looked down at his talons and wished they weren't shaking so much. He was half afraid that he'd tremble himself off balance and into the lava, but that wasn't even in the top twenty things he was worrying about right now. *What are they planning?*

He glanced up at the screen where the queen was hidden. She hadn't spoken at all yet. But he could feel her watching; from the way his skin prickled, he thought she hadn't taken her eyes off him since he'd entered the cave.

All at once, the dragon with the diamonds leaned towards the screen, tilting her head.

A hush fell instantly around the room. Nothing moved except the *bloop-bloop* of bubbles in the lava. Every NightWing present seemed to be holding his or her breath.

Starflight didn't hear anything – no queen's voice issuing

regally from her hiding spot – but the diamond dragon nodded and straightened up again.

"Queen Battlewinner says to shut up and ask *him*." To his horror, she pointed at Starflight. "That's why he's here. Make *him* tell us what they know and what they're going to do next."

The listening dragons all swivelled their heads towards him.

Falling into the lava suddenly sounded like a pretty great option.

"Um," Starflight stammered several times. "I – I – um—"

"Speak or I kill you right now," Morrowseer growled behind him.

Starflight pressed his front talons together and took a deep breath. "Her name is Glory," he blurted.

The dragons all hissed. This was not something they cared about.

"She – she said you have RainWing prisoners." *Please tell me she's wrong. Tell me it's all a mistake.*

But no one corrected him.

Should he tell them Glory's plan? That she was trying to become queen of the RainWings so she could build an army to come rescue their lost dragons? That they shouldn't underestimate her?

Would he be betraying his friends if he said all that to the NightWings?

31

Or would he be betraying his tribe if he didn't?

The close, smoky air of the cave pressed down around Starflight.

What if I can fix everything?

This is the chance you wanted. You asked Glory to let you talk to the NightWings. You wanted to give them a chance to explain themselves – you wanted to find a peaceful solution, so you wouldn't have to pick sides in a war.

But now that he was here, facing their dark eyes, he couldn't find any of the brilliant words he'd meant to use.

Suddenly one of the nearest dragons snapped, "Just tell us if they're planning an attack!"

"Yes," Starflight blurted. "I mean – I think so."

This met with such an uproar that Starflight had to sit down and cover his head with his wings. He'd said the worst possible thing. He'd made everything worse for Glory and the RainWings, and he couldn't even bring himself to speak up and try that famous "diplomacy" he'd always thought was such a good idea.

They wouldn't listen to me anyway, he told himself, but he didn't know if that was true. He wasn't brave enough to find out.

"It doesn't matter," rasped a hoarse, wet voice. "RainWings are no match for us."

A horribly disfigured dragon pushed past Morrowseer,

slithered into the cave, and glowered at the other dragons. His snout was twisted and deformed by a terrible scar that had closed one nostril, melted several scales, and left nasty oozing bubbles along his jawline.

The dragon with the diamonds frowned. "Vengeance, you were not invited to this council."

"Yeah, I noticed," he hissed. "And yet I know more than any dragon about RainWings and what they can do." He gestured to his face. "And I can tell you that this was a fluke. RainWings are too stupid and cowardly to be dangerous. Most of you know I got this when I grabbed their queen – well, turns out, just one of their queens – stupid tribe – and she had no idea what she was doing, or I'd be dead. She didn't even mean to spray me. They never do." Vengeance shook his head, breathing loudly through his mouth. "They have Pyrrhia's most powerful weapon and they're too pathetic to use it."

"Maybe they were before this *Glory* came along," said one of the other dragons. "From what Morrowseer says about her, she's not as weak as the rest of them."

You have no idea, Starflight thought.

"And it's your fault they found out about us," the diamond dragon said. "You're the one who brought her here, even though Deathbringer warned us the dragonets were in the forest, and that we should stay away until they were gone."

33

"Deathbringer." Vengeance smirked. "Oh, yeah. How is your pet, Greatness? I've heard a very interesting story about him." He turned and beckoned with his tail.

Starflight recognized the NightWing assassin who was dragged into the cave by four guards. It was starting to get crowded on the ledge by the door. Vengeance seized Deathbringer's ear and virtually threw him on to the stone outcropping with Starflight. They knocked into each other and flung out their wings for balance.

Deathbringer wasn't much bigger than Starflight, after all – he'd looked larger when he was attacking Queen Blaze and threatening Glory. But here, in the same lava predicament as Starflight, with everyone looking just as displeased with him, he seemed a lot less intimidating.

"Ah," he said to Starflight in a friendly way. "You're here, too." His eyes looked as if he wanted to ask something but didn't dare.

"This dragon," Vengeance bellowed, pointing at Deathbringer. "*This* pet assassin of Princess Greatness was actually *conspiring with the enemy. He* is the one who brought the MudWing here and *he* helped them both to escape."

Princess, Starflight thought. *So the diamond dragon – Greatness – speaks for her mother, for some reason.*

"Hang on," Deathbringer said, hopping neatly over

Starflight's head so the dragonet was between him and Vengeance. He looked around at the other dragons and spread his wings with an innocent air. "Conspiring with the enemy? Do you have any proof?"

"Yeah, I have witnesses," Vengeance hissed. "One of the guards she attacked on the way out saw you helping them. And the guards you distracted from the tunnel so the MudWing could come through – they can tell us all about that."

A terrible silence followed. Starflight wondered whether they were all searching Deathbringer's mind to find out what was true. He kept his own mind carefully blank, just in case.

"Deathbringer," said Greatness, twisting her diamond necklace in her front claws. "That kind of betrayal . . . the punishment is death."

The NightWing assassin spread his wings and bowed deeply towards the queen. "I swear I have only ever done what I thought would be best for my tribe."

"Oh, yeah?" Vengeance coughed wetly. "So why are all the dragonets still alive, then?"

Deathbringer glanced under his wing and met Starflight's eyes. There was a question in them, and this time Starflight guessed what it was. *Are they? All still alive?* Starflight nodded as imperceptibly as he could, and a look of relief flitted across Deathbringer's face, then was gone.

"My mission is not complete, it's true," Deathbringer said. "I need to return to the rainforest and—"

"And betray us some more," Vengeance suggested. "I bet you do."

Starflight noticed Greatness leaning towards the screen again, but most of the dragons were staring at Deathbringer and didn't notice this time.

"I assure you I'm a loyal NightWing," Deathbringer said, his voice rising. "Perhaps I think it's worth discussing whether we really *need* to kill these dragonets, but—"

"You see?" roared Vengeance. "He's—"

"Vengeance!" Greatness shouted, cutting him off. She stood up on her ledge and spread her wings, revealing the silver scales glittering underneath like echoes of her diamonds. She puffed up her chest and contorted her face as if she was trying to appear menacing and regal, but it looked like a performance. Starflight still couldn't see a future queen in her.

"The queen has spoken," Greatness said into the perilous silence. "Vengeance. You endangered the whole tribe. You disobeyed orders. You brought a viper to us disguised as a simple garden snake."

"Wait," Vengeance cried. "What he did was worse! I just grabbed a RainWing, same as always! How could I know – she didn't look no different than the others!"

"And in addition," said Greatness, "you are irritating the queen." She flicked her tail, just the tiniest movement, at the guards in the doorway.

"NO!" shrieked Vengeance. His wings flapped open, but he'd barely lifted off when the four guards grabbed him. With one swift heave, before Starflight even had time to blink, they hurled the scarred dragon into the lake of lava.

CHAPTER 3

Deathbringer shot up and out of the way as lava splashed all around them. Starflight didn't move fast enough, and a bright orange droplet splattered on his foot. Burning pain flared through him, and he thought he might faint.

Then a shape surged out of the lava – Vengeance, screaming and trying to escape as he was boiled alive.

Deathbringer's talons yanked Starflight into the air just in time. Lava sprayed in all directions as the dying dragon flailed his wings.

"DON'T DO THIS! SAVE ME!" Vengeance howled.

The guards stepped forward with expressionless faces. They were wearing a sort of armour, including helmets and thick plates over their underbellies, and they were all carrying wicked pronged spears like the one Glory had brought back to the rainforest.

It was these spears they used to shove Vengeance back under the lava, and to hold him there until the thrashing stopped and the dark shape of the scarred dragon finally sank all the way below the bright gold-red surface and disappeared.

After a long moment, Starflight remembered to

breathe again. He glanced at Deathbringer, hovering in the air beside him. There was an unusually sombre look on the assassin's face, as if he'd just seen a glimpse of his possible future, and not in a magical prophetic vision sort of way.

"Thank you, Majesty," Deathbringer said at last, bowing towards the hidden queen.

"Don't, Deathbringer," Greatness said, her voice cracking. She cleared her throat and looked away. "We're not done with you." She addressed the guards. "Take him to the dungeon. We'll investigate the charges and then Her Majesty will decide what to do."

Deathbringer flew down to the guards and allowed them to push him out the door, only glancing back once to meet Starflight's eyes with a look Starflight couldn't decode.

Maybe he expects me to have mind-reading abilities. Maybe he's trying to send me a message.

If so — sorry, Deathbringer. You picked the wrong dragon.

Greatness rubbed the ridges above her eyes, looking tired. "All right, we need a break. If it's your turn to eat this week, go do that now, and we'll reconvene tonight." She glanced around the room, leaned towards the screen again, and added, "The queen says to return at dusk with possible defensive and offensive strategies. Morrowseer, see if you can claw some more information out of the dragonet before then."

Morrowseer dipped his head, flexing his talons. Starflight hoped uneasily that she meant "claw" in a metaphorical way.

The NightWings began to disperse, most of them through holes in the ceiling. Morrowseer jerked his head, and Starflight reluctantly followed him back into the tunnels.

The mention of eating had reminded him of how hungry he was, although he couldn't really worry about food when he wasn't even sure if he was a prisoner or a spy or just a failure. And after what had happened to Vengeance, Starflight was pretty nervous about what the NightWings might do with a failure.

Morrowseer's wings billowed like thunderclouds as he stormed ahead of Starflight. Soon Starflight realized that they weren't going back to the dormitory – Morrowseer had taken a turn somewhere, and now Starflight could see dim grey light up ahead.

They emerged on to a shelf of rock that jutted from the side of the fortress. Below them was a weird landscape of rocks that looked like giant lumpy grey-black dragon scales with a fiery orange glowing underneath, filling in the cracks. *A lava field,* Starflight thought.

He remembered a little about volcanoes from one of

the scrolls he'd studied back under the mountain, what felt like a lifetime ago. But there weren't any active volcanoes on the mainland of Pyrrhia, so he hadn't memorized it like the other scrolls. It had never occurred to him that the NightWings, who'd written most of the scrolls, might have first-hand knowledge of volcanoes; might, in fact, be living on one.

Starflight couldn't see any caves or a lava river like the one Glory had described, so he guessed they were on the other side of the volcano. But the air was as smoky and grey as she'd said, and as hard to breathe. He still felt that raw scraped feeling all the way down his throat.

Far overhead in the ashy sky, a pair of black dragons wheeled and circled, around and around, like vultures. Starflight wondered if they could see the mainland from up there. How far was the island from the rest of Pyrrhia? Did the NightWings have a way to get there other than the secret animus-made tunnels to the rainforest?

So many questions. His whole life, he'd been full of questions about the NightWings and their secret home, and now perhaps they could all be answered. He took a moment to think, *I'm here. This is my home. This is my tribe. This is what I was looking for.*

But it didn't feel true. This awful place was nothing like the NightWing utopia he'd always imagined. He'd pictured a beautiful hidden place full of art and music and dragons who loved to read, with spires reaching to the clouds, and waterfalls and sunlight and a library around every corner. Not this – the smoke and stench and hostility and gloomy surroundings.

And even a million answers, even all the answers to all the questions he could think of, wouldn't be able to take the place of Sunny and the other dragonets.

Morrowseer stared across the lava field and inhaled several times, his nostrils flaring and his tongue slithering in and out. He did this for so long that Starflight began to wonder if there was something wrong with his nose.

"Um," Starflight squeaked at last.

Morrowseer glared at him in the middle of a giant sniff.

"J-just, um," Starflight said. "I just want you to know I don't know anything else. Really. About the RainWings attacking." Almost immediately, his traitorous brain started clamouring, *Except that Glory might be queen by now! And that RainWings are normally pacifists! And—*

He fixed his eyes on the mountain behind them and tried to think of nothing but lava.

Morrowseer snorted. "That doesn't surprise me," he said. "You're just about the most useless spy I've ever met." He spread his wings and inhaled once more. "Let's go."

His tail nearly knocked Starflight off the ledge as he leaped into the sky.

"Down there?" Starflight called, glancing at the molten cracks in the rocks below them. "Is it safe?" He flapped to catch up to Morrowseer.

"Of course it isn't," Morrowseer snapped. "Several dragons have made the mistake of trying to land down there, only to break the crust and fall right through." He nodded at a white shape sticking out of the rocks. Starflight peered at it until he realized what it was, and then wished he hadn't. His stomach twisted as he spotted a few others: dragon skulls, their mouths open in an eternal scream.

"I wouldn't suggest a closer look," Morrowseer said drily. "We're going over there." He nodded to the far side of the lava rocks, where Starflight now saw a tangle of grey, ash-covered trees.

"So." Starflight cleared his throat. "When Greatness said 'if it's your turn to eat this week' – what did that mean?"

Morrowseer hissed. "There's a rotating schedule. All NightWings are allowed to hunt or gather for about five days out of every month. Naturally, I am exempt."

"Naturally?" Starflight echoed, although he hadn't meant for it to sound so much like a question. *Only five days a month? No wonder they're all so thin . . . they must be running out of food on this island.*

The older dragon frowned down at him. "My role in the tribe's future makes me indispensable."

"Oh," Starflight said, not daring to ask any more questions.

As they got closer to the trees, it turned out to be a bigger forest than Starflight had expected, covering about a quarter of the island, from the edge of the lava to the ocean.

"I see," he said with relief. "I wondered where you hunted." Surely there couldn't be much prey on an active volcano.

"Here, when we have to," Morrowseer spat. "For instance, when we can't get to the rainforest or the Kingdom of Sand." His forked black tongue hissed in and out.

Oh. That must be another reason they're so angry right now — they've been using the rainforest to find extra prey, he thought. *Like that sloth Glory, Clay and I found by the river.* He'd had trouble getting the stench of that dying sloth out of his nose. For a moment, Starflight thought the memory of it had brought the smell back, until he realized a similar smell of decay was coming from the forest below him.

"The whole island was like this when we got here," Morrowseer said.

"You mean, covered with trees?" Starflight asked. "What happened? The volcano?" *Stupid question. Of course it was the volcano.* He looked back at the mountain, which must have sent a river of lava this way that covered almost all the trees, turning the island into a mostly barren rockscape.

Morrowseer didn't answer him. They circled overhead once and Starflight spotted a few other NightWings prowling through the trees. Morrowseer glowered at them, then flicked his tail at Starflight.

"Quickly," he snapped. "Before one of them finds my prey."

"Your—" Starflight started curiously, but Morrowseer had already tucked his wings and was arrowing down to a patch of stunted trees not far from the beach.

The older dragon landed with a *thud* that sent grey dust billowing around his talons and immediately dropped his nose to the ground. With a horrible snorting noise, he charged across the clearing, taking deep breaths and flicking his tongue rapidly in and out.

Starflight had never seen hunting like this. Dune had taught them what he could in the caves under the mountain, and sometimes it had involved scent trails – Starflight was always decent at those – but usually it also involved being quiet, waiting to spot your target, and then attacking swiftly, before they even knew you were there.

But from the noise Morrowseer was making, Starflight thought every animal on the island must know he was coming.

He followed the large black dragon, thinking about Dune and his hunting lessons. Their SandWing guardian hadn't been particularly kind to the dragonets, although he'd never been as cruel as Kestrel. But he'd always noticed how hard Starflight studied, and sometimes he gave him special tutorials on scrolls that Starflight found confusing.

Their other guardian, Webs, had often made an effort to bring back more scrolls for Starflight on his trips outside. They'd both been more cautious with him than the other dragonets – perhaps wary that his NightWing mind reading or prophecy skills might suddenly manifest.

Something I'm still waiting for, he thought, hunching his wings.

Morrowseer made a guttural, triumphant noise and swiped a leafless bush out of his way.

Underneath it was something half dead.

More than half dead, Starflight thought. *Almost all the way dead.* It looked like a pile of grey and white feathers as big as a dragon's head. When the giant NightWing hooked one claw in it to drag it out, it let out an awful pathetic squawk.

"What is it?" Starflight asked, trying to remember a bird like this from his scrolls. His curiosity made him forget about being too afraid to talk. "It's bigger than any seagull I've seen."

"A giant albatross," Morrowseer said, flipping it over. "I was sure it would be dead by now." With a shrug, he sliced one claw across the bird's throat.

Starflight covered his snout with one of his wings. The toxic smell of the dead bird was almost overwhelming; he wanted to run to the ocean and bury his head in the salt water to make it go away.

As Morrowseer prodded it a few more times, Starflight spotted a bite on the bird's neck like the one on the dead sloth in the rainforest. It looked infected and disgusting, crawling with insects.

"Are you sure that's safe to eat?" he asked.

"I'm the one who killed it," Morrowseer growled. "I'm certainly going to eat it."

"But won't it make you sick?"

Morrowseer gave him a dark look. "NightWings don't get sick. Don't tell me you have a weak stomach in addition to everything else wrong with you."

"N-no, I don't think so," Starflight said, hoping he wasn't about to throw up and prove himself wrong. "But look, there's probably horrible bacteria all through that wound."

"Of course there is," Morrowseer said. "How do you think it died? My bite infected it. That's—" He paused, frowning at Starflight. "Isn't this how you hunt, too?"

Starflight glanced down at the horrible-smelling bird.

He had a feeling he shouldn't admit that so far Clay had done most of the hunting since they left the mountain. But he also didn't want to admit that he didn't understand this at all.

Use your brain, he told himself. *You can figure this out.*

"You bite your prey," he said slowly. "And then you wait for it to die. And then you find it and eat it – once it's already dead and rotting. But it doesn't make you sick." He squinted at Morrowseer's teeth. "There's something in your mouth that kills them, even if the bite itself wasn't fatal. Is it venom?"

Morrowseer shook his head. "Some NightWings think so, but none of our scientists have been able to find any when they examine our tribe's corpses. Nor have we had any success replicating RainWing venom shooting." He scowled at the bird and abruptly ripped off one if its wings. "You may have this," he said ungenerously, tossing it at Starflight.

Starflight jumped back to avoid catching it, and the wing splatted to the ground in front of him. Several wriggly things crawled out of it and he closed his eyes quickly.

"Um," he said. "No, thank you."

Morrowseer already had his teeth buried in the underbelly of the albatross. He tore off a mouthful and chewed for a moment, staring narrowly at Starflight.

"What do you think you're going to eat?" he barked. "This is the NightWing way."

"I'll catch something else," Starflight said. He glanced around. "A turtle or a lizard or something."

"I'm starting to see why you're so useless," Morrowseer hissed. "No one's ever taught you to be a NightWing. We assumed you'd be born superior like the rest of us, but perhaps you're defective. Well, we don't have time for delicate sensibilities and a lengthy turtle hunt. Eat the wing or starve."

Starflight was too intrigued by this strange biological phenomenon to register that he'd just been called defective as well as useless.

"Listen, it might not make you sick, but I think it would make *me* sick," Starflight said. He wished he could write all this down. Were there any scrolls about NightWing bites and what they did to their prey? Maybe he could study the tribe and write the first one. "I'm not used to eating infected carrion. Scientifically I would assume it's something you have to adjust to over time, as your dragonets will have done, growing up with a diet like this. But I won't have the correct antibodies to keep me safe. It's not worth the risk."

The enormous black dragon had paused mid bite and was staring at Starflight with his mouth open.

"Well," he said after a long moment, "that answers that question."

"What question?" Starflight asked.

Morrowseer picked at his teeth with one claw and lashed his tail.

"Now I know who your father is."

CHAPTER 4

The wind off the ocean seized the tree branches and rattled them fiercely.

Starflight dug his talons into the ground.

It wasn't that he'd forgotten to wonder who his parents were – it was more that he was terrified to hear the answer. A father like Morrowseer or Vengeance, or a mother like Greatness or Fierceteeth . . . perhaps it would be better never to find out, rather than have his dreams meet the inevitably awful reality.

But suddenly, the idea that a real dragon, somewhere on this island, was connected to him and might care about him was almost too much to bear.

It's what Sunny and I always talked about – finding our parents.

"My father," he whispered. "Didn't you know who he was before?"

"There were a few possibilities," Morrowseer said grimly. "But only one other dragon I know talks like you."

He talks like me.

"Well, this is guaranteed to make him even more insufferable," Morrowseer muttered, shredding the other albatross wing and stuffing scraps of meat in his mouth. "He's been claiming it was his egg for the last six years."

"Can I meet him?" Starflight asked.

"Oh, there's no getting out of that." Morrowseer's tail twitched. "I'm surprised he didn't track you down the moment you were dragged in. Must be in the middle of another big experiment. Nose in his scrolls . . . probably hasn't even noticed that we're about to go to war."

He wants to meet me. He'll be looking for me.

"What about my mother?" Starflight asked. "Could – could I meet her?"

"No," Morrowseer said, plucking a feather off his tongue. "Dead. Died a few years ago."

"Oh." Starflight didn't understand the wave of sadness that seemed to punch him in the chest. He hadn't known her. She'd agreed to give up her egg for the prophecy, so she couldn't have been very attached to him. She was probably as bad as Coral, or Clay's mother.

Still.

"How did she die?" Starflight tried not to look at the mess Morrowseer was making of the albatross. Dune and Kestrel had always insisted on strict table manners and cleanliness, since they were all trapped under the mountain together, in just a few caves with nowhere to escape to if someone ate their prey in a loud, annoying way.

"She got herself involved in a battle – tried to help a SeaWing who'd been attacked by two SkyWings."

Morrowseer grunted. "Idiot. So obviously you didn't get that brain from *her*." He narrowed his eyes at Starflight and waved one of the bird bones at him. "Enough. I have questions for you."

"I really don't know anything," Starflight said in a hurry.

"How dangerous is that RainWing?" Morrowseer asked, ignoring him. "Our studies indicate that most RainWings care only about themselves and prefer everything to be easy. Accurate?"

Starflight nodded. He really desperately didn't want to betray Glory in any way. But he couldn't think of a way to avoid Morrowseer's questions or lie to him when Morrowseer was sure to read the truth in his mind.

To his surprise, Morrowseer's shoulders relaxed. "That's what I thought," he said. "So perhaps they won't do anything. Perhaps they'll roll over and go back to sleep."

Starflight realized that Morrowseer had misunderstood him — he'd only meant that laziness was true of most RainWings, but the NightWing had heard that it was true of Glory as well.

"Maybe," he said non-committally. He tried not to think about how Glory would never let this go — how she would fight tooth and claw to rescue the RainWing prisoners. It had been strange seeing her like that, as if she'd borrowed Tsunami's ferocity for a day. For years Glory had acted as though she didn't care about anything. But apparently imprisoning and torturing members of her tribe was one way to get her attention.

He remembered what the council had said. "What plan was the council talking about?" he asked. "What is it we don't want the RainWings to know?"

He stumbled over the words, trying to say "we" as if he could be part of this tribe. But he wanted Morrowseer to feel as if Starflight was on his side, that he could be trusted. It was a trick he'd seen Sunny use a few times when Glory and Tsunami were fighting – "Why are we mad at Tsunami today?" "Now what has Glory done to us?" – and it often worked.

Not this time, though.

"The less you know, the better," Morrowseer snapped. "You'll get in less trouble that way."

That wasn't generally Starflight's philosophy. He'd say knowing more was always better than knowing less.

Morrowseer ripped the last chunk of flesh off the bird and spat out several more feathers. "If you're determined to starve," he muttered, and devoured the wing he'd thrown to Starflight in a few bites. "Very well," he grumbled, "let's go see Mastermind." He flung the remains of the bird into the bushes and jumped into the sky. "Then I'll take you to the alternates," he said over his shoulder.

"The what?" Starflight asked, but Morrowseer was winging away quickly and didn't look back.

Starflight followed him, still thinking about the way NightWings hunted. It explained a few things, including the bad breath on all the dragonets in the dormitory. Oddly, Deathbringer didn't seem to have the same smell. Starflight wondered if the assassin spent more time on the continent than other NightWings and had learned to prefer live prey over carrion, like most dragons.

Ahead of them, the NightWing fortress loomed, black against the grey sky. It was massive, built in layers that wrapped halfway around the mountain. But it also looked somehow precarious, as if one rock shelf could shift underneath it and the whole thing might suddenly slide all the way into the ocean.

In fact . . . Starflight squinted. It was hard to see at first, black on black in the dark smoky air, but as they got closer he was sure. Part of the fortress had been swallowed by lava, clearly some time ago. A whole corner of the building, at least as big as Queen Scarlet's gladiator arena, was covered by a hardened mass of black rock bubbles. It looked like a giant dragon had reached out of the mountain and slammed its talons down over the walls.

Starflight glanced up uneasily at the plume of steam rising from the top of the volcano. Orange-gold fire glowed from inside, and he knew that streams of molten lava ran down at least one face of the mountain, towards the caves where the RainWings were trapped, if Glory's description was right. Surely another eruption could come anytime, endangering the rest of the fortress.

That thought made him even more nervous about following Morrowseer back inside, but he didn't have much choice. The large NightWing ducked into a mouth-like opening on the highest level of the fortress. The tunnels here were lit with hanging chandeliers of torches as well as the niches of coals Starflight had seen before. The stone under his talons felt smoother and more polished, as if it was frequently swept or mopped, unlike the lower tunnels.

Starflight thought of the gold dragon prints in the Sky Palace, the emerald-studded throne in the Kingdom of the Sea, and the colourful flowers that wound all around the RainWing village. There was nothing like that here – nothing to break up the monotony of the stone walls, nothing to showcase the wealth and power of the NightWings.

Then again, I guess no one ever comes here, he thought. *Instead of trying to impress other dragons with opulence, they do it with mystery.* He could see how that would make sense. But it would have been nice to see something besides fire and rock in all directions.

As they turned a corner, Starflight paused and looked back. He thought he'd heard – but maybe he was imagining things. But – it had sounded like claws *tip-tapping* on the stone behind them.

He stared along the dark tunnel, and suddenly had a shivery feeling of hope. *Maybe it's Glory,* he thought. *Maybe she's here and camouflaged; maybe she's come to rescue me.* He couldn't imagine how she would have got past the NightWing guards who must be posted around the hole. In fact, if he were in charge, he'd have stuck a NightWing *in* the tunnel at all times, just to be sure no one could invisibly squeeze by. But maybe the NightWings weren't that smart.

There it was again. *Tap tap tap.* Definitely talons, although whoever it was wasn't doing a terrific job of being stealthy. *Glory is much better at sneaking than that. Maybe Clay?*

It was awful how much his chest hurt with hope. If only it were Clay! If only that big brown head would poke around the bend, see him, and grin. Starflight promised the universe that he would never, ever make fun of Clay again, if only the MudWing would suddenly be here, rescuing him.

"Keep up!" Morrowseer growled from up ahead.

Starflight realized that he was really being an idiot. If someone were trying to sneak up behind them to rescue him, it wouldn't much help if Starflight stood there staring at them. He started to turn to follow Morrowseer – but just then a head *did* poke around the last corner.

It wasn't Clay. Or Glory or Tsunami . . . or Sunny.

It was just a NightWing dragonet.

She stared right at him for a startled moment, and

then he shrugged and turned away – but at the same time she yelped, "Oh my gosh, it's you!" and bolted up to him, grabbing his front talons.

"I had a vision about you," she declared grandly. He froze in the act of trying to pull his talons away. "Have you had any visions about me?"

"You did?" Starflight said, blinking. She appeared to be his own age. So if she was having visions, that meant dragonets *did* develop their powers before they were full-grown. Which meant Starflight should have *something* by now.

But he didn't. Whenever he tried to read minds or see the future, it was like staring into the night sky – empty and cold and meaningless.

He hadn't admitted that to Morrowseer yet.

Speaking of whom – the floor now trembled ominously as the older NightWing came thundering back along the tunnel to them. His eyes nearly popped out of his skull when he saw the new dragonet.

"FATESPEAKER!" he roared so loud that Starflight thought the volcano might erupt right then. "I told you to stay in your cave with the others!"

"I know, I heard you," she said cheerfully. "But I got bored and I wanted to explore and I saw you flying by, so I thought I'd come, too. I can't believe I'm in the NightWing fortress at last! I've had lots of prophetic dreams about it, you know," she said conspiratorially to Starflight. She still had his front talons pressed between hers. "Although in those it was actually bigger and lighter and smelled way less terrible, plus it had a lot more treasure and seriously less grouchy dragons." She thought for a moment. "Hmm. Maybe they were just regular dreams."

"Fatespeaker," Morrowseer hissed. "What did I say about keeping your visions to yourself?"

"You said, 'Shut up about your visions. I'm not remotely interested,'" Fatespeaker answered. "But that doesn't mean *this* dragon isn't interested. Aren't you interested?" she said to Starflight.

He was, but he did not think it would be wise to admit that in front of Morrowseer, who had smoke rising from his nostrils. Starflight tried to study the dragonet without obviously staring.

Fatespeaker's black scales shimmered with underscales of deep blue and purple. Like Starflight's wings, hers were scattered with silver scales on the underside, so they looked like part of the night sky. But unlike his, Fatespeaker had several extra silver scales – one at the outside corner of each eye, a band circling one ankle, and a few lone ones sparkling along her tail like starry freckles.

"Anyway, I just know you're terribly important," she said to him, releasing his talons. "And that we have a great destiny together."

We do? he thought hopefully. Perhaps he was going to survive the NightWing fortress after all. *Am I actually useful in this great destiny? Are my friends there? Am I with Sunny?* He wished he could ask her questions without Morrowseer breathing furiously over their heads.

"Go back to the others," Morrowseer ordered.

"Oh, can't I come with you?" Fatespeaker asked. She gave Morrowseer a pleading look. "I foresee that I'll be *really helpful* with whatever you're about to do! Also that I'll find it totally interesting!"

"I – don't think that counts as foreseeing," Starflight said. "It sounds more like guessing."

Morrowseer growled deep in his throat. "Very well. Keep your mouth shut and don't get in the way."

"As if I would!" Fatespeaker said happily, immediately tripping Starflight with her tail.

Morrowseer stomped away, muttering. Fatespeaker gave Starflight an enormous smile that reminded him of Sunny. He wondered if Sunny missed him, and whether she felt anything like the ache that filled his chest whenever he thought of her.

"Oh my, sad face," Fatespeaker said, nudging Starflight's wing as they walked. "Cheer up. What's your name?"

"That wasn't in your vision?" Starflight tilted his head curiously. He'd always wondered how much detail the visions had. The prophecy Morrowseer had delivered years

60

ago was remarkably cryptic, but perhaps there was more information in the seer's head that he hadn't shared.

"Um. . ." Fatespeaker wobbled her head back and forth, squinting thoughtfully at him. "Oh, of course – Bigtoes!"

"What?" Starflight glanced down at his talons, a little offended. "No, no. It's Starflight."

"Oh," she said. "Are you sure?"

"Quite sure."

She shrugged. "Well, I was close. Hi, Starflight! I'm Fatespeaker. You're probably wondering why you've never seen me before."

Starflight paused midstep and frowned at her. "Am I?"

"It's because I didn't grow up here," she carried on blithely without noticing his reaction. Morrowseer's growl echoed down the corridor and they both started walking faster. "I only got to the island yesterday. I know this is going to sound crazy, but I was raised by the Talons of Peace!"

Starflight walked straight into a chandelier. He staggered back, his head spinning.

"Oh, ouch," Fatespeaker said. She patted his shoulder gingerly. "That looked painful. Anyway, so it turns out I'm part of that big dragonet prophecy everyone is so excited about. Can you believe it?"

No, Starflight thought.

"I'm the 'wings of night'," she said proudly. "Morrowseer

says it's up to me to stop the war. For some reason he seems kind of grumpy about that."

Starflight felt all his hope flicker and go out. He'd been praying quietly that maybe this was another NightWing intervention to point him in the right direction. He'd hoped perhaps he'd be given another lecture and then sent back to his friends.

But apparently Fierceteeth was right: he was here because he'd failed.

And Fatespeaker was his replacement.

CHAPTER 5

It made sense. Fatespeaker had powers and Starflight did not. He'd failed to follow Morrowseer's orders more than once. He was a useless NightWing and a useless dragonet of destiny.

"Wow," Fatespeaker said, finally noticing his expression. "You look like someone just ate your only walrus. Are you all right?"

"I—" Starflight began. "I just thought—"

They came around a bend in the tunnel and nearly stepped on Morrowseer's tail. He gave them a glare that shut Starflight up in a hurry.

Fatespeaker, however, was undaunted.

"LABS," she read off the door in front of them. "Oooo, what does that mean?"

"It means *don't touch anything*," Morrowseer said grimly. "We are here so Starflight can meet his father. If we're very unlucky, he'll have time to give us a tour of all the experiments he's working on." He hissed. "Let's get this over with."

The door swung open to reveal a huge room, more brightly lit and cleanly kept than any other part of the fortress that Starflight had seen. They were standing on a balcony; there was a level above them and a level below them, and a criss-crossing network of strange pipes stretching across the space in front of them.

"No, no!" cried a voice. A whip-thin black dragon shot down from the top level and hovered in front of them. He wore an odd helmet over his whole head, with only a few small holes poked in it for him to see out – rather like the queen's council screen, Starflight thought. "I must not be interrupted! This experiment is at a critical juncture! And Greatness says I might be shut down at any moment! Everyone please leave!" He flapped his wings and front talons at them.

"Mastermind," Morrowseer said coolly. "It seems you were right all along. The dragonet from Farsight's egg is apparently your son, and he's here now, so I've brought him to meet you."

Starflight tensed, expecting the other dragon to shrug and shoo them away.

But instead Mastermind reached up and removed his helmet, revealing a snout pockmarked with little scars and curious bloodshot eyes.

"My son?" he said, and Starflight felt a happy shiver at the tone of wonder in his voice. Mastermind landed on the balcony beside them, set his helmet on the floor, and took Starflight's shoulders in his talons. "Three moons," he said. "What a handsome dragonet. He does look like me; I knew he would. As I suspected, this jawline is genetically dominant." He gestured to the same spot on himself and on Starflight. "Ah, and yes, see the way the star scales on our wings spray outward, like a splash of water, whereas Morrowseer's, for instance, curl inward, more like a snail shell." He flared one of his wings and then reached for Morrowseer's, but the larger NightWing batted him away with a snarl. "All theories at this point, of course," Mastermind said, and Starflight found himself smiling back at his father's toothy grin. "A larger data set would naturally be essential for proving anything, but one is much better than none; entirely wonderful, in fact, especially compared to most of the rest of the tribe. Including yourself, right, Morrowseer? No dragonets as yet?"

Morrowseer's face indicated he did not intend to dignify that with a response.

"But *I* have a son," Mastermind said proudly. "I, of all dragons! Let's see Strongwings laugh now! Just wait until everyone sees my handsome offspring." He clapped Starflight's shoulder again. "So strong and healthy! You can be the assistant I've been looking for. What are you interested in, son?"

Son. Starflight's knees felt as if they might not hold him up very well for much longer.

"Um, everything," he stammered. "Scrolls. I like scrolls."

"Fantastic!" Mastermind said. "I have lots of scrolls. How about desalinization? Know anything about it?"

Starflight perked up. "A little – taking the salt out of seawater to make it potable, right?"

"Potable?" Fatespeaker interjected. She was watching them with wide, startled eyes, and Starflight remembered that she didn't know yet that he'd been raised away from the island, too.

"Drinkable," Starflight explained. "Is that what those pipes are for?"

"Very good," said Mastermind, waving his talons excitedly. "We have only one freshwater source on the island, and it's become rather contaminated with ash over the last few years, so I invented this magnificent contraption to provide safe water for the entire tribe. . ."

He talked on and on, pointing to the various pipes and explaining the science behind the process. Starflight listened with fascination. He'd never met a dragon who seemed so full of information – like a walking library of scrolls.

"Come, come," Mastermind said eagerly, gathering his helmet and leaping off the balcony. "I'll show you what else I'm working on."

Starflight glanced at Morrowseer for permission, and the large NightWing rolled his eyes and sat down with a yawn. Fatespeaker didn't wait to be invited; she flew behind them as Mastermind led the way down to the bottom level.

"Here is where I do all my vulcanology," he said, striding between tables laden with cauldrons of lava and steaming holes dug right into the ground. "I'm testing for materials that can withstand eruptions, and working on scale models of barriers, and outlining possible implementation systems. No wonder I need an assistant, right?"

"This place is pretty cool," Fatespeaker said, glancing around at the volcano experiments.

"It's amazing," Starflight said. He peered down at the smoke issuing from a deep hole. He wanted to study each section of the lab in careful detail. There was a strange contraption in the corner that looked as if it was designed to fit entirely around a dragon and then be filled with something – water, maybe? He couldn't even imagine. He already had a million questions and a couple of ideas about lava that might be worth testing, if his dad didn't mind some suggestions.

Mastermind flicked his tail at a corner of the lab where tiny versions of the mountain had been constructed with little fortresses stuck on the side. Several of them were already smouldering ruins. "Not going well, as you can see!" He laughed a little, almost nervously. "Queen Battlewinner isn't pleased about that. Of course, she has her own ideas about where I should be focusing my attention. Come, come!"

He lifted off towards the top level. Starflight took

one more look around, wondering what could be more interesting or important than protecting the tribe from the volcano. *I wonder if he's done any research on NightWings infecting the prey they bite. Maybe I could help him study it.*

He shook himself, blinking. *Sounds like I'm planning to stay.* He glanced at Fatespeaker, then quickly away at one of the smoking jars of lava. *I might not have any choice about that. But – they have to let me see Sunny again. If I'm trapped here for ever, without her, without even a chance to say good-bye—*

"Come on!" Fatespeaker interrupted his thoughts, tugging him into the air.

They hurried after Mastermind and discovered that the third level was another balcony with several doors ranged around it, each one marked with three or four different symbols.

Starflight's father stopped in front of one door and rubbed his front talons together. "About a year ago, we discovered a truly, truly astonishing natural phenomenon. You won't know about this. The Talons of Peace have no idea; none of the other tribes do. Our understanding of this biological anomaly is as yet so new and incomplete that we haven't even put it in any scrolls – certainly not the ones we distribute on the mainland, but also not even the ones that are For NightWing Eyes Only. I'm preparing a treatise on the subject, but there's still so much to learn that I have no idea when I'll think it's ready for publication.

"You see," he said, leaning towards them, "it turns out one tribe of dragons has evolved an unusual defence mechanism. They can shoot *venom* from their *fangs* – deadly, toxic venom that essentially melts any animal or plant matter it comes in contact with. And you'll never believe which tribe!" He didn't wait for them to guess. "*RainWings!*"

"RainWings!" Fatespeaker echoed in a surprised voice. Starflight's heart was sinking. He suddenly had a feeling he really did not want to see what was behind these doors.

"Let's see – we'll start here," Mastermind said. He opened one of the doors to reveal a long, narrow stone room. A set of silver shackles with very short chains was bolted to the floor near the entrance. And all along the length of the room, black marks scarred the floor and walls, with indecipherable notes scribbled beside each one in chalk.

Starflight stared at the shackles, feeling ill.

Mastermind hopped down the room, avoiding the black patches, although they all seemed to be hardened and harmless, like old lava. "This was one of our first questions, naturally, when we first learned that RainWings could shoot venom. How far? Was it a short-range weapon or a long-range weapon? Would we be able to approach and incapacitate them if we developed projectiles that could be fired from a safe distance?"

He stopped at the far end of the room and indicated a mark on the floor. "This is as far as I've seen any one dragon shoot. An older male RainWing, so my hypothesis is that it's a skill that gets stronger as they age." He rubbed the horns on his head, frowning in thought. "I wonder if they have any elderly dragons we could bring over and test."

"Bring over," Starflight thought bitterly. *As if they're invited guests instead of abducted prisoners.*

Fatespeaker was eyeing the shackles nervously, too. She looked as if she didn't know quite how to ask about them.

"The next obvious question is: what materials *aren't* affected by the venom? Anything we could use as armour or a shield?" Mastermind went on, hopping back up the room towards them. "Come, come!" He ushered them out and over to the next door. "We had to devise ways to study the dragons without placing ourselves in danger, naturally. Very few RainWings have ever deliberately tried to shoot their venom at us, but it goes very badly when they do – it's quite horrifying, really."

He opened the door and swept his talon towards the tables inside. Items of different shapes, sizes and materials were arranged in related groups. One table contained a gathering of sad little plants in pots, drooping yellow flowers dripping with black. Another was all rocks. And a third – Starflight looked away quickly when he realized that the trays all contained remains of living things:

sloths, lizards, fish – that hadn't survived the experimental process.

"Ew!" Fatespeaker cried.

"We've tested it on everything," Mastermind said proudly. "Turns out it doesn't affect metal, so." He banged on his helmet, which gave out a muffled *clang* in response. "But anything alive, plant or animal, it just destroys. If it gets in your eyes or your bloodstream, you're dead within minutes. If it only hits your scales, you'll wish you were. We have a couple of recent victims I'll be getting to study as soon as they're released from the healers." He rubbed his talons together again. "If you're lucky I'll let you take a peek," he said to Starflight. "A once-in-a-lifetime opportunity to see what RainWing venom can do."

"I know what it can do," Starflight choked out. "I've seen it kill two dragons." *Possibly three, if Queen Scarlet is dead.*

He thought of Fjord, the first dragon Glory's venom had killed – the IceWing who had been about to kill Clay in the arena. Some of the poison had landed on the open wounds on Fjord's neck; that must have been why it killed him so quickly. And Crocodile, the MudWing who had betrayed the Talons of Peace and led the enemy right to the Summer Palace – when Glory killed her so they could escape, her venom had gone right into the dragon's eyes.

But Queen Scarlet. . . He shifted uneasily. If he

remembered right, Glory's spray of venom had landed on the side of the queen's face. So she really might still be alive. Alive and looking like Vengeance, which didn't bode well for the dragonets.

Mastermind stared at him avidly. "*Two* dragons? *Killed* them? Are you sure? How incredibly careless; we haven't picked up any RainWings with that little control yet."

"It wasn't careless. It was on purpose," Starflight said, annoyed on Glory's behalf.

Fatespeaker sucked in an astonished breath.

"Well, I never – are you sure?" His father's wings flared. He looked equal parts alarmed and enthralled. "That changes things entirely! A variable I hadn't considered! You'll have to tell me all about it. What prompted the attack, what it looked like, how long it took the victims to die, whether there was any time to fight back—"

Starflight realized, too late, that he shouldn't have said anything. If this information got back to the council, they'd know how dangerous Glory was. He had to hope that Mastermind was too wrapped up in his experiments to tell anyone.

"My, my, my." Mastermind headed towards the next door. "Well, knowing the venom only worked on certain substances led us to the next project: constructing armour that could withstand a RainWing attack, if necessary."

"But it isn't necessary," Fatespeaker chimed in. "RainWings

don't attack other dragons. Everyone knows that." She looked at Starflight. "Well . . . they're not *supposed* to."

"Even a RainWing will defend herself sometimes," Starflight said.

"Hmm. Not often, in my experience," said Mastermind. "But why don't you stand back just in case." He waved them a few steps away, settled his helmet over his head again, and flung open the door.

Inside, a dragon was pinned to the wall.

CHAPTER 6

Starflight was lucky his stomach was empty; it heaved perilously, and he had to cover his eyes and take a few deep breaths before he could speak again.

The RainWing was the sad grey colour of the chains that had bound Starflight in the Sky Kingdom, the first time he'd been separated from Sunny. She drooped against the wall, her wings outstretched and secured in place. When he was able to look again, he saw that what he'd thought were pins were actually clamps, holding her where she was, but not going straight through her wings as he'd first thought.

Not that anything about this is all right.

"What are you doing to her?" Fatespeaker cried. She bolted into the room and lifted the RainWing's snout gently in her talons. The trapped dragon barely responded.

"This one is done for the day," Mastermind said. "We were testing to see whether they run out of venom at some point, if they shoot it for long enough, but she fainted before we could get any really useful data."

"She needs water," Fatespeaker said, glancing around the room, then looking straight at Starflight.

He hesitated, remembering Fjord and Crocodile again. If this dragon did suddenly spray venom at them, he wouldn't blame her – but he didn't want to be in the way when it happened.

"Starflight," Fatespeaker said, and the tone of her voice reminded him again so much of Sunny that he couldn't say no to her.

"I'll get some." He flew to one of the pipes on the desalinization machine, where he'd seen a faucet earlier, found an empty cauldron that smelled clean, and filled it up.

Fatespeaker had one of the prisoner's wings unclamped by the time Starflight got back. Mastermind stood in the doorway, watching through the holes in his helmet but neither interfering nor helping. It was hard to know what he was thinking with his face completely hidden.

Starflight brushed past him and set the cauldron down, then unclamped the dragon's other wing. She slumped forward so suddenly that both Fatespeaker and Starflight were nearly knocked over, but they managed to catch her and lean her wings over their shoulders. Fatespeaker held the cauldron up and the RainWing revived enough to drink a little.

"What's your name?" Starflight asked her.

She coughed and looked sideways at him. "No NightWing has ever asked my name before," she whispered hoarsely. "It's Orchid."

"Oh!" Starflight gasped, then closed his mouth quickly and glanced at the door.

Mastermind was leaning into the hallway, yelling, "Strongwings! Strongwings, you blockhead, get up here!"

"Mangrove is looking for you," Starflight whispered hurriedly. "He hasn't given up. He'll be here to rescue you soon."

Fatespeaker stared at him as if he'd just peeled off his scales and revealed a hippo underneath. But Orchid lifted her head, her eyes flooding with hope. A shimmering rose pink spread over her, starting on her chest and drifting out to her wingtips.

"Soon," she said softly. "Then I can hang on until he comes."

I hope it'll be soon, Starflight thought. *I hope he doesn't die on his way here. I hope Glory survives, too. I hope my friends are planning to rescue me as well.*

Fatespeaker's expression was ten kinds of confused. She tilted her head as if she was listening, and Starflight realized with a jolt of panic that he'd been having several unguarded thoughts since they'd started this part of the tour. He'd forgotten – *how could I forget?* – to worry about having his mind read.

But his father hadn't reacted to any of his thoughts; Mastermind looked as pleased as ever. *Not a mind reader, then, perhaps. Maybe those kinds of powers aren't "genetically dominant" in us. Maybe it is enough just to be smart like him.*

He'd always thought all NightWings could read minds

and all NightWings could see the future. That's what it sounded like in the scrolls he'd read. But Glory thought maybe it was only some of them, and perhaps she was right. *Maybe I'm not completely defective.*

"Three moons!" Mastermind barked from the doorway. "How did you turn her that pink colour? I've never seen any of them look like that before."

That's because it's the colour of happiness, and there's no happiness on this twisted island.

Starflight met Fatespeaker's eyes.

"I think she's just grateful for the water," Fatespeaker said, blinking at him. He didn't have to read minds to guess she was thinking, *We'll be talking about* this *later.*

"Fascinating." Mastermind came over and prodded the scales on Orchid's neck with one claw. She closed her eyes. Her colour didn't change. "Utterly fascinating."

A burly NightWing slouched grumpily in from the balcony. Half a lizard hung from one corner of his mouth, and his shoulders were almost too wide for his wings to fit through the door.

"What?" he mumbled, chewing.

"This one can go back," said Mastermind. "Oh, and Strongwings, guess what? *This* is my *son*." He waved gleefully at Starflight. Starflight wished he could go back half an hour in time, to when he'd been just as happy about those words as Mastermind was.

Strongwings gave Starflight a dubious look. "Heh," he said. "All right. So when do I get a helmet like that?" He nodded at the thing on Mastermind's head.

"This is just a prototype," Mastermind said. He turned to Starflight. "As you can imagine, the hardest part of creating venom-resistant armour is coming up with a solution that protects the eyes but still allows one to *see*. I'd love to hear your thoughts, because I must admit I'm stymied. This is a thoroughly imperfect solution." He tapped on the helmet with his talons. "Peripheral vision is negligible at best, and of course, venom could still splash through the holes if one were unlucky." He shook his head. "There must be a more ingenious approach."

"Whatever," Strongwings grumped. "Where's her band?"

Mastermind waved at the corner, and the muscular NightWing picked up a heap of metal and one of the spears. He brought it over and fitted a kind of muzzle around Orchid's mouth, twisting the lock into place with a practised flick of the spear tips. Then he shooed Starflight and Fatespeaker aside, snapped a chain around the RainWing's neck, and gave it a yank. Without protesting, Orchid followed him out of the room.

"But why are you doing this?" Starflight blurted. "Why study their venom at all?"

Mastermind pulled off the helmet and gave him a

confused look. "It's science! We're expanding dragon knowledge!"

"There's got to be more to it than that," Starflight said. "Why is this so important? Why do you *need* venom-resistant armour? The RainWings would never have bothered you if you left them alone."

His father shrugged. "The queen has her reasons, I have mine. I don't get involved in her plans. For me, scientific discovery is reason enough."

Starflight looked at the clamps on the wall, then down at the floor, too sickened to ask any more questions.

"Well, I wish I had time to show you more," Mastermind said, setting his helmet up on a shelf. "But my daily scheduled meeting with the queen is upon me."

"Do *you* get to see her?" Starflight asked.

"No, no," said Mastermind. "Three moons, no. No one *sees* the queen. Not for the last nine years or so. She's very private."

Really, Starflight thought.

"I wish I had some more progress to report," Mastermind mused. "But telling her about you will certainly be a triumph. Come back tomorrow and we can get to know each other better, yes?" He wrapped his wings around Starflight and hugged him, not waiting for an answer. "It was fantastic to meet you, son. I am so very proud."

He ushered them out the door and locked it, then

slid away towards a tunnel at the far end of the balcony. Starflight glanced along the row of doors, imagining tortured RainWings behind each one.

"Wow," Fatespeaker said. "So. Turns out we might be *horrible*. I did *not* foresee that at all."

Starflight sat down, his shoulders slumping. "I believed everything I read – about NightWings being so noble and brilliant and perfect. This . . . I can't understand this."

"So where have you been?" she asked curiously. "You're not like them. And who's Mangrove?"

"I was raised by the Talons of Peace, too," he said, hoping he could avoid the Mangrove question by distracting her. "Actually, I'm the one in the prophecy. Or I was. I guess I'm expendable, since they're replacing me with you."

"What?" She took a step back, fluttering her wings. "Wait, I never saw you. I lived right in the Talons of Peace camp."

"We were kept hidden," Starflight explained. "Under a mountain. No one was supposed to find us."

"There you are." Morrowseer landed beside them with a *thump*. "If you're quite finished with your little chat, there are other pressing matters we could attend to."

"*I'm* not finished," Fatespeaker said, whirling towards him. "He's all special and chosen, too! How can we both be in the prophecy?"

"Only one of you will be," said Morrowseer. "But that's why you're both here. So that we can decide which one."

So there's still a chance, Starflight thought.

"Don't you know? Didn't you deliver that prophecy?" Fatespeaker asked, wrinkling her nose.

"Prophecies can be complicated," Morrowseer said coldly.

"Oooo," Fatespeaker said. "Good comeback. I should write that down and use it on Viper."

"The real problem," Morrowseer went on, "is that neither of you are suitable candidates whatsoever, but we have no other dragonets of the right age we could use, so it must be one of you." He growled. "We apparently made a grave error allowing you to be raised outside the tribe, where we thought you'd be safe from – well, just in case. It has always been our assumption that NightWing superiority is something every NightWing is hatched with."

He looked down his nose at the two dragonets. "Evidently we were wrong."

"But why aren't I suitable?" Starflight asked. He hated the plaintive tone in his voice, but he couldn't seem to quash it. "What have I done?"

"You have no leadership qualities," Morrowseer said. "You make NightWings look like cowards and followers. And you antagonized our ally."

"Blister?" Starflight said, uncomfortably remembering his interaction with her in the Kingdom of the Sea. He'd tried to find reasons to support her as the next SandWing queen – really, he'd tried – but she was too manipulative and too untrustworthy. And he didn't like the way she'd looked at Sunny, as if the little dragonet would make an excellent snack.

"You have placed our whole plan in jeopardy," Morrowseer said.

"*What* plan?" Starflight cried. "How am I supposed to make anything happen when I don't even know what you really want?"

To his surprise, Morrowseer actually paused and thought about that.

"No," he rumbled finally. "Dragonets can't be trusted with secrets. Perhaps if you are the one chosen, we can reveal more. But all you should really need to know is how to follow orders." He scowled. "Now come."

Morrowseer swept away, lashing his tail.

Starflight and Fatespeaker exchanged glances. "Have your visions given you any hints?" Starflight asked. "About whatever their secret plan is, I mean?"

She scratched her neck, the anklet of silver scales glittering as she moved. "Let me think." She closed her eyes for a moment, then opened them again. "Oh, absolutely! It involves us! But both of us! And we're going to be heroes and the whole tribe will help us stop the war and maybe they'll even make us king and queen."

Startled, he blinked at her. King and queen? But he couldn't – she wasn't – well, she wasn't Sunny. And he'd been in love with one dragon his whole life.

"MOVE NOW OR I WILL KILL YOU BOTH, PROPHECY OR NO PROPHECY," Morrowseer bellowed from the tunnel.

The dragonets scrambled up and hurried after him, tripping over each other. Fatespeaker bounded into the lead, and Starflight was left trailing behind, his mind a whirl of confusion.

He didn't want to think about a possible future as Fatespeaker's king, so he focused on his father's experiments instead. *Why are they torturing the RainWings? I can figure this out. Think, Starflight, think.*

His first guess was that the NightWings wanted to use RainWing venom themselves. As Vengeance had said, it was one of the most powerful weapons in Pyrrhia. If they could somehow replicate the venom or adapt it for their own purposes, that plus their telepathy and precognition would make the NightWings unstoppable.

Maybe their secret plan involved joining the war once they had this new kind of weapon for themselves. Starflight already knew they'd chosen a side – Blister's – although why her, and why they were thinking of fighting the war now, eighteen years into it, he couldn't figure out.

Perhaps Blister had promised them something, the way Blaze was giving up territory to the IceWings in exchange for their help.

Territory.

Starflight stopped in the middle of the rocky tunnel as understanding flooded over him.

That's what they need. More than anything, the NightWings need a new home.

The volcano was extremely dangerous – maybe it had been dormant when the tribe moved here, but it certainly wasn't any more. The NightWings were living under its threat every day. And the island *was* a horrible place to live. They must be running out of prey, with hardly any freshwater to drink, no view of the sky through the thick cloud cover, and nowhere to go except through the tunnel to the rainforest.

The rainforest, which was the opposite of here: the perfect place to live.

That's their plan. Starflight clutched his head. Why hadn't he figured it out sooner? The NightWings weren't trying to reproduce the venom – Mastermind's experiments were all about how to defend against it. Because the NightWings were planning to invade the rainforest and steal it from the RainWings. But they were afraid of the

RainWings fighting back. Even the famously peaceful tribe would surely have to defend their home.

So the NightWings were figuring out how to protect themselves from RainWing venom, in preparation for the day when they stormed into the rainforest and took it over for themselves.

Is that what Blister has promised them? The tunnel from the rainforest to the Kingdom of Sand. . . *That's for a SandWing army, once she is queen, so they can come through and help the NightWings fight the RainWings, if need be.*

The RainWings were in awful danger. This wasn't a matter of a few dragons disappearing here or there. *Glory was right, and Queen Magnificent was wrong. They have to fight back, or soon they'll all be dead.*

And I'm the only one who knows.

But he was just Starflight, the weakest, most cowardly dragon ever chosen for a prophecy. How could he save the RainWings? How could he stop his own tribe from destroying them?

Fatespeaker came charging back down the tunnel.

"I keep thinking he can't get any more grumpy, and then he DOES," she said. "Come on, hurry up! He says you have to meet the others, in case you're the dragonet in the prophecy instead of me." She waved her talons in front of his face. "Wake up, dreamy face."

Starflight shook himself as hard as he could. "Coming," he said, although he felt like he could barely string words together.

Maybe I'm wrong. But he knew he wasn't. All the pieces fit together too well.

I've figured out the NightWings' secret plan, he thought. *But now . . . what do I do about it?*

PART TWO
THE QUEEN'S SECRET

CHAPTER 7

Others.

What Fatespeaker had said didn't sink in until Starflight was actually standing in the cave a short flight from the fortress, facing four unfamiliar and unfriendly faces. Red, green, brown and white-gold.

They have a SkyWing, Starflight thought. *And a SandWing who looks like a real SandWing.* He hadn't met many SandWings in his life, but this one's scowl and restless hostility made her look like the opposite of Sunny.

"The alternate dragonets of destiny," Morrowseer growled, scanning them with a displeased expression.

"Who is that?" said the emerald-green SeaWing, squinting at Starflight. "Looks like *her*. Is he going to be annoying like her?" He jerked his head at Fatespeaker.

"This is Starflight. Starflight, these are my friends," Fatespeaker said, blithely ignoring him. The SkyWing snorted and the SandWing rolled her eyes. "Over there is Flame, the SkyWing, obviously. The fat MudWing is Ochre, the SandWing with the sour expression is Viper, and the shrimpy SeaWing is Squid."

"Did she get in trouble?" Squid asked Morrowseer. "I

told her she'd get in trouble if she left the cave. I hope you thumped her."

"Where have you been?" Viper demanded at the same time, jabbing her poisonous tail towards Morrowseer. "We've been here for a whole day and a half and no one has checked on us or fed us anything but what appears to be leftovers from a meal three months ago."

"Most of which he threw up," Flame said darkly, pointing at Ochre.

"It was awful," Ochre said. "Probably food poisoning. You're lucky I'm still alive."

"Quite lucky," agreed Flame. "Since I was extremely tempted to kill him."

"That's why it smells so bad in here," Fatespeaker offered. "Can we move to a different cave? Or, oooh, into the fortress!"

If there's a whole other set of dragonets – with all the elements that are really in the prophecy – then nobody needs us at all. Starflight's head was spinning. *But if the Talons of Peace had these all along, then why treat us the way they did? Why keep us around? And why would the NightWings send an assassin after us?*

Pieces started to fall into place in his head. *They wanted us dead so they could replace us with these five. It wouldn't do to have two sets of dragonets running around claiming destiny.* Then he thought about the timing, and a shudder ran through his scales. *We had a chance until we angered Blister – until I angered her. It was after that when they decided to kill us. Because I failed to convince the others to pick her as the queen.*

Morrowseer was watching his face intently, as if he might be listening to the thoughts running through Starflight's mind.

"So Deathbringer was coming for all of us," Starflight said to him.

"His primary target was the RainWing," said Morrowseer. "Secondary, the SeaWing. The rest of you are still negotiable."

Starflight shook his head. "You can't kill Glory and Tsunami. I – I won't do anything you say if that happens." His talons trembled as if the volcano were rumbling under his feet. He half expected Morrowseer to slash his throat right then.

"We'll see," said Morrowseer. He didn't look very worried.

"Your real problem is that my friends are never going to let you replace me," Fatespeaker said to Morrowseer. "We were raised together! We're loyal to each other! They'll fight back if you try to take me out and put someone else in!"

"Replace her?" Viper said alertly. "We can do that?"

"Do it," said Flame. "I vote yes."

"Me too," said Ochre. "He looks quiet. Quiet would be *great*."

"Can I be the one to shove her off the cliff?" Squid asked.

Fatespeaker gave them all an injured look. "Very funny, guys."

Starflight got the distinct impression that they weren't joking. *Poor Fatespeaker,* he thought. *She really thinks they're her friends.*

"Do you have annoying visions all the time, too?" Squid asked Starflight.

Starflight shuffled his talons awkwardly, but Morrowseer cut him off before he had to answer.

"You may *all* be 'replaced'," he said as if the word tasted disagreeable in his mouth. "Except for you." He nodded at Flame.

The SkyWing dragonet puffed out his chest. "Ha. And don't you all forget it."

Viper hissed at him. "Then why'd you bring us here?" she asked Morrowseer.

"And when can we go back?" Squid asked.

Morrowseer frowned at Squid. Starflight could sense that he found the SeaWing unusually irritating. He wondered if that meant the NightWings might change their minds about Tsunami. If they kept her alive, they wouldn't have to deal with this dragon as the alternative.

Then again, Tsunami could be pretty unusually irritating, too.

Too bad it didn't work out more neatly for Morrowseer,

Starflight thought with a twinge of satisfaction. *Two unsuitable NightWings. Two annoying SeaWings. But two perfectly fine MudWings and SandWings.*

He thought Sunny was more than perfectly fine, of course. Who needed a poisonous tail when she was funny, smart and kinder than any other dragon in the world?

"If you want to be part of this, what I need to see from all of you," Morrowseer growled, "is that you can take orders, work together and do as you're told."

"'Take orders' and 'do as you're told' are the same thing," Fatespeaker said to him.

He glared at her. "That's how important it is." His dark eyes scanned the dragonets in front of him. "So. Your first test. You," he said to Starflight. "All you have to do, if you can, is stay alive."

"What?" Starflight said.

"The rest of you," said Morrowseer. "Kill him." He flicked his tail at Starflight.

The dragonets all stared at him for a long, awful moment.

"Can't we kill her instead?" Viper asked, pointing at Fatespeaker.

"Oooo, yes. I volunteer," said Flame.

"No," Morrowseer nearly shouted. "What are you waiting for? That was an order! I said kill him!"

He's serious, Starflight realized. And then Viper lunged

at him, her poisonous tail arching forward like a scorpion's. On his other side, Ochre's claws slashed at his wing, missing by a hair. And Flame made the fire-is-coming hissing sound Starflight remembered from his terrible training sessions with Kestrel.

Morrowseer was probably hoping to see Starflight's fighting skills in action, but Starflight didn't care. He knew better than to rely on those. He also knew he couldn't do what he normally did, which was freeze and hope nobody noticed him.

Starflight ducked under Ochre's wing, shoved Squid into Viper, dodged around Fatespeaker, and leaped out of the cave.

Wind whistled through his wings as he sailed down the cliff. The shouts of the dragonets echoed behind him. He knew they'd be right on his tail.

He had to find somewhere to hide.

CHAPTER 8

Starflight shot down the cliffside and banked towards the ocean. His eyes scanned the ground below him frantically.

The good news was, if he'd understood them right, the dragonets hadn't been on the island very long and probably didn't know its geography at all.

The bad news was, neither did he.

Right now he was on the other side of the volcano from the forest. Here, there were no trees. Everything below him was dark rocks or rivers of glowing lava – nothing to hide behind.

Ahead of him there was a strip of black-sand beach that seemed to circle the island. He remembered Glory saying that the tunnel to the rainforest was in a cave above a black-sand beach.

He wondered for a moment if he could find it, but there wasn't time with the dragonets coming after him. He couldn't outfly them for long either – Flame, like most SkyWings, had enormous wings, which made them faster than dragons from any other tribe.

He risked a glance over his shoulder and saw the bright

colours of four dragonets flash through the sky, much closer than he would have liked.

Only four.

Fatespeaker was nowhere to be seen.

Disobeying orders? Or sneaking up on me some other way?

He didn't have time to think about it. Starflight twisted into a dive and swooped as close to the ground as he dared. His black scales would make him harder to see against the rocks than if he were up in the sky.

A blast of steam shot out of one of the vents in the ground and he flapped hastily aside, barely avoiding the heat. From this close, the rocks below looked even more like black dragon scales, but all melted and fused together. *Like mine will be if Flame and Viper get their claws on me.*

The problem was, the dragonets were so close behind him that they'd see anything he did. They'd be able to follow him straight to any hiding place. It was too risky to try to lose them in the water or the clouds, not with a SeaWing and a SkyWing among them.

He beat his wings faster, trying to think. *Use your brain, Starflight. That's all you've got.*

There was only one place to hide: the fortress. Maybe he'd find a room he could lock himself into, or maybe his father would help him. He swooped into an arc, heading towards it, hoping the dragonets wouldn't cut him off before he reached it.

Another blaze of heat brushed his tail, and he twisted to see where the steam had come from this time.

To his horror, Flame was only a few wingbeats behind him, with fire curling out of his nose.

The sight of the SkyWing propelled Starflight forward, the dragonet beating his wings as hard as he could. But his muscles already ached with exhaustion, and he knew he'd never make it to the fortress before Flame caught up.

Then he spotted the caves that lined the lava river below.

The RainWing prisons! Glory had described hers in vivid detail.

Suddenly a blast of thick smoke shot out of a vent in the ground below him. This was a chance he couldn't miss.

He dropped behind the smoke, hoping it looked as though he was still aiming for the fortress, and then spiralled tightly down and dived into the first cave he found.

A NightWing guard was lying across the entrance. Starflight shot over her head and tumbled on to the stone floor. The guard sat up in a hurry, blinking as if she'd been asleep. Further into the cave, Starflight heard scales shifting as the imprisoned RainWing peeked out at the commotion.

"Hey!" said the guard. "What are you doing here?" She lashed her tail, looking very large all of a sudden, despite the ribs visible through her underscales. Starflight staggered up to his feet again, trying to look calm and ordinary and like he wasn't being chased.

"I – I – I came to see the RainWing," Starflight stammered.

"The prisoner?" The guard frowned suspiciously. "Why?"

"Um. . ." Starflight flipped through scrolls in his head as fast as he could. There were a few stories about dragonets in his favourite scroll, *Tales of the NightWings*. This couldn't possibly work, but – "School project?" he tried.

To his astonishment, the guard completely relaxed. "Ah," she said. "Assignment from Mastermind, right? That weirdo is all about 'field studies' and 'live observation'. Drives my daughter crazy. All right, go ahead, just be careful."

Starflight bowed gratefully and fled towards the back of the cave.

The RainWing prisoner was chained to the floor and the wall, and his snout was wrapped in an iron band like the one Strongwings had put on Orchid. He watched Starflight

98

with a resigned, mournful expression. His scales were grey and dark blue.

Starflight wondered if extra chains had been added to all the dragons after Glory and Kinkajou escaped; as far as he remembered, Glory had been muzzled but not chained to the wall. He was tempted to tell the sad RainWing that he would be rescued soon, too, but it was dangerous enough that he'd told Orchid. He had no idea whether RainWings could keep secrets, and if the NightWings found out that he'd been going around saying reassuring things to their prisoners . . . well, he couldn't imagine they'd like it very much.

A commotion of wings sounded outside. Starflight turned to the back of the cave, which overlooked a huge, dark abyss. Glory had said that all the prison caves were connected by this chasm, which was how Kinkajou got from one to the other.

The last thing Starflight wanted to do was jump into that darkness. Well, no. The very last thing he wanted to do was face Flame and Viper in talon-to-talon combat, so, given those choices, leaping off a cliff into the pitch-black was the clear winner.

He spread his wings and hopped off the edge, flapping to lower himself down slowly. He kept thinking he was about to crash into something sharp and pointy, but only empty space yawned below him, as if it were trying to suck him down.

Finally, several dragon lengths down from the top, he felt a shallow ledge below him and gently rested his talons on it, folding his wings in. Even if someone peered into the chasm, his black scales should keep him well hidden in the shadows.

Voices started shouting up above.

"Where is he?" That sounded like Flame.

"Who are you?" roared the NightWing guard. "Intruders! A SkyWing! And a MudWing! They've come back for the rest of our prisoners!" She started banging on some kind of metal alarm gong that reverberated painfully off the rocks around Starflight.

He covered his ears, but even over all the noise he could still hear Flame bellowing, "No! We're supposed to be here!"

And Ochre: "We're with Morrowseer!"

"We're trying to kill a NightWing dragonet!" Flame shouted. "Did you see where he went?"

Wow, that was the wrong thing to say, Starflight thought.

"THEY'RE HERE TO KILL OUR DRAGONETS!" shrieked the NightWing guard.

An almighty crash followed, as if she'd smashed the gong over Flame's head. Starflight hoped she had. Every time he thought of the SkyWing's smug face, he thought of how Flame was meant to take Glory's place in the prophecy.

Morrowseer has been trying to have Glory killed since the first moment he saw her, he thought. *Because she's a RainWing, and he was afraid she'd figure out the plan and warn her tribe. It's not that he thinks she's weak and useless. He's actually worried about what she might do.*

As he should be.

The crashing and shouting finally ended with sounds of what appeared to be several guards arriving and carting off Flame and Ochre. Starflight hoped Viper and Squid had met a similar fate, maybe searching for him in the fortress. Just in case, he decided to stay hidden for a while longer.

I could try to escape, he thought. *Now, while no one is watching me. I could try to get back to the rainforest to warn Glory and the others. I have an idea where the tunnel is . . . but surely it's guarded, and surely they'd stop me, and even more surely, Morrowseer would be furious and most likely he'd kill me himself.*

He closed his eyes, picturing the island. *Or I could fly away across the ocean. Just pick a direction and go.* He already knew he'd never be brave enough to try that. There was no way to know where the nearest land was, or how to find the mainland from here. This island had not been on any of the maps of Pyrrhia he'd ever seen, that was for sure.

Starflight wrapped his wings around his talons, rested his head against the rock wall behind him, and sighed.

"Starflight?" a voice whispered above him.

He froze. The shadows would hide him if he kept still.

"Starflight, it's me, Fatespeaker," she called softly. He realized her voice wasn't coming from the cave he'd come through – she must be in the cave next to it, also overlooking the abyss.

"I'm pretty sure you're down there," she said. "Because it's a crazy-smart and crazy-brave thing to do, which sounds like you."

HA, Starflight thought. *Crazy-brave is the opposite of me. Crazy-brave is Tsunami. Crazy-brave would have been turning around to fight all four dragonets at once, which is what she would have done. Sitting in a dark hole? Waiting for someone else to deal with my problem? She's right about one thing: that does sound like me.*

Fatespeaker sat quietly for a moment, but he could still hear her breathing. "Of course, if you're not down there, I sound totally insane right now," she said. "There's a RainWing sitting next to me who is giving me the weirdest looks. Hey there. What's happening? Nothing weird, just talking to a pit. Carry on looking miserable, don't mind me. "Oooo, his ears went a little yellow," she reported. "Does that mean amused or terribly annoyed? What do you think?"

Amused, Starflight thought, if his very limited study of RainWing scale-shifting was any guide.

"I wish I could let you go, sad dragon," she said to the RainWing. "I'd need one of those long pointy sticks, though. Starflight, come on, get up here so we can talk about how to help all these sad dragons. I checked a few of the other caves and there are at least ten of them here, can you imagine?"

Fourteen, according to Kinkajou.

"Oh, I promise I'm not going to kill you," she added. "Is that what you're worried about? Pffft. My visions say we're going to do amazing things together. That's hardly going to happen if you're dead, right? I don't mind telling Morrowseer that *my* prophecies are just as good as *his* prophecies and *my* prophecies say you get to live *for ever, so there.*"

Starflight smiled into the dark. He would love to be present for *that* conversation.

"All right," he said. "I'm coming."

Together they flew back to the cave, where Viper and Squid were huddled sullenly against the wall and Morrowseer was pacing back and forth.

"Oh, did you lose some dragonets?" Fatespeaker said to him with mock sympathy. Morrowseer glared at her.

"It's not funny," Squid hissed. "There were about a thousand NightWing guards chasing me!"

Viper rolled her eyes. "Try four," she said.

"They nearly burned my tail! One of their spears could

have taken an eye out! And when I told them I was a dragonet of destiny, they got even *more* mad. I want to go home." Squid folded his wings and sulked. "Plus I haven't seen any sign of the treasure I was promised."

"We keep our treasure safe," Morrowseer rumbled, "instead of on ostentatious display like the other tribes." He rubbed his forehead. "Perhaps I could have done a better job of warning my tribe that you were here."

"Perhaps you could have," Viper snapped.

"The council has been told, but apparently the news hasn't spread. It's going to take some explaining to get Flame and Ochre out of the dungeon." Morrowseer tapped his claws on the rocks and tipped his head at Starflight. "A clever way to foil your attackers. Whether you intended it or not. It's not what I would have done, but it worked."

"*Now* can we kill Fatespeaker instead?" Viper asked.

"Sometimes you're just horrible," Fatespeaker said to her.

"Seems like *you* had an opportunity to kill him and didn't take it," Morrowseer said darkly.

"Look, destiny is destiny," Fatespeaker said. "I don't know why you're so worried about who's in the prophecy. You delivered it; now you can sit back and watch it happen. Whether it's me or Starflight, who cares?"

"The NightWings care," said Morrowseer. "The queen

has decreed that I should choose one of you and then kill the other."

Fatespeaker opened and closed her mouth a few times. "Really?" she finally said in a small voice. Starflight felt sorry for her. Starting with what Glory had told him in the rainforest, he'd had a few days to adjust to how different NightWings were from his expectations. Fatespeaker was getting it all thrown at her at once.

"Not today, though," said Morrowseer. "For now, I'm moving you all to the fortress so I can keep an eye on you."

He ended up dumping them in the same dormitory where Starflight had first woken up. Then, to Starflight's relief, Morrowseer stomped off to the evening council meeting without him.

"Are you sure you don't want to take me?" Fatespeaker asked him. Starflight guessed she was hoping to meet other NightWings – ones who might give her a better impression of the tribe than Morrowseer and Mastermind.

"Very sure. Stay here," Morrowseer growled at her. "And try to speak as little as possible."

She watched him leave, her wings drooping. "I was hoping to see the queen," she said to Starflight.

"You heard Mastermind. Nobody sees the queen." He shook his head. "It looked to me like she does everything through her daughter, Greatness." Which was something

105

else Starflight needed more time to think about. He suspected there was more to that story.

He wondered if he should try talking to Fatespeaker about the NightWings' plan. Maybe she'd be willing to help him stop it – he knew she felt sorry for the trapped RainWings she'd seen. But no matter how sympathetic she was, would she be willing to betray her tribe?

There was no time to talk to her anyway. As soon as Morrowseer was gone, Starflight and Fatespeaker and Viper and Squid were swarmed by the NightWing dragonets who lived in the dormitory.

"Hello!" Fatespeaker chirped. "Hi! Hi! It's so nice to meet you all!"

"Oh, so you're the other one," Fierceteeth said, sniffing her. "You don't look that great either."

"Look at all the colours!" Mindreader said, poking Squid's green wings. "Shiny!"

"Don't touch me!" he whined. "Viper! Make them stop!"

The SandWing ignored him. She brandished her tail until the NightWing dragonets got out of her way, then stormed to a sleeping spot at the farthest end of the dormitory and curled up on the stone.

Exhaustion was starting to overwhelm Starflight. He left Fatespeaker while she was introducing herself to everyone and lay down in the same place where he'd woken up a few hours before.

He missed his friends. He wanted to be eating boar with Clay, arguing with Tsunami, telling Glory about all his strange new discoveries and warning her about the NightWings. But mostly he missed Sunny. He missed her warm scales leaning against his, her green eyes watching him while he talked. He wanted to tell her about everything that had happened today – about the strange hunting habits of the NightWings, the terrifying council chamber, the mysterious behaviour of the queen, and what he'd figured out about their secret plan.

He wanted to tell her all about his father.

And the alternate dragonets.

And. . .

His eyes closed, and sleep came for him.

CHAPTER 9

Starflight was dreaming, but it wasn't so much a dream as a memory.

He was waiting by the cave entrance when Webs rolled the boulder aside and came in. His wings unfurled and he leaned forward, trying to see the guardian's claws.

"Just one this time," Webs said, untangling a scroll from the net full of fish he was carrying. He tossed it to Starflight, who caught it and turned it reverently between his talons. It was damp around the edges and smelled like fish, but he didn't care.

He carried it to the study cave and found Sunny curled in the small beam of sunlight that came through the hole in the roof. His heart skipped a beat as she opened her green eyes and smiled at him.

"A new scroll?" she said. "What's this one about?"

He sat down next to her and unrolled it carefully. "It's about us." His eyes scanned the text quickly. "Oh, weird. This must have been written recently. It's all theories about where we are and who might be part of the prophecy and how it might come true."

Sunny sat up and peered over his shoulder, her warm golden scales pressing against his. "Wow, I'd like to know all that myself."

"It says there were seventeen SeaWing dragonets who hatched on the brightest night, but only six of them were from blue eggs, and maybe it's none of them because perhaps there were other SeaWing eggs outside the Kingdom of the Sea. Like children of the Talons of Peace, it says."

"Or an egg that was stolen by the Talons," Sunny pointed out.

"Right. It doesn't mention that possibility." Starflight went quiet, reading a little further.

"Does it say anything about the SandWing egg?" she asked nervously.

"The author seems confused about that." Starflight rolled the scroll along, searching for references to SandWings. "He says if a SandWing dragonet hatched on its own in the desert somewhere, it couldn't have survived. So it must be someone's egg — maybe from the Talons of Peace again. That would explain 'hidden away from the rival queens'."

"I wish the guardians would tell us more about where our eggs came from," Sunny said with a sigh.

"Maybe I should skip ahead to the part about stopping the war," Starflight said, rolling the scroll through his talons.

"Good idea. We're taking suggestions!" she joked. "Any war-stopping tips are welcome over here."

Starflight paused on the word SkyWing. "It says something about how there aren't any SkyWings left who were hatched on the brightest night . . . what? That's weird. There must be some in the Sky Kingdom. Maybe this author doesn't know what he's talking about." He kept reading, hoping to keep Sunny close to him for as long as possible.

"We don't need a SkyWing anyway," she said. "We've got Glory. Isn't it exciting that there are dragons talking about us all over Pyrrhia?" she added dreamily. "Right now there are soldiers camped on battlefields talking about how we're the ones who'll save them from the endless fighting. There are dragonets who want their mothers and fathers to come home, and they know we're the ones who'll make it happen. We're going to make so many dragons happy, Starflight." She shifted her wings and shrugged like she was trying not to sound too dramatic. "I mean, I don't know. It's just nice to know for sure that we're here for a reason, and we're going to do something important."

Starflight liked the way Sunny thought about the prophecy. The idea of that many dragons relying on him always made Starflight feel overwhelmed and anxious. But for Sunny, the prophecy was a promise, not an order. Listening to her talk about it was comforting.

"Here," he said. "Possible ways for the dragonets to fulfil the prophecy. Um . . . all right, the first theory is that all the dragonets are royal daughters, so they'll all become queens of their tribes and stop the war that way."

Sunny smothered a giggle. "I can totally see Clay as a MudWing princess."

He grinned back. "It doesn't make sense, though, without

an IceWing — and it means you'd have to be the next SandWing queen."

"No, thank you!" Sunny said firmly. "I'm not Tsunami. I would never want to be queen."

Starflight didn't like the idea either, although the part that bothered him was the thought of Sunny being challenged by vicious SandWings who wanted to be queen in her place.

"All right, let's find the next—" he started, when suddenly a commotion of running claws sounded from the tunnel.

They both looked up as Kestrel burst into the room with Dune and Webs right behind her.

"Give me that," Kestrel snarled, snatching the scroll out of Starflight's talons. He let out a cry of dismay as it tore between their claws.

The SkyWing peered at the scroll, then whipped around to glare at Webs. "What were you thinking? Handing them any piece of trash you find on the beach?"

"The fish trader gave it to me," Webs said defensively. "She knows I'm always looking for new scrolls. I didn't have time to read it, but I didn't think it sounded that bad."

"Where Are the Dragonets of Destiny?" Kestrel read off the title. "That doesn't sound dangerous to you? Filling their heads with questions and ideas?"

"Our heads are already full of questions and ideas," Sunny piped up.

"We'll tell you what you need to know about the prophecy,"

Kestrel growled at Sunny and Starflight. "You don't need a pile of gossip and rumours and speculation cluttering up your tiny little minds."

"Starflight's mind isn't at all tiny or little," Sunny objected. She glanced at Starflight, and when he didn't say anything, she whispered. "Hey, your line is, 'Neither is Sunny's.'"

Starflight knew she was trying to make him feel better, but he was too nervous to speak. Why were the guardians so mad? Had he done something wrong?

"This is not for you," Kestrel snapped, waving the scroll. She pointed it at Starflight. "You. Battle training, now." She turned and stomped out of the cave with the other guardians close behind her.

Sunny ran to the entranceway, then turned back to Starflight with a comically outraged look on her face.

"Are you just going to let her do that?" she said. "She took your scroll! That's so unfair!"

Starflight thought so, too, but he definitely was not going to argue with Kestrel. "It's all right," he said, looking down at the grey rocks below his talons. "Hopefully Webs will bring a new scroll next week."

"Oh, Starflight. I know you're trying to hide it, but you're so sad now," Sunny said. She came and sat in front of him, reaching to touch his tail with her own. "Listen, that scroll wasn't going to have all the answers anyway. You know that, right? Nobody knows how the prophecy will unfold. We just *have to always do what we think is right and fate will take us in the right direction."*

"Maybe," he said. "But a map on how to get there would be helpful."

"You don't need a map," she said, "when you have excellent travelling companions. Like Clay and Tsunami and Glory. And, of course, me." She beamed at him.

"That's true," he said, feeling again how lucky he was. Of all the caves in all of Pyrrhia – of all the eggs that could have been chosen – somehow his and hers had wound up here, and two dragons who never should have met were together.

And that's how we'll always be, he thought.

Starflight woke up to find a claw poking his snout. "Mmmmf?" he mumbled. Everything was still and dark in the dormitory. The coals smouldered in the wall niches like the half-closed eyes of slumbering dragons. The skylight looked out on to a night with no stars.

The warmth from his dream faded instantly. Sunny was far away, and he had no idea when he'd ever see her again.

"I can't sleep," Fatespeaker whispered in the dark. Her wings rustled as she edged closer to him and poked his shoulder again. "What are you doing?"

"Um," said Starflight. "Sleeping?"

"Let's go explore," she said. "I want to know more about our tribe, don't you? We can go look around the whole fortress while they're asleep."

He rubbed his eyes and blinked at her. "Won't we get in trouble?"

"Why?" she said. "Nobody's told us not to. We're NightWings, aren't we? Isn't this our fortress, too? Let's explore it before someone tells us we can't."

There was a kind of logic to that, although Starflight wasn't sure Morrowseer would agree with it. But really, she was right. Why should they get in trouble for acting like they belonged here?

Besides, it was what Tsunami would do. And wasn't he always thinking he wanted to be more like her?

He rolled off the bed on to the floor next to Fatespeaker, and they padded softly out into the tunnels. She picked a direction apparently at random and they started to walk the empty halls. The only sound was the tapping of their own claws and the slithering of their tails on the stone.

Don't be scared, Starflight told himself. And then told himself again, a few more times. *You're not doing anything wrong. There aren't any dangers lying in wait for you. You're not being treated like a prisoner. You're a NightWing dragonet. This is your tribe. This is where you could have grown up.* He glanced at the bare walls, not so very different from the cave where he *had* grown up. *This is where you're supposed to be.*

No. I'm supposed to be where Sunny is. I'm supposed to be helping my friends stop the war. He stopped walking for a minute to take a deep breath, then hurried after Fatespeaker.

All the torches had been extinguished, so the only light came from the glowing red coals in the walls. Starflight couldn't even see any of the moons when he looked out the windows. The sky was too hidden by clouds and smoke from the volcano.

He knew they wouldn't find much that might be useful unless he was brave enough to open a door sometime, but he was terrified of waking up any sleeping NightWings. He kept imagining walking straight into Morrowseer's room and stepping on his tail by accident, and the death or dismemberment or both that would no doubt inevitably follow.

He was glad to see that Fatespeaker wasn't going in the direction of his father's lab. Mastermind was surely sleeping like the rest of the tribe, but Starflight didn't want to risk encountering him – or get any closer to the things he'd seen in there.

Every once in a while, as they walked, they heard a quiet snore from the rooms they were passing. But they saw no one awake. No guards anywhere.

"I guess they're used to not needing guards," Starflight whispered. "Since no other tribe could find this place, they were always safe from attack." He thought for a minute. "And even now that they *might* be attacked, they only need to post guards at the tunnel."

"I'm surprised everyone is asleep, though," Fatespeaker

whispered back. "I always thought being a NightWing meant you wanted to be awake all night. I mean, that's true of me. I can never wake up in the morning, but once it's dark, I'm full of energy. Does that happen to you? I really thought that was a NightWing thing. But maybe my friends are right and I'm just weird." She kicked a rock sticking out of a crack in the floor.

"Or maybe it is a NightWing thing and they're all muddled here because they can't really see the night sky any more," Starflight said. "Maybe you're more of a NightWing than any of them."

She fluttered her wings, looking sceptical.

"As for me, I lived in a cave with no sky most of my life, so I was on whatever schedule our guardians told us to be. But once we were free . . . well, it's been a strange few weeks, so it's hard to say. But I do feel more alive when the stars are out. Does that make sense?"

"It does," she said, smiling at him. She paused at an intersection, thinking, and then purposefully turned right.

"Are we going somewhere?" he asked her.

"Did you see the part of the fortress that collapsed?" she asked. "I want to see what it looks like from inside."

He stopped, his heart rattling nervously. "Wait," he said. "It collapsed because it was covered in lava. That *can't* be safe to explore."

She flicked his nose with her tail. "Oh, stop worrying.

Mightyclaws told me it happened, like, eleven years ago. It's just a bunch of rocks now, and he said it's kind of neat-looking. I guess it covered the part of the fortress where they used to keep their treasure, so they had to blast tunnels into it to get their treasure out. Tunnels! In lava rocks! It'll be awesome. Come on!"

She bounded ahead and he followed, more slowly, wishing he'd listened to his original stay-in-bed instincts.

Fatespeaker's sense of direction turned out to be better than her sense about dragons, and before long they found themselves in a part of the fortress where the roof was partly gone. What looked like thick black bubbles of rock filled the hall ahead of them. Chilly air whistled through the gaps in the walls, battling with the heat from the volcano below their talons.

"There," Fatespeaker whispered, darting up to where the petrified lava met the wall. A tunnel just big enough for a dragon had been chiselled and blasted and dug out of the rocks. Without any hesitation, she headed inside.

What am I doing? Starflight asked himself. He really desperately wanted to melt into the shadows and stay there waiting for her. But he also felt as though she couldn't go in there alone. And this time there was no Clay or Tsunami or Glory to do the brave thing for him. He was the only dragon Fatespeaker had.

Taking a deep breath, he forced himself to step into the

small tunnel. Jagged rock pressed in from all sides, scraping his wings and the top of his head.

The tunnel twisted quickly downward, so they had to dig their claws in to avoid sliding. Fatespeaker breathed a small plume of fire, but all that did was illuminate the thick dark walls that encircled them. The air was hot and stuffy, and Starflight began to wonder if anyone had ever died exploring these tunnels.

Suddenly the tunnel turned directly down and dumped them out into an empty space. Fatespeaker fell first, letting out a shout of surprise, so Starflight had a minute's warning and was able to open his wings as soon as his claws lost their grip on the floor. Still, he tumbled several feet and landed on top of her.

"Ooof," she said. He scrambled away, and they both lit up the air with their fire at the same time.

The room was small but intact; the lava had crushed the upper floors but left this one preserved. Starflight could see a small hallway outside the door, with more rooms beyond that. He looked up uneasily, thinking about the weight of everything above them.

Fatespeaker was already hurrying to the doorway as their fire faded into complete darkness. "Mightyclaws said the old treasure room is three doors down on the left. Come on!"

"But isn't it empty?" Starflight asked, following her with

his front talons outstretched. "Are we just going to look at an empty room?"

"A *fascinating* empty room," she insisted. "It used to be *full of treasure*, just imagine. I've never even seen *any* treasure before."

"Oh, right," Starflight said. "The Talons of Peace wouldn't have any, I guess, unless some dragons brought it with them when they left their tribes."

"If anyone did, they keep it hidden," she said. He felt her tail flick against his snout accidentally as they both felt their way along the walls. "You didn't have treasure in your hiding-under-the-mountain place, did you?"

"No, but I've been to the Sky Kingdom and the Kingdom of the Sea," Starflight said, "and I saw enough treasure there to know that having lots of treasure doesn't make you a good queen, or a happy tribe."

"I thought Queen Coral *was* a good queen," Fatespeaker said, sounding surprised.

"Well, keep in mind she wrote a lot of the scrolls you've probably read about her," Starflight said. "But she's not terrible. She's better than Queen Scarlet, that's for sure. Or Blister." He shuddered, remembering the SandWing dragon who had been so disgusted with him.

"I bet the SandWings would be happier if they could find the treasure that scavenger stole, though," Fatespeaker said.

"Maybe," Starflight said. "There were some really

famous pieces of treasure in there, including stuff that was rumoured to be animus-touched."

"Animus-touched?" Fatespeaker stopped and breathed fire again. They were standing under a tall archway with two black metal doors, one of which was propped open just enough for a dragonet to slip through.

"*Animus-touched* means an object that's been magicked by an animus dragon," Starflight explained in the helpful-teacher voice he sometimes used with his friends. "So the object is left with some kind of power – like a necklace that can make you invisible, or a stone that can find anyone you're looking for." *Or a statue that'll kill any heir to the SeaWing throne it can get its claws on.* "It's sort of an archaic term because supposedly there aren't any animus dragons any more, but that's clearly not true – there's at least one among the SeaWings, and there must have been one not long ago among the NightWings."

"Really?" Fatespeaker pushed lightly on the metal door, and it groaned open another inch.

He realized he didn't know how much she knew about the NightWing island. "Yes – there's a tunnel from here to the rainforest, and one from the rainforest to the Kingdom of Sand, which must have been made by an animus dragon," he said. "I guess I can't be sure how long ago it was, but none of the RainWings knew about them. Isn't that how you got here?"

She shook her head. "We flew across the ocean. It was *so* long and *so* boring. I swear I nearly fell asleep and ended up in the sea a couple of times."

He perked up, full of geography questions, but she was already squeezing into the room and making "Oooooh!" noises. He squashed himself through the door behind her and saw, in the plume of fire she sent out, a couple of wooden sticks on the floor. He picked one up and lit it so they could look around more easily.

But when he lifted it up, the first things they both saw were the shrivelled corpses of two dead dragons.

CHAPTER 10

Starflight clapped his talons over Fatespeaker's mouth midshriek.

"You'll bring the mountain down on top of us," he whispered, and she snapped her mouth shut. He glanced down at the two midnight-black bodies. "Don't worry, these two have been dead a long time," he added. "Probably since the volcano erupted."

When he released her, she whispered, "How did they die?"

Starflight lifted the torch again and peered a little closer, although he really didn't want to. A spear lay beside one of the NightWings, but it was an ordinary spear, not the creepy hooked-and-pronged kind all the guards carried now. Neither of them wore armour either.

"Suffocation, I bet," he answered. "Or starvation. Or heat, although dragons can withstand a fair amount of heat. My guess is they were guarding the treasure when the eruption happened and they were trapped here. Nobody could come find them until the lava cooled enough to make the tunnel we crawled through, and by then it was too late."

Fatespeaker shook herself from horns to tail. "How incredibly awful."

Starflight turned to look around the room, which, as he'd predicted, was otherwise empty. Bare shelves lined all the walls, reaching up to the ceiling, and large urns stood in the two back corners. He could imagine that they had once been filled to the brim with gold and jewels.

He caught himself thinking, *A giant urn full of gold and jewels would be kind of cool to have.* Which was ridiculous – just his dragon instincts talking. What would he do with that much gold? Unless it could get him back to his friends or stop the war, it would be useless to him.

Something went *ping* at the back of his mind, but before he could figure it out, Fatespeaker said, "Maybe we should go."

"I think so," Starflight said. "I don't know how much air is down here, but I don't want to find out by running out of it."

"Yikes," she said, her eyes widening. "That's all you had to say!" She turned and scooted out of the room faster than he'd ever seen her move before.

He took a step to follow her, and the torchlight flashed on something small and bright in one of the corpse's talons.

Starflight hesitated.

A piece of treasure that was left behind? Something they missed, because who would want to search a corpse. . .

Well, not him – not particularly.

But – he felt as if it was calling to him, as if it had been waiting for him these eleven years, hiding from anyone else who came along until the right dragon arrived.

Now you sound like Sunny, with her faith in fate and destiny and signs and magic.

So if taking the lost jewel was what she'd want him to do. . .

He braced himself, reached down, and plucked it from the dead guard's claws. Rough dead scales scraped against his, and he shuddered so badly he nearly dropped the gemstone, but instead he gripped it harder and jumped back, knocking against the shelves behind him. The claws were left clutching the air, as if hanging on to the memory of treasure would have to be enough.

Now Starflight felt fairly sick, but when he held up the torch and glanced down, he realized he'd done the right thing.

The blue star-shaped sapphire glinted in his talons with a tiny inner spark of its own light.

He'd only ever read about these. There were supposedly three of them in the world, all lost – all created hundreds of years ago by a SandWing animus dragon.

A dreamvisitor.

He closed his claws around it.

With this, he could see his friends again.

"Starflight?" Fatespeaker called.

"Coming," he said. He couldn't risk anyone finding the

dreamvisitor and taking it from him. Not even Fatespeaker could know about it.

He put it in his mouth, tucked down between his teeth and his scales, and pressed his tongue over it.

On the way back to the dormitory, Fatespeaker asked why he was so quiet, but he just shook his head and mumbled that he was tired. She shrugged and headed off to her own bed once they were back inside.

Starflight pulled out the rough blanket he'd been given and arranged it so he could huddle underneath it. The heavy brown fabric caught on his horns and smelled like smoke, but it would keep him hidden from any eyes that might still be awake. He cupped the dreamvisitor in his talons and stared at it, trying to remember if he'd read anything about how they worked.

Perhaps I just think of the dragon whose dreams I want to visit?

Surely Sunny would be asleep right now, in the middle of the night. If he remembered right, he should be able to step into whatever she was already dreaming about – and if she were in the deepest level of dreamsleep, she'd see him and they could talk to each other. But if her sleep was shallow or uneasy, he might be able to see in, but she wouldn't know he was really there. And if she were awake, it wouldn't work at all, of course.

He closed his eyes and pictured Sunny – her laugh that

125

made everyone else laugh, too, her flares of temper that vanished as quickly as they came, her small claws and fierce protective face, her scales like rippled sunshine, the way she looked like no other dragon on Pyrrhia. If she were here, she'd know exactly what to say about his father. She'd tell him what to tell the NightWings about Glory, and how to talk them out of hurting RainWings, for ever.

But no matter how hard he concentrated, his mind stayed firmly in the NightWing dormitory instead of finding her dreams.

Maybe she was awake. Maybe she was in the rainforest somewhere, looking at the moons and wondering if he was looking at them, too.

He tried Glory next, then Clay, then Tsunami. Nothing happened. He couldn't reach any of them.

Starflight squeezed the dreamvisitor between his claws, grinding his teeth. This *had* to work. Unless it wasn't really a dreamvisitor, but it certainly looked like one.

Try a RainWing. They're always *asleep.*

The first RainWing who came to mind was Kinkajou, the little dragonet Glory had rescued from the NightWings. Starflight focused on her enormous dark eyes and quick-changing scales. He pressed the dreamvisitor to his forehead, praying that this would work.

And suddenly he was perched on a branch in the rainforest.

Starflight took a deep, relieved breath, but he still inhaled the smoke of the dormitory. He could see the rainforest, but he couldn't smell it, unfortunately for him.

Kinkajou was curled on a giant leaf beside him with her eyes closed. There was a bandage of soft leaves and moss wrapped around one of her wings, and piles of red and yellow and purple fruits all around her, like offerings to a statue. Her scales were a strangely pale shade of blue in the moonlight, and she breathed shallowly, as if even in her sleep she knew a deeper breath would make something hurt.

"What happened to you?" Starflight wondered aloud, but she didn't wake up.

He turned to find another dragon staring right through him. For a startled, terrifying moment, Starflight thought the dragon could see him, but then he realized she was just watching Kinkajou. She was old, older than any of the guardians or queens he'd met so far, and she had that royal elegance about her that he'd noticed Greatness lacking.

Starflight turned back to Kinkajou. How could he get inside her dreams? He looked down at the dreamvisitor and remembered pressing it to his own forehead. Carefully he leaned over and rested the sapphire between Kinkajou's eyes.

The first time he tried, he nearly fell right through her; since he wasn't really there, he couldn't touch her or anything around her. But when he tried a second time, holding the dreamvisitor where he thought it should go, he felt a thrum of energy radiate from Kinkajou through the jewel to him and back again, and then he saw what she saw.

In Kinkajou's dream, she was standing in bright sunlight in a wide green bowl laced with brightly coloured flowers, surrounded by thousands of RainWings – more RainWings than there could possibly be on the whole continent – all of them staring at her with expressions of disdain that Starflight had never seen in real life on any RainWing.

Glory was there, in the centre of the bowl, but this Glory was impossibly big and impossibly beautiful, and a crown of orange hibiscus, gold chain and rubies sparkled atop her head. *That's how Kinkajou sees her,* Starflight thought. This Glory smiled more, too, at least at Kinkajou.

A crown, he thought suddenly. *Does that mean Glory won? Is she now queen of the RainWings? Or is this a wishful dream?*

Kinkajou backed away from the stares of the dragons until she reached the far edge of the bowl. Suddenly she turned and leaped off, spreading her wings.

But instead of soaring away through the trees, she fell, plummeting like a coconut towards the ground below. Her wings flapped helplessly, and when she twisted to look at them, giant holes appeared all over her wings, spreading as though acid was eating them away.

Kinkajou screamed and clawed at the air.

Starflight watched helplessly from above as the greenery

swallowed her up. *It's just a dream,* he told himself, but his racing heart didn't believe him. *Just a dream. Nothing you could do. She didn't even see you here.*

He wouldn't be able to reach her in a dream like this, where her emotions were so strong. It was really strange to be in someone else's nightmare, so different from the ones he had almost every night. His own anxiety dreams usually involved the NightWing queen telling him that dragonets who weren't telepathic were not welcome in the tribe.

The dreamscape around him shuddered and then suddenly went dark.

She's waking up. Starflight dug his talons into the tree branch below him, even though he couldn't see it now and he also knew it wasn't really there – or rather, he wasn't really there. He wanted to hold on to the rainforest as long as he could. He didn't want to go back to the gloomy NightWing dormitory.

Stay asleep, he thought desperately. *Please see me. I need to send a message to my friends.*

Now he could see faint outlines of shapes in the darkness, as if it was very early morning and the sun was rising far away. In front of him, Kinkajou was curled on the leaf again, still asleep but twitching restlessly. A silvery shaft of moonlight lit up the expression of pain on her face. She'd snapped out of the nightmare into a shallow sleep with no dreams, where she was half aware of everything around her without being fully awake. He could be here, but she wouldn't see him, not now.

"Another nightmare?" said a quiet voice behind him.

Starflight whirled around, his heart leaping into his throat.

Sunny.

The SandWing was just landing on the branch beside the queenly RainWing. Her golden wings folded in and she flipped her tail over her back talons the way she always did. A moment later, a glint of blue scales appeared through the trees behind Sunny: Tsunami, flapping down to land next to her.

"I think so," said the older RainWing. "I wasn't sure whether to wake her. How is the queen?"

"Mad," said Sunny. "*Super* mad. I keep telling her there's no way Starflight went to the NightWings on his own, but she's convinced he's betrayed us."

Shock rippled through Starflight's wings. It hadn't occurred to him that his friends would think he'd left them on purpose. *The queen – does she mean Glory?* Glory *thinks I betrayed them?*

Then he remembered telling the NightWing council that the RainWings were planning to attack, and his scales felt hot with shame. He may have been abducted, but he hadn't done anything to help his friends since he got here. He hadn't tried to escape. He hadn't even argued with Morrowseer or tried to stop the NightWings.

Maybe he really didn't belong in the prophecy. Maybe Fatespeaker was the better dragon to save the world.

"*Starflight,*" Tsunami snorted. "Of all dragons, like he'd ever betray us. Can you actually imagine how it could have happened? First, making a decision. Not exactly Starflight's forte. Then, actually *doing* something instead of sitting and waiting for it to happen to him. And not just anything: jumping into a dark hole with angry dragons on the other side. *Starflight.* Are you kidding me? STARFLIGHT."

"Oh my gosh, stop it," Sunny said. "You've been arguing with Glory all day. You don't have to convince *me* that Starflight wouldn't do something like this." She hopped down to Kinkajou's side, nearly passing right through Starflight. He shivered and leaned towards her. He could almost imagine he felt the warmth of her scales as she went by.

"You don't think he chose to go to the Night Kingdom?" asked the dragon Starflight didn't know.

Sunny looked up at the two moons that were visible through the canopy, then back down at Kinkajou. "If he went, then I'm sure it was for a good reason. But if he didn't choose to go – then he needs our help, right, Tsunami? Isn't that the important thing? Shouldn't we go get him right now, before something terrible happens to him?" She bent to examine the bandage on Kinkajou's wing.

Yes, Starflight thought frantically. *Please. Hurry.*

"If it were up to me, the four of us would be there now, tearing that place apart," Tsunami growled. "Instead of wasting our time here."

"Combat training didn't go well?" asked the other dragon.

Tsunami lashed her tail so hard she nearly fell off the branch. "General, may I take a nap? General, I need a papaya! General, my claws are tired! General, look, a butterfly! SOMEBODY IS GETTING STABBED IN THE FACE IF YOU DON'T SHUT UP."

Sunny smothered a giggle.

"When does the queen want to attack?" The older dragon bared her teeth as though she was ready to go right now.

"Oh, look," Sunny interrupted, touching her front talons lightly to Kinkajou's head. "She's waking up."

No. Starflight saw Kinkajou's eyes flutter. He reached out, holding the dreamvisitor, trying to send her back into dreamsleep, but it was too late.

With a wrenching sideways jolt, the rainforest – and Kinkajou and Tsunami and Sunny – was ripped away, and Starflight found himself lying on cold stone once again. The thick canvas lay heavy on his horns and the dim red light of the coals pulsed beyond it, making his eyes ache.

Sunny had been right there, inches from him.

So close, and yet she might as well have been on one of the moons.

He stared down at the dreamvisitor that glowed faintly in his talons. Seeing them had somehow been even worse than not seeing them.

My friends think I betrayed them – or if they don't, they think it's because I'm too much of a coward to do something like that.

He closed his eyes, feeling lonelier than he had ever felt in his life.

CHAPTER 11

The blanket was ripped off Starflight's head with such force that he tumbled on to the floor. His head spun for a moment, but his first thought was that he was glad he'd hidden the dreamvisitor well the night before.

"Up," Morrowseer snarled. His breath was fiercely awful this morning. At least, Starflight assumed it was morning, although the sky was barely lighter than it had been the night before.

Flame and Ochre stood sullenly behind the giant NightWing, glaring at Starflight. He hoped they had had to spend the night in the dungeon.

Fatespeaker came bounding over to join them, followed more slowly by Viper and Squid. All around the dormitory, NightWing dragonets were poking their heads out of their blankets, watching. Fierceteeth looked openly envious; smoke rose from her snout and her tail twitched angrily.

Morrowseer didn't even look at the other NightWing dragonets. "Let's go," he ordered. His tail nearly knocked Starflight over as he turned and swept out of the room.

"Where are we going?" Fatespeaker asked cheerfully. She seemed to have recovered from the news that either she or Starflight were slated for death.

"To see if it's worth spending any more time on you," said Morrowseer. "Certain dragons think we should lock you all up until we sort out our RainWing problem, but I think you need as much training as possible starting as soon as possible. So. Today we'll have another test."

"A test?" Starflight echoed, flapping his wings. "On what? We haven't had time to study! Shouldn't we review the material first?"

Morrowseer looked over his shoulder at Starflight. "Sometimes it is very hard not to bite you," he growled.

Well, that's hardly fair, Starflight thought, but he decided not to say anything else. Usually he was pretty good at tests. Maybe this was finally his chance to earn a place in the prophecy. *Especially if it's about history. I read all the history scrolls several times each.*

He noticed that Flame was still glaring at him with resentful orange eyes. Carefully, Starflight manoeuvred so that Fatespeaker was walking between him and the hostile SkyWing dragonet.

The six of them trailed after Morrowseer all the way to a roof of the fortress that faced the small island forest. Morrowseer spread his wings and narrowed his eyes at the sky, which was dark grey and flickered with faraway lightning. In the distance, the clouds seemed to be pouring down into the ocean. *A storm out at sea,* Starflight thought.

He shuddered, remembering the storm that had nearly

flooded the cave in the Kingdom of the Sea. Clay had been chained to the wall, and Glory and Sunny had been so determined not to leave him. If Tsunami hadn't come for them, they probably would have decided to drown along with Clay. Starflight wasn't sure he'd have been able to do that. He'd been too scared to say anything, watching the water slowly rising towards them.

"Stay close to me," Morrowseer growled. He jabbed Starflight in the neck with one claw. "Don't try anything."

And then he lifted into the sky without any more explanation or instructions.

It took Starflight a moment to figure out that they were leaving the island. *Back to the mainland?* He leaped into the air, his heart jumping hopefully at the same time.

"Wait," Squid called in a complaining whine, flapping after Morrowseer. "We haven't even had *breakfast*. You're not going to make me fly on an empty stomach, are you? Because I will *die*. I will *literally die*."

"You won't, actually, not for a while," Starflight informed him. "Most dragons can naturally survive for up to a month without eating, if necessary, according to *A Natural History of Unnatural Dragon Abilities*."

"Listen to the scrollworm," Flame said nastily. "Isn't he clever?"

"I will never never *never* go a whole month without eating," Ochre said passionately.

"Is one of the 'unnatural abilities' being really annoying?" Viper asked. "Because there should be a whole chapter on you and Fatespeaker."

"You don't even know me," Starflight pointed out. "I was just trying to help."

"*I* thought it was interesting," Fatespeaker said. "And probably useful, if the NightWings keep feeding us the horrible stuff they've been bringing so far."

"Oh, I have a theory about that." As they flew over the forest and out across the ocean, Starflight told her about how the NightWings hunted and his ideas about the bacteria in their mouths, and how he and Fatespeaker probably didn't have it, since they'd grown up eating live or recently killed prey and hadn't developed the bacteria like the NightWing dragonets on the island would have.

"Wow," said Fatespeaker, looking genuinely fascinated.

"Is this the test?" Viper asked. "Listen to you for as long as we can without dying of boredom?"

"Nobody's talking to you, Viper," Fatespeaker said. "Go be grumpy at Squid and leave Starflight alone."

Starflight glanced down at the waves rushing below him. The island was disappearing behind them, visible only as a red glow in the sky. Ahead of them was nothing but sea as far as the distant horizon. He had no idea how Morrowseer was navigating – there were no landmarks and the sky was still hidden behind the clouds.

I should pay attention so I can fly this way if I ever get a chance to escape.

Actually, what he should do was try to escape once they reached the mainland. *Just fly away. Hide. Try to get back to the rainforest.*

He could not in a million years imagine doing any of that by himself. Maybe with Tsunami and Clay and Glory and Sunny, but alone? It sounded much safer to stay with the NightWings and hope someone came to rescue him.

Rain began to fall. Or rather, they reached the edge of the storm, and Starflight realized that Morrowseer planned to fly right through it.

"My wings are getting wet," Squid griped.

"Boohoo, you poor SeaWing," Flame snapped.

Starflight wasn't about to say anything aloud, but the rain made his wings heavier and it was much harder to fly. He didn't have the strongest flying muscles anyway – being raised in a cave meant not much opportunity to practise.

He clenched his jaw and flew on. If this was the test, he refused to fail. He would fly until his wings gave out and he would not let anyone see how much it hurt.

Think of Sunny. Think about being the dragon you want her to think you are.

The sea kept getting closer, which he knew meant he was drooping. The rain pelted down harder and harder, battering his scales and making it almost impossible to see Ochre flying just ahead of him. Morrowseer was a dark blur in the clouds. Starflight hoped they didn't lose him. He hoped Morrowseer wasn't *trying* to lose them, because it wouldn't be hard in this weather.

A bolt of lightning sizzled through the sky, followed instantly by the loudest thunderclap Starflight had ever heard. His whole body shook with the vibrations.

I hope we get there soon. I hope we get there soon.

He blinked away raindrops and realized with a sickening lurch that the sky ahead of him was empty.

Where are the other dragons?

For a horrible moment, he was completely lost.

Then Fatespeaker appeared at his side and nudged his wing. "Down there!" she shouted over the wind.

What looked like a small smudge on the ocean turned out to be a tiny, rocky island. Morrowseer and the others were perched there already. Starflight landed awkwardly next to Squid, who had his wings over his head and was muttering angrily.

"Halfway there!" Fatespeaker grinned at him.

Only halfway? Starflight's resolution wavered, and he stared down at his claws. He was too exhausted even to ask all the questions brimming inside him. How had the NightWings found their island, if it was this far from the mainland? How often did they go to the mainland – and did they usually use the tunnel to the rainforest, or fly over the sea like this?

He guessed most of them would choose the tunnel if they could, rather than risk this exhausting flight.

Morrowseer allowed them to rest for a short while. He didn't speak. His dark eyes glowered at all of them, and occasionally he glanced back in the direction of the volcano.

All too soon, he gathered himself and said, "Let's go," and then they were all flying once again.

Rain. Thunder. Aching wings. Raindrops filled Starflight's eyes. Lightning blazed too close to his tail.

Off to his left, Squid was complaining loudly, but no one could hear him over the storm, or else no one had any energy to respond.

Starflight was starting to think that drowning wouldn't be such a bad way to go, after all, when he saw Morrowseer tilt his wings and begin sailing downward.

Land had appeared in front of them quite suddenly; Starflight hadn't been able to see it through the clouds and rain. Now he saw a coast lined with jagged cliffs, steep and rocky and plunging straight into the sea. Behind them jutted sharp peaks like dragons' teeth, some of them tipped with snow, extending in a relentless line across the horizon.

The Claws of the Clouds Mountains.

His heart sank. He'd hoped they were near the southern coast and the rainforest, but this had to be Pyrrhia's northern edge, where the SkyWings ruled. Too close to Queen Scarlet's palace. Too far for him to fly back to his friends. . . It would take days, and he'd have to travel alone through the Sky Kingdom and the Mud Kingdom.

I'm sorry, Sunny. I can't do it. I can't find my way back to you.

His wings felt like glaciers, slow and heavy and dragging him down, as he followed Morrowseer and the others to the clifftop in the driving rain. Bare rocks scraped beneath his claws when he landed, and he bent forward, gasping for breath.

Squid sprawled out flat on his back, groaning with pain, and Ochre immediately began sniffing the rocks as if he were hoping to startle out some prey. Flame was the only dragonet who wasn't breathing heavily.

Starflight looked up and caught Morrowseer studying the sea behind them again. He had a weird flash of intuition that made no sense.

"Is someone . . . following us?" he asked Morrowseer.

"That's none of your concern," Morrowseer answered. He spread his wings and pointed down the coast. Through the storm, Starflight could barely see the glow of firelight coming from a cave in the cliffside.

"What is it?" Fatespeaker asked.

"The most remote outpost of the SkyWing army," said Morrowseer. "Their assignment is to guard against attacks from the north, in case Queen Glacier ever decides to try this approach to the palace. There are no other dragons for miles. This is your test."

They all stared at him, uncomprehending.

"What is?" Starflight finally asked. The wind ripped his voice away.

"You want us to kill them," Viper guessed. She arched her poisonous tail and flexed her claws. "All of them?"

"I don't want to," Squid whined. "What if someone bites me?"

"Shut up or *I'll* bite you," Flame said. He looked deeply rattled, as if he'd never expected to be asked to kill members of his own tribe. Starflight wondered suddenly where all their parents were, and whether these dragonets dreamed of home and family the way his friends had.

"No, you're not here to kill them," Morrowseer snapped. "You're the dragonets of the great prophecy, remember? Your test is to act like it." He pointed to the outpost. "Go in there, tell the guards that you are the real prophesized dragonets, and convince them to switch their alliance from Burn to Blister."

In the shocked silence that followed, a hurricane-force wind came howling up and tried to throw them all off the cliff. Starflight dug in his talons and made himself as small as he could.

"Just — convince them," Viper shouted at Morrowseer,

raindrops flying as she shook her head. "A bunch of strange SkyWings. So instead of killing them, we're going to ask them to kill us."

"I foresee that this is going to go really, really badly," Fatespeaker yelled over the wind.

"Me too," cried Ochre. "Maybe I have special NightWing powers, too."

"They're going to kill me!" Squid shouted. "SeaWings and SkyWings are enemies! If you send me in there, I'm dead!"

Morrowseer's expression suggested that he wouldn't be terribly devastated by that.

"If you can't survive this," he rumbled, "then you're useless for the prophecy anyway." He pointed at Fatespeaker. "You, stay here. We'll see how well that one does, this time." He flicked a claw at Starflight.

Starflight wanted to melt into the rocks. He wanted to leap off the cliff into the sea. He wondered how far he would get if he bolted for the mountains right now. Would the journey to the rainforest be any worse than walking into a SkyWing guardhouse and announcing himself as one of the dragonets Queen Scarlet had lost not long ago?

"Won't they just take us prisoner?" he asked Morrowseer. "And take us back to the Sky Palace?"

"Not if you're convincing enough," Morrowseer said,

baring his teeth. "Now go." He shot a blast of fire at Squid, who barely leaped out of the way in time.

"I don't want to," Squid complained again, but Viper and Flame were already shoving him forward. Ochre trailed after them and Starflight reluctantly brought up the rear.

He glanced back once and saw Fatespeaker huddled into her wings, a small drenched shape beside the vast bulk of Morrowseer. He hoped his friends would welcome her as the new NightWing when he was gone.

I'm about to die, he thought, *and I never got to tell Sunny I love her. I'm going to die without saving the world, without stopping the war . . . without ever doing one brave thing in my life.*

CHAPTER 12

As they approached the firelight, Starflight's dread grew heavier and heavier.

Loud dragon voices spilled from the cave, along with a column of smoke that rose from a hole in the stone wall.

"What if someone's on watch?" Starflight whispered when they were a few lengths away.

They all froze. Starflight searched the darkness around them with his eyes, trying to move as little as possible.

Lightning flashed, and Starflight's heart seized up. Perched on a clifftop above them was a dragon with enormous wings, staring out to sea.

"There," he whispered. Surely he could see them? Why hadn't he called out to warn the other soldiers yet?

Starflight squinted at the shape, at the rise and fall of its shoulders and the curve of its neck, and he realized that the guard was asleep – despite the rain pouring down on him, despite the booming thunder, despite his whole job being to stay awake.

"We're all right," he whispered to the others.

They crept towards the cave, staying closer to the shadows now. A wooden door blocked the entrance.

"Wait," Starflight whispered.

Flame paused with his front talons raised to knock. He frowned at Starflight.

"Let's be smart about this," Starflight said. "We don't have to charge right in. Let's listen for a minute and see if we hear anything that might be useful."

"Fine by me," Ochre said with a shrug.

"But it's wet out here," Squid grumbled.

Flame and Viper exchanged glances, and then, to Starflight's surprise, they both nodded. Perhaps fear made them more agreeable. The two of them put their ears up to the wooden door, so he crept along the wall and crouched below the smoke hole. He tried to arrange his wings in a way that would shield him at least a little bit from the rain.

There seemed to be several arguments going on inside. Starflight could only catch snatches of one that seemed to be closest to the fire.

"If Queen Ruby says we can return to the palace, you better believe I'm going home," growled one dragon.

"You'd be obeying the orders of a false queen," snarled another. "Queen Scarlet is still alive, and she'll have us all killed if we abandon our posts."

"Then where is she?" challenged a third voice. "What kind of queen leaves her kingdom in chaos like this?"

"It's not chaos. We have Ruby now," said the first voice. "And she says we can leave."

"But Queen Burn says we shouldn't," said another dragon.

"She's not *our* queen," snapped more than one voice.

"That's enough. No one's going anywhere today," boomed someone authoritative-sounding. The hubbub of voices stilled. "Not in this storm. We'll discuss it again tomorrow."

After a moment, a murmur of grumbling and muttering started, but nothing that Starflight could pick out. He crept back to Flame and Viper.

"Useless," Flame hissed.

"Perhaps not," Starflight said. "Did you hear how some of them are dissatisfied with Burn? We can press that, I think. If she's trying to act like *she's* their new queen, I bet a whole lot of SkyWings would be willing to reconsider their alliance."

"Fancy talk," said Viper, flicking her tail at him. "Now let's see you actually do it." She shoved Squid away from the shadow of her wings, where he was trying to huddle.

Flame rapped on the door before Starflight could think of another way to delay.

All the noise inside abruptly stopped. Stamping feet approached the door and it was flung wide open.

Starflight found himself facing a room full of SkyWings.

Most of them were clumped in small groups, eating

or rolling prey bones in games of luck. Red, orange and gold scales gleamed in the firelight. Savage-looking spears leaned casually against the wall, and a map next to the fireplace showed the continent of Pyrrhia, with an X where the outpost was located and arrows showing possible attack routes from the Ice Kingdom.

"What in the. . ." said the guard who'd answered the door. He trailed off, staring at them. The whole room — about seventeen dragons, Starflight estimated — turned to stare as well.

Starflight could easily imagine how they looked: five bedraggled dragonets, soaking wet and exhausted, in five different colours that were normally not seen together.

One of the SkyWings inhaled sharply. "It's them!" he hissed.

"It can't be," said another.

For some reason, Flame, Viper and Ochre all glanced at Starflight. But his power of speech had abandoned him. All he could think about was the cold spire where he'd been imprisoned by SkyWing guards just like these only a short time before. He wanted to cower behind the others' wings the way Squid was doing.

Flame let out a small snort of fire and drew himself up as tall as he could get. "It *is* us," he said. "From the prophecy."

"The dragonets of destiny," said one soldier in an awestruck voice.

"Wow, dragons actually call us that?" Viper said. "Lame. I hereby forbid anyone to use that phrase again."

"Is that a roasted seagull?" Ochre asked, shoving his way forward and pointing at a half-eaten carcass on one of the tables. "Is anyone going to finish that?" Without waiting for an answer, he snatched the bird and sank his teeth into it.

Behind Starflight, Squid let out a small whimper.

A few of the SkyWings exchanged glances, looking a little more sceptical than they had a moment ago. Starflight could feel panic rising in his chest. He had to speak up; he had to be convincing. But his jaw felt like it was welded shut.

"Why are you *here*?" asked one of the soldiers. "After you escaped – why come back? To here, of all places?"

"And what did you do to the SeaWings?" asked another. "No attacks, no raids, no sign of them since we destroyed their Summer Palace. We know plenty of them must have survived, so where's the counterattack?"

"Do *you* have Queen Scarlet?" demanded a dragon leaning on the wall by the fire. "What have you done with her?"

Flame waved his front talons as if none of these questions were important. "We're here to tell you you're supporting the wrong SandWing." He tilted his head arrogantly. "Burn isn't going to be queen. Like the prophecy says, she's going to die. We've chosen Blister."

The uproar was immediate. Several dragons sprang to their feet, knocking over tables and scattering bones and ashes everywhere.

"How dare you?" somebody shouted.

"We're not taking orders from some puny dragonets!"

"We'll never let the SeaWings win!"

One of the guards shoved Flame in the chest. "Traitor!" The red dragonet stumbled back, stepping on Starflight's claws.

"Blister killed my brother!" roared another soldier. "She will never be queen. Her fate is to die beneath my talons!"

"We're the dragons from the prophecy!" Viper yelled over the din. "You have to listen to us!"

"No, you're not," said the same authoritative voice Starflight had heard from outside. An orange dragon with a long, scarred neck stepped forward, peering intently at the dragonets. Starflight had a feeling he'd seen this SkyWing before – probably in the queen's palace.

The other SkyWings quieted as the soldier reached around Starflight, seized Squid's ear, and dragged him into the middle of the room. Squid yelped with pain, flung his wings over his head, and sat down, gibbering.

"That is not the SeaWing we captured before," said the orange dragon contemptuously. "You saw the marks she left on the guards she fought with. And I do mean *she*. Also *she* was *blue*. This snivelling creature is no dragonet of destiny." He looked around at the others, his eyes

150

gleaming with suspicion. "I say we kill him. Perhaps we kill them all."

"No!" Starflight blurted. "I am the NightWing the queen held prisoner. I swear I am. Remember she had me fight scavengers? And then the other NightWings came and took me?" He held his breath. *Please believe me.*

The dragon breathed a plume of smoke at him, then narrowed his eyes at Ochre, who had moved on to gnawing on a large leg bone he'd found on the floor.

"I suppose that could be the MudWing," he muttered. "And we never saw the SandWing or the SkyWing." He studied Flame and Viper. "We assumed the queen was holding them elsewhere in the palace, in case they could be fixed and allowed to rejoin us." His gaze stopped on Flame. "But perhaps living with the Talons of Peace will ruin any dragon, even from the best of tribes."

He jabbed Squid sharply with his tail, and the small green dragon moaned unhappily. "If you're the NightWing from the palace," he said to Starflight, "what happened to the SeaWing who was with you before?"

"She's—" Starflight felt hopelessly stupid. Why hadn't Morrowseer guessed this might happen? Did he think this outpost was so remote that no one from the palace would be here? But if he really wanted to replace Tsunami with Squid, he had to know *someone* would notice and object sooner or later.

He knew he should act like Squid was the real prophecy dragonet, especially if they all wanted to get out of this cave alive. But he couldn't bring himself to betray Tsunami, who, if you asked him, in all of Pyrrhia was the dragon most likely to fulfil a prophecy and save the world.

He braced himself and looked the orange dragon in the eye. "She's gathering an army." This was true. No need to mention that it was an army of RainWings. "We're going to end this war." He turned to the other SkyWings in the cave. "Soon you'll be able to go home to your families. Soon you will all be safe. Soon there will be peace."

He caught a look of longing on some of their faces. Even the fierce, bad-tempered SkyWing tribe wanted a chance to live peacefully, he was sure of it.

"Was that a prophecy?" one of the soldiers whispered to another.

Starflight shook his head. "It was a promise," he said.

Viper let out a muffled impatient snort. Starflight knew even his real friends got fed up with the way he sounded like an epic scroll sometimes, but he couldn't help it – when he thought about prophecies and acting like a hero, that's how he thought they should all sound.

"But what about Blister?" asked the orange dragon. "Have you really chosen her? Is she the next SandWing queen?"

Several of the SkyWings hissed, rattling their wings.

Flame and Viper and Squid and even Ochre were watching Starflight now. He could guess that they were willing him to say the right thing here – to convince everyone that Blister was the choice of destiny, that she was going to win, and nobody could do anything about it.

But he remembered Blister's menacing stillness and the glint of evil in her eyes. He remembered the way she manipulated the SeaWing queen, and he remembered that she'd killed Kestrel and tried to kill Webs, although there wasn't any good reason why—

Oh.

He glanced at the alternate dragonets. If Blister wanted to pick and choose her dragonets of destiny, she needed the original guardians dead so they couldn't dispute her version of history. His mind was racing. *She knew about Glory when we met her – she even said she had NightWing friends. She's conspiring with them.*

Which meant she was almost certainly part of the plan to assassinate Glory and Tsunami, too.

He coiled his tail. He *couldn't* make her the next queen of the SandWings. If his voice had any power, he couldn't let her use it.

"No," he said, wincing as his voice cracked. He sounded like a one-year-old dragonet pretending to be a queen. "We haven't chosen anyone yet."

"So choose Burn," said one of the soldiers. Several others nodded.

"Burn is cruel," Starflight said. "You know she is. She lives for war. Even if she wins, she won't stop killing and fighting. She'll probably turn on all of you and try to take your kingdom next."

There was no uproar this time, only shocked silence. They may not have wanted to admit it to themselves, but what he'd said was true. Burn was not a safe ally to have, and she'd be a very dangerous queen of the SandWings.

"Yeah," Flame said half-heartedly. "What he said."

"So, was *that* a prophecy?" the same soldier whispered.

"Let's take them back to the palace," said the orange dragon decisively. "We'll turn them over to Queen Ruby and let her decide. If they know anything about Queen Scarlet's whereabouts, she'll get it out of them." He lashed his tail.

No, Starflight thought, backing towards the door. Back to the SkyWing palace – that would be even worse than staying with the NightWings. Queen Scarlet had tried to make him fight to the death in her arena. He still had nightmares about scavengers with sharp weapons climbing his neck, determined to stab out his eyes. Or about a horde of IceWings descending to destroy him, even though Morrowseer had taken him away before that happened in reality.

But this wasn't a dream. The SkyWing claws reaching

for him were real, and his legs really were not moving, and he couldn't remember a single training move that might help him fight back, and he was about to be captured and imprisoned once more.

And then the door burst open.

And the NightWings came blazing in.

CHAPTER 13

That's who was following us, Starflight thought with a jolt of shock as eight NightWings came through the door, breathing flames in all directions. He saw the tables and the map catch fire, and he saw flames engulf the orange dragon, and then he felt talons seize his tail and he was dragged out the door into the pounding rain outside.

Flame, Viper, Ochre, and Squid were tossed on top of him, howling.

By the time Starflight struggled free and looked up, the door of the outpost was ablaze. Inside the cave, fire raged from wall to wall. SkyWings were shrieking in agony. A troop of black dragons blocked the way out, killing any soldier who tried to escape.

"No!" Starflight yelled. "I promised them! I promised them!" He flung himself at the back of the nearest NightWing, but the dragon shrugged him off easily. "You can't kill them!"

Starflight hadn't wanted to be taken prisoner, but these soldiers were just ordinary dragons, following their queen and doing their jobs. They wanted peace as much as he did. They didn't deserve to die like this.

"Morrowseer!" Starflight cried. "Stop them!"

"You are peculiar," Morrowseer said from the shadows right beside him. Starflight jumped. "They're only a handful of SkyWings. Why would you care?"

"Can't you spare them?" Starflight said desperately. "Please let them live."

"It's much too late for that," said Morrowseer.

Starflight turned to face the flames and realized that this had been Morrowseer's plan all along. That's why he'd chosen a remote location with a limited number of dragons. That's why he didn't care if the soldiers questioned Squid's presence – it was all part of the test. But whether the dragonets passed or failed, he'd planned to kill all the SkyWings, no matter what.

To erase any evidence that we were here – by murdering any witnesses who might wreck our story.

He stared hopelessly into the fire, certain that he'd be hearing dragons screaming in his dreams for the rest of his life.

"They nearly killed me!" Squid shouted at Morrowseer. "Just like I said they would! I quit! I don't want to be in the prophecy any more! There's no treasure and it's boring and stupid and I'm hungry and I hate your island and I want to go home!"

"Fine," Morrowseer snarled coldly at him. "I've never met a dragonet more pointless than you. Go snivelling back to the Talons of Peace. See if you can find them by yourself.

I hope you die on the way." He shoved Squid forcefully in the chest. "Get out of here! Go!"

Squid stumbled back, slipping on the wet rocks. It took him a moment before he could talk. "By myself?" he squeaked. "But – but you wouldn't – my dad is the leader of the Talons – you *have* to be nice to me. You can't send me off—"

"I certainly can," Morrowseer hissed. Lightning flashed in the sky above him, illuminating the dark mountains looming over them all. "Leave or I will kill you. I never want to see you again."

Three moons, Starflight thought. *He really hates Squid.*

"Wait," Fatespeaker said, reaching towards the SeaWing. "Morrowseer, wait. He's one of us. We can't lose him." Squid grabbed her front talons and squeezed, looking desperate.

"We have another one," Morrowseer said. "We just have to retrieve her from the rainforest. But she's clearly made an impression on any dragons who've run into her, so we're stuck with her. Whereas this one is nothing but useless."

"It's not fair," Squid whined. "It's not my fault some other SeaWing is better than me."

That's true, Starflight thought, feeling an unexpected stab of pity for the snivelling green dragonet. *No one could live up to Tsunami.*

"You *can't* do this," Fatespeaker cried. "Flame! Viper! Tell him!"

Viper shrugged, and Flame hunched his wings. His eyes were fixed on the cave where his fellow SkyWings were burning.

"He said he doesn't want to be in the prophecy anyway," Ochre said to Fatespeaker.

"I didn't mean it," Squid cried.

Morrowseer whipped his tail around and smacked Squid hard over the head. "Leave. Now. Be grateful I'm not killing you instead."

Whimpering, Squid backed away, spread his wings, and lifted into the storm-soaked sky. Starflight watched him flap slowly towards the Claws of the Clouds Mountains. A SeaWing alone in SkyWing territory – Squid wouldn't last a day. Starflight's head pounded and he felt nauseous. Every time he thought he'd seen the worst of Morrowseer and the NightWings, they did something even more horrible.

Fatespeaker was crying, tears and raindrops together soaking her face. She pressed her talons to her eyes as if she wished she could claw them out.

Starflight put one of his wings around her and she leaned into his shoulder, shaking.

"Maybe he'll be all right," he whispered. "Sometimes dragons surprise you."

"Don't get comfortable," Morrowseer said to Starflight. "You are running out of chances to show me you can obey orders."

Starflight wound his tail around Fatespeaker's, thinking, *Why should I have to? Who decided you get to order me around?* He realized he didn't even care if Morrowseer read his mind, and he stared at the big dragon, waiting for a reaction.

Morrowseer looked away first. "Back to the island," he ordered. "The others will clean up this mess." He flicked his tail at the ruined guardhouse, then leaped into the sky.

Fatespeaker turned towards the mountains, as if she was thinking about going after Squid. Starflight wished he were that kind of dragon. Would he disobey Morrowseer and chase after one of his friends if this had happened to them? He thought he would for Sunny. He would never let her fly away alone into death. He thought perhaps he could be brave for her, if he ever needed to be.

Not brave enough to escape right now, though, he realized. *But maybe they're coming to rescue me. Maybe I should wait for them anyway.*

Or maybe I'm looking for excuses to do nothing.

"Come on, before anything worse happens," he said gently to Fatespeaker. She wiped her eyes and followed him into the rain-soaked sky.

The flight back to the island was even more exhausting than the flight out, and the storm was relentless the entire way. Starflight's whole body felt numb by the time they touched down in the NightWing fortress. None of the dragonets spoke as they trudged back to the dormitory behind Morrowseer.

"Training at dawn tomorrow," Morrowseer said, stopping at the doorway. The room was empty; the other NightWing dragonets were nowhere to be seen. He eyed Starflight and Fatespeaker, then turned to go.

"So . . . nothing to eat?" Ochre ventured in a woebegone voice.

It had now been days since Starflight's last meal – tiring, energy-sucking days. But he didn't think he had the strength to eat anything tonight anyway. He just wanted to close his eyes and try to forget the sad, dripping shape of Squid flapping away into the mountains.

"No," Morrowseer rumbled. And then he was gone.

Ochre sighed pitifully. Viper hissed and marched to the sleeping hollow she'd chosen, burying herself immediately in a thick canvas blanket.

Flame lashed his tail for a moment, studying the room. "Not much better than last night's dungeon," he muttered. He and Ochre found spots beside Viper at the far end of the room, and soon the MudWing was snoring. But the SkyWing dragonet sat and stared into the coals, unmoving.

Starflight was half asleep already, but the minute he curled on to his bed, Fatespeaker hopped up beside him.

"Mmph," Starflight objected sleepily.

"I know what we have to do," she whispered. "We have to talk to the queen."

"We?" Starflight asked.

"You and me. Without Morrowseer. Maybe she has no idea how awful he is. I bet he's lying about her ordering him to kill one of us. I bet he came up with that himself."

Starflight coiled his tail, feeling uneasy. He wondered how involved Queen Battlewinner was in decisions about the dragonets and the prophecy. Had she ordered their trip to the mainland and the deaths of those SkyWings?

"*I* bet," Fatespeaker said fiercely, "that she won't be too happy with Morrowseer for sending Squid away."

"Maybe she trusts him," Starflight pointed out. "Maybe she lets him do what he wants without direct orders. In which case we could get in really big trouble for going behind his back."

"Or maybe she has no idea what he's up to," Fatespeaker pointed out. "And maybe if we talk to her, she'll let us both live, free the RainWings, stop the experiments, and let the prophecy happen however it's supposed to without Morrowseer ruining everyone's lives."

Starflight tilted his head at her. "That's a lot of hope piled on to a very slim possibility."

"It's worth a try," she insisted.

He thought for a moment. His brain felt sluggish and

confused. He needed real food and he needed sleep and he really needed his friends.

"Maybe we can ask for a private audience tomorrow," he suggested.

"No!" Fatespeaker said. "Morrowseer won't allow it. We have to go find her ourselves."

"She doesn't want to be found," Starflight pointed out. "Maybe she keeps herself hidden for a reason." He hadn't come up with any good theories about that yet.

"Right, and maybe we need to know what that reason is," Fatespeaker said.

She had a point. More knowledge would make them more powerful. If they found out something they could use. . .

"All right," he said with a sigh. "We'll go look for her."

Fatespeaker shook out her wings and smiled at him. "Tonight," she said.

"Tonight?" Starflight covered his head with his aching wings. "Don't make me leave this bed before dawn. Please."

"This is important, Starflight. Sleep now and I'll wake you later. Deal?"

He sighed again. "Deal."

He felt her hop off the bed. Listening to her footsteps patter away, his tired brain began spinning in hypothetical circles.

What is the queen's secret? Why doesn't she let herself be seen?

He thought of Queen Glacier and how she kept her SandWing ally, Blaze, cozily confined in a fortress built just for her, under instructions never to leave or do anything risky.

What if Queen Battlewinner is being controlled by someone, like Blaze is? What if staying hidden isn't her own choice?

If something was wrong . . . if he could help Battlewinner, maybe she could help him in return.

Stop thinking and sleep, he told himself. He could see the thin trail of smoke from where Flame sat, hunched and brooding just like he was.

But despite the exhaustion that seemed to weigh down every bone in his body, sleep was a long time coming for both of them.

CHAPTER 14

Starflight was surrounded by scrolls. Stacks of scrolls, walls of scrolls as high as ten dragons, scrolls as far as he could see in every direction.

His intense joy – so much to read! Surely everything he could wish for had to be in here, all the answers to all his questions – warred with deep, paralysing anxiety. How would he ever learn all this? How could he possibly get through it all before the test?

What was the test? Something about wings of fire. There had to be a scroll on wings of fire in here.

"Oops," said a voice from the next aisle as a pile of scrolls went tumbling, scattering all around Starflight's talons. Clay's face poked out of the wreckage and he grinned at Starflight. "Oh, hey. There you are."

"Clay, be careful," Starflight said. He started picking up scrolls and re-stacking them as neatly as he could. "We need all this."

"Do we?" Clay wrinkled his snout. "Does the prophecy say 'A bunch of scrolls are coming to save the day?' Funny, I don't remember that part."

Starflight gave him a look and picked up the next scroll. *How to Free the RainWing Prisoners.* "See?" he said, waving it at Clay. "All the answers we need." He unrolled it eagerly, only to find it completely blank inside. Smooth, empty parchment stared back at him, indifferent to his disappointment.

"Come on outside," Clay said. "We could use your help."

"I can't. I have to read all of these first." Starflight started to spread his wings, knocked over another stack of scrolls, and turned in an agitated circle. Had the walls of scrolls got taller? He picked up another scroll: *Secrets of the NightWings.* "That's what I need," he muttered, rolling it open. But it was blank, too.

Clay was still waiting. "I can't help you until I know everything," Starflight told him. "I should stay in here. It won't take long. Soon I'll know a lot more than I do now. But I can't go out there yet." He pulled a shimmering golden scroll out of a pile. Surely something so beautiful had to have something useful in it.

How to Tell Sunny That You Love Her.

Starflight sighed. He knew before he unrolled it: blank, blank, blank.

"Starflight," Clay said. "Starflight. Come on. Hurry. Starflight, he's going somewhere, come on."

It wasn't Clay's voice any more – and someone was shaking his shoulder – and Starflight blinked awake, muddled and still sleepy.

"Come on," Fatespeaker whispered again. "Flame just snuck out. Let's follow him, quick."

"Why?" Starflight mumbled, rubbing his eyes. "He won't know where the queen is."

But Fatespeaker was already hurrying to the doorway. He stretched, knowing he definitely had not got enough sleep, and followed her.

Flame's red tail was just disappearing around a corner at the far end of the hallway. Fatespeaker and Starflight scurried quietly after him. She didn't speak, so he kept silent as well. His dream had left him feeling disturbed, like he'd forgotten something really important . . . someone he had to warn.

Soon Flame found a long staircase that wound down, and down, and down through the fortress, each level darker than the last despite the coals glowering in the walls. He stopped a few times, listening, and Fatespeaker and Starflight stopped, too, ducking their heads and letting the shadows envelop their black scales.

Finally they reached the bottom of the staircase and Flame chose one of the tunnels, which seemed to lead directly into the rock of the volcano. Heat pulsed beneath their claws. Starflight paused to touch the walls, worried that he was feeling rumbles of movement from deep within the earth.

And then they came to the first cage.

It was empty, but Starflight could guess what the bars and the shackles were for. This was the NightWing dungeon, where Flame and Ochre had been imprisoned overnight.

Most of the cages were empty, but in the fourth one was a skeletal, drab grey RainWing, fast asleep. Fatespeaker and Starflight paused outside her cage, looking in. Starflight wondered why this RainWing was kept separate from the others in the caves outside.

"What are you doing here?"

Flame's accusing face appeared from the shadows, making Starflight jump.

"Following you," Fatespeaker said breezily. "What in the three moons are you up to?"

"None of your business," Flame snapped. "Go away."

"What if a guard catches you down here?" Starflight pointed out. "You'll be in much more trouble as a SkyWing alone, prowling the fortress, than if you're with two NightWings."

The red dragonet considered that for a moment, smoke rising from his nostrils.

"Fine," he said ungraciously. "Do whatever you want, I don't care." He turned and stomped away. Fatespeaker and Starflight exchanged a glance and followed him.

The last cage in the hallway contained a NightWing. This was where Flame stopped and rapped on the bars with one claw.

Not just any NightWing: Deathbringer.

The assassin lifted his head and regarded them. His wings rose and fell as he breathed, and the cage seemed too small for him. "Hello, SkyWing. Glad to see you on the outside of the cages this time."

"What does it take to become an assassin?" Flame blurted. "I want to know the best way to kill another dragon fast."

Deathbringer stood up and took a step towards the bars. "You mean, the best way to kill another dragon and not care," he said.

Flame hissed and lashed his tail.

"You have to be doing it for a really good reason," said Deathbringer. "And you have to believe in that reason completely. You also should avoid talking to your targets, in case you find out that they're beautiful, sarcastic and fascinating. For instance."

"Is that what happened to you?" Flame asked with a snort. "Is that why you're in here?"

The silver scales under Deathbringer's wings glinted faintly in the torchlight as he shrugged. "Perhaps. But it's not a terrible thing to question your orders, if you ask me."

Flame flicked his tail and fidgeted with one of his wings.

"What orders?" Fatespeaker asked Flame and Starflight. "Who is this?"

"Can't one of your visions tell you that?" Flame asked snidely.

"This is Deathbringer," Starflight explained. "He was sent to kill my friends, but instead he let us go and he saved Glory from the other NightWings."

"Three moons, keep your voice down," Deathbringer said, looking nervous for the first time. "I think I'm the only dragon down here – apart from Queen Splendor – but you never know."

"That's Queen Splendor?" Starflight asked.

"The first RainWing captured by the tribe," said Deathbringer. "She's the one who accidentally scarred Vengeance. The idea was, once we had their queen, they'd do whatever we wanted. Little did we know that not only do they have multiple queens, apparently they can go for months without noticing one is missing either."

"Yikes," said Fatespeaker.

"Doesn't surprise me," Flame said.

"That's all going to change," Starflight said. *Glory will make sure of it.*

"Because of Glory?" Deathbringer asked. Starflight jumped. Had the other dragon read his mind?

They stared at each other for a moment.

"Yes," Starflight said finally.

The look on Deathbringer's face was so obvious – so real

and sad – that Starflight had the weird experience of being able to see what his own expression must be every time he thought of Sunny.

"Who's Glory?" Fatespeaker asked.

"That's . . . a long story," Starflight said.

"I'm going back to bed," Flame growled. A small burst of fire curled out of his snout as he pushed past Fatespeaker. "This is pointless."

"Wait," Deathbringer said. "Just – remember that you're your own dragon. You don't have to do what you're told. You can at least ask questions."

"So I can end up like you?" Flame snapped. "Behind bars, soon to be dumped into a pit of lava? That does sound like great advice."

Deathbringer shrugged. A ghost of a smile crossed his face. "It could be worse."

"Like if you'd killed any of my friends," Starflight said. "That would be worse."

Flame snorted again and slithered away up the tunnel. Starflight watched the flickers of fire around his snout moving through the shadows, past Splendor's cage, and back to the stairs.

"So Glory's all right?" Deathbringer said to Starflight. "She made it back?"

Starflight nodded. "But she's pretty mad about all the imprisoned RainWings." He hesitated, thinking that he really shouldn't trust this NightWing, no matter how much he'd helped them.

"Of course she is," said Deathbringer with another half smile. "I never thought that was a good idea, for the record."

The niches for the coals down here were rough, hacked out of the jagged rock walls instead of neatly carved and chiselled like the ones on the upper floors. So the shadows all had sharp edges, like talons trying to claw their way out of the stone. The heat was even worse than the blazing sun in the Kingdom of Sand, and Starflight's head was starting to ache.

"You don't – um, you don't seem. . ." Fatespeaker started, then trailed off.

"Like a typical assassin?" Deathbringer finished for her. "Well, a lot of energy went into training me. But then I was sent to the continent and . . . I guess when you're on your own for a while, you start thinking your own thoughts instead of anyone else's. I'm afraid that makes me quite a disappointment to the queen."

Fatespeaker grabbed the bars. "You've met the queen?"

He tilted his head at her. "No, not face-to-face, of course. She watches us through screens and speaks through her daughter, Greatness. It's been like that as long as I've been alive anyway."

Starflight's scales prickled. What if the queen had

screens like that all over the fortress? What if she was always watching her tribe without any of them realizing she was there? He looked around uneasily, thinking that the dungeon shadows could easily hide a few holes in the walls.

"We need to talk to her," Fatespeaker said. "How can we find her? I've spent all night searching the whole moonsbegotten fortress and I can't figure out where she might be."

"You have?" Starflight said, surprised.

"While you were sleeping," she said. "I told you, I'm wide awake at night. I wanted to get started."

"I'm the same way," Deathbringer said to her. "Listen, it's not safe to seek out the queen. She wouldn't like it."

"We don't have to invade her magical privacy or whatever," Fatespeaker said. "Does she have a throne room? Somewhere we could talk through the wall and probably find her?"

Deathbringer hesitated. "This isn't a good idea. I don't think she'll help you."

"*I* think she will," Fatespeaker said. She pressed her front talons to her forehead dramatically. "I saw it – in a VISION!"

Deathbringer gave her an extremely odd look. "Really."

"My visions are never wrong," Fatespeaker said breezily. "Although, I wish they'd warn me about more useful things sometimes." She glanced down at her claws, and Starflight guessed she was thinking of Squid.

"Well," Deathbringer said slowly, "if you really want to try the throne room – it's on the far side of the fortress from here, two doors past the library if you're coming from the council chamber. But even if she's behind that screen in the middle of the night, which she won't be, she won't speak to you without Greatness there."

"She doesn't have to speak," Fatespeaker said passionately. "She has to *listen*."

Deathbringer met Starflight's eyes and then shrugged again. "Well, good luck. But hurry – it'll be dawn soon."

"How can you tell?" Starflight asked. There were no windows in the dungeon, nothing to mark the passage of time. Nothing but pockmarked black rock surrounded the prisoners.

"I can sense it," Deathbringer said. "Spend a few months sleeping out in the open, and you'll get the knack of it, too."

"What were you doing on your own on the continent for so long?" Starflight asked.

"I had a list," Deathbringer said. "And regular meetings to receive new orders. Did you ever notice that whenever one side appeared to be winning the war, one of their top generals would mysteriously die? Not that I'm taking credit for anything, of course."

"I did notice that!" Starflight said. "At least, from what I could figure out from the newest history scrolls. But if that was you – well, it seemed to happen to all three sides, so I thought it had to be a coincidence."

Deathbringer spread his wings. "We only chose a side recently." He paused. "I was not consulted in that choice."

"You don't like Blister either," Starflight realized.

"Starflight, we have to go," Fatespeaker said, tugging on his tail. "I want to find the queen tonight. Before Morrowseer can do anything else awful. Come *on*."

Starflight stepped back reluctantly. He felt as if he still had so many questions for Deathbringer – and this might be the first NightWing who would actually give him real answers. "I'll come back," he promised. "Soon. I'll – I'll see what I can do to help you."

"Don't get in trouble," said Deathbringer. "I'll be all right. Good luck." He tipped his wings towards Fatespeaker.

Starflight wished he could do something. He should try to save Deathbringer the way the NightWing had saved Glory – both from assassination and from the prison caves. He should do something brave, something bold and kind and heroic. But he had no idea how to even begin.

Instead he followed Fatespeaker back into the fortress,

back through the tunnels and hallways, in search of the throne room and the queen who might or might not be there, who might or might not listen, and who almost certainly would not help them.

CHAPTER 15

"Two doors past the library," Fatespeaker muttered. "Something about a council chamber." She paused at an intersection, looking down both tunnels and pressing her claws together.

"I think I remember where the council chamber is," Starflight said. He'd been trying to create a map of the fortress in his head every time they left the dormitory. "That way, if I'm right." He pointed.

"Then we go this way," she said. "I think we'll pass the library this way."

"Library," Starflight echoed, finally hearing what Deathbringer had said. "There's a library! Fatespeaker! Have you seen it? How many scrolls do they have?"

"Like a million," she said.

"A *million*!" Starflight felt momentarily faint, thinking of a million scrolls he'd never read. It would be just like his dream.

"That wasn't a real guess," Fatespeaker said, stopping to give him an amused grin. "I just meant 'lots,' really. I didn't try to count them."

"Lots is exciting, too," Starflight said. He felt a little silly getting so excited over scrolls. But there had never been enough of them under the mountain. He'd read the same ones over and over and over again. Something new . . . something with more answers, more of the information he needed . . . that would be everything.

"Here it is," Fatespeaker said, pausing at a tall open archway.

Starflight peered inside, his heart pounding. The room was cavernous, even bigger than the council chamber. Instead of coals lying open in wall niches, here the light came from fire that was carefully trapped in metal globes and kept away from the scrolls. Square nooks were carved out of the wall, all the way up to the ceiling, and in each square there were between three and six scrolls, neatly rolled and labelled and organized – organized! – with a mark next to the square and a large scroll rolled out on a main table as a catalogue. He could see how it worked in the first glance and his talons ached to rush inside and start reading.

"You are so cute," Fatespeaker said. "Look at your face – like someone just opened up a giant treasure box and it's all for you."

That was exactly how Starflight felt, looking at all these scrolls. He took a tentative step inside and Fatespeaker immediately grabbed his tail.

"Oh, no you don't," she said. "We find the queen first. You can come back and moon over scrolls tomorrow."

"If Morrowseer lets me," Starflight said wistfully.

Fatespeaker dragged him away from the library and stopped two doors down, in front of a round stone room that was completely empty, with no windows and no furniture and only one niche for glowing coals. The wall opposite the door was a strange lattice of stone studded with diamond-shaped holes no bigger than ladybugs.

"I did see this room," Fatespeaker said. "I just didn't guess it was the throne room. Shouldn't a throne room have a throne in it? Even if no one plans to sit on it?"

"Maybe there's a throne behind the screen," Starflight suggested.

"Hmm," she said. "Still seems like it shouldn't get to be called a throne room, then." She stalked up to the lattice wall and pressed one eye to one of the holes.

"Fatespeaker!" Starflight said, shocked. "We're not supposed to try and look at her!"

"Don't panic," she said. "It's all dark back there anyway." She tilted her head and tried another hole lower down. "Maybe there's something glowing, but it just looks like fire. I can't see the queen. Do you think she's there?" She rapped on the screen. "Hello? Your Majesty?"

Silence from the wall.

"Queen Battlewinner?" Fatespeaker tried again. "We really need to talk to you. It's us, the dragonets from the prophecy."

"Well, the two NightWing options," Starflight amended.

"Hello?" Fatespeaker said.

Nothing. Fatespeaker knocked and kicked the wall a few times, but there was no response.

"That is SO FRUSTRATING," she growled. "Your Majesty! I'm not impressed!"

"It *is* the middle of the night," Starflight pointed out. "She's probably not even there. She must sleep somewhere."

Fatespeaker hunched her wings, then sighed and nodded. "All right. We'll sneak away from Morrowseer and try again tomorrow."

Starflight did not love the sound of that plan. But he already knew better than to try arguing with Fatespeaker.

They turned to go . . . but just then, Starflight heard a noise.

A noise like scraping, coming from behind the wall.

He looked at Fatespeaker and saw that she'd heard it, too. They both returned to the screen.

"Your Majesty?" Fatespeaker said.

When there was still no answer, Starflight said, "If she's back there, she doesn't want to talk to us."

Fatespeaker folded her wings in close and scowled. "Then we should *make* her see us." She started pacing along the wall with the screen. "There must be a door here somewhere. She has to get in and out somehow, right?"

"Unless she always stays in the same room," Starflight said. His mental map of the fortress started clicking together. "I think – I think the room behind this wall could also overlook the council chamber. Maybe that's where she lives."

"So we just have to find a way into it," Fatespeaker said, charging into the hallway.

"Is that a good idea?" Starflight asked. His claws caught on the rocks as he hurried behind her. "I'm pretty sure she won't be pleased."

"Too bad!" Fatespeaker cried. "We're her subjects, too! She has to listen to us!"

Clearly Fatespeaker didn't know very much about queens or tribes and how they worked. Perhaps the Talons of Peace camp was a little more open to input from all dragons. Or perhaps Fatespeaker would have been like this no matter where she was raised.

She stopped abruptly, frowning and tipping her head from side to side. "How do we *get* there?" she muttered to herself. She closed her eyes and took a deep breath.

"Having a vision?" Starflight asked, recognizing the expression on her face.

"Trying to," she said. "But all I can see is walls. Rrrgh."

"Let's try this way," Starflight suggested.

They followed winding passages that seemed to be circling the council room, but he couldn't find any doors that might lead to the place where the queen had been hidden.

But he did find one room with the door open, and it was empty when he peered inside. It was a strange room, too. The space was dominated by a giant map on the wall – Pyrrhia, but with more detail in it than he'd ever seen on any map before. Every inlet, every fjord was drawn with scientific precision. Even the rainforest sparkled with information: the location of the main RainWing village, all the rivers and streams that criss-crossed the jungle, and the two tunnels that led to the Kingdom of Sand and the NightWing island. Each was marked and carefully labelled.

Starflight noticed that the SeaWings' Summer Palace was noted on there as well, in ink that looked darker and newer than some of the other marks, and he wondered whether the NightWings had only learned of its location when it burned. The Deep Palace was not on there – still a SeaWing secret, apparently.

But strangest of all, the map was covered with tiny squares that were each labelled "Scavenger Den." There were seven of them, from the outer islands of the Kingdom of the Sea to the peninsula below the Kingdom of Sand; there was even one among the snowy wastes of the Ice Kingdom. And each one had a careful, deliberate X slashed across it in green ink.

What are they doing? Starflight thought, staring at the map. *Why track scavengers? What do the X's mean?*

"What's a scavenger den?" Fatespeaker asked from behind him.

"Have you ever seen a scavenger?" Starflight asked. She shook her head. "They're these little creatures with hardly any fur, and they run around on two legs, and they love to steal treasure – kind of like magpies or raccoons, but bigger. And sometimes they get pointy sticks and poke dragons with them, which means they can't be very intelligent."

"Oh," Fatespeaker said, "right, like the scavenger who killed Queen Oasis and started the whole war in the first place."

"Exactly," Starflight said. He shivered, remembering the only ones he'd ever encountered – the two who'd tried to kill him in Scarlet's arena. In his nightmares they always stared at him with big, dragonlike eyes, and even though he found them terrifying, he couldn't help thinking, *They're in the same situation I am. They're just trying to survive this arena.*

"So these dens – that's where they live?" Fatespeaker reached up and traced the outline of one of the dens with her claw.

"I guess so," Starflight said. "I've never seen one. I always imagined warrens of tunnels – the scrolls say they like to live in big groups, like meerkats. But they try to keep their dens hidden, according to what I've read. They're safer from predators that way."

"Predators like us," Fatespeaker said cheerfully.

"I have no idea why the NightWings would care about them," Starflight said, scratching his head. A theory was bubbling at the back of his mind, but before he could put it together, Fatespeaker slid her talons along to the outer edge of the map and let out a yelp.

"Look! There's something behind here!"

She unpinned one corner of the map and lifted it up, and sure enough, there was a small tunnel hidden behind it.

"Let's go," she whispered, ducking into it with no hesitation.

Starflight's heart was trying to clamber up his throat and strangle him. But what else could he do? If this tunnel led where it looked like it might – he couldn't leave Fatespeaker to face Queen Battlewinner alone.

If only Tsunami were here, or Clay! They'd at least be some use in a fight, unlike him.

His claws shook as he lifted the corner of the map and slid into the dark tunnel behind Fatespeaker.

"I'm having a vision!" Fatespeaker whispered dramatically in his ear, nearly making him leap out of his scales. "Of us standing in front of Queen Battlewinner! This is going to work!"

"You scared me half to death," he said, clutching his chest.

"Sorry," she said, and even in the dark he could sense her grinning.

"So," he whispered as they started creeping forward, "in your visions, there *is* a Queen Battlewinner. She's alive? She exists?"

"Of course," Fatespeaker said. "What?"

"Nothing," Starflight said. "It's just – I've been wondering, since no one ever sees her and apparently no one even hears her except Greatness . . . well, if she were dead, this would be a pretty clever plan, is all. As long as Greatness claims Battlewinner is alive, she can issue orders and do all the things a queen might do – in Battlewinner's name – but no one can challenge her to try to take the throne."

"That is way sneaky," Fatespeaker said. "I would never have thought of that."

"I could be wrong." His nose bumped suddenly into stone. He stood up on his back talons and poked the low ceiling above their heads, then breathed out a plume of fire. The tunnel ended at a large boulder right in front of them.

Fatespeaker hissed. "No way! This *has* to be it!"

Starflight gingerly felt around to the back of the boulder and realized there was empty space under his claws. "The tunnel keeps going, only smaller, I think," he said.

There was a hole in the wall, hidden by the boulder, barely big enough for a dragon to fit through. He reached his talons inside and guessed that the hidden tunnel led up in the right direction.

"Oooo," Fatespeaker said, sniffing at the darkness. "I foresee that this is going to be mad scary. You go first."

It felt like a volcano was about to explode out of Starflight's chest. *Well, if anyone does catch us, they can't kill both of us. They need at least one of us alive.*

He didn't find that thought very reassuring as he climbed into the dark tunnel and felt sharp black rocks digging into his talons. The only thing that was oddly comforting was the sound of Fatespeaker clambering behind him, close enough to step on his tail a few times.

The tunnel sloped up and around in a kind of spiral. When a last twist suddenly left them standing in an open cave, they were both caught by surprise.

Starflight froze and Fatespeaker blundered into him.

This is it.

On one wall, the circle shape punctured with holes, looking out over the council chamber. On another wall, the screen that faced the throne room. And then there was a third wall with only a few carefully hidden eyeholes, for spying on something or someone or somewhere without being noticed.

But no queen.

There were no dragons here, no signs of life.

Where else could she be? Or am I right – is she dead after all?

In the centre of the cave was an enormous cauldron full of lava, big enough for two Morrowseers. It looked like a jagged black bowl that had been yanked and pummelled out of the volcanic stone. Molten lava filled it to the brim, bubbling and spitting and gurgling weirdly. A few drops spattered over the side, and Starflight took a cautious step back, remembering the stinging burn on his foot.

The room was stiflingly hot, almost painfully so. Starflight slid around the cauldron, hugging the walls, to peer through the secret eyeholes across from the tunnel entrance. Fatespeaker followed him, uncharacteristically quiet.

Starflight didn't recognize the room on the other side of the third wall, but he could see a low table, and the leftover bones of prey were strewn around the floor.

"I bet this is where the council members eat," he said quietly to Fatespeaker. "It's a good time to spy on dragons – when they might say anything, if they don't realize she's watching." He glanced at the other two screens and shook his head. "Then again, it looks like she's not doing much watching right now." He leaned in to peer through at the dining cave again.

"Maybe you're right about—" Fatespeaker started, then

cut herself off with a cry of terror and seized Starflight's shoulder at the same time, clutching him so hard he thought she might draw blood.

"Ow, what—" he began, then turned and saw what she saw.

A dragon was rising up out of the lava.

CHAPTER 16

Starflight had been terrified plenty of times since leaving the caves where he grew up. He'd thought nothing could ever be worse than the moment Queen Scarlet walked in with her guards, killed Dune, and took all the dragonets prisoner. But then there was the moment he stood in her arena, knowing that she intended for him to be violently dead by the end of the day. That was followed by the moment Queen Coral had them thrown in her prison, Tsunami's plunge through the electric eels, the SkyWing attack on the Summer Palace, their frantic escape right through the middle of a battle, and perhaps the actual worst, when Sunny had disappeared right in front of him in the rainforest. Not to mention all the scary things he'd faced since being abducted by the NightWings. In fact, he'd spent most of the last few weeks in a state of near-constant terror.

This was a whole other level. A level of *that's not scientifically possible* and *has it been under the lava this whole time?* and *THAT'S NOT POSSIBLE* and *now this is really it and there's no one to protect me and I'm definitely absolutely one hundred per cent going to die because THAT IS A DRAGON WHO LIVES IN LAVA.*

Its head and wings came first, in a fountain of golden molten lava, and then a set of claws shot out and clutched the side of the cauldron. The dragon shook itself, sending splatters of lava flying. Slowly the lava poured off her head, revealing a thickset neck, a battle-scarred snout, and black scales that gleamed like polished ebony against the orange-yellow pool around her.

"Starflight, Starflight, Starflight," Fatespeaker whispered in a panicked rush, shaking his arm violently. "Do something!"

"Like what?" he whispered back. The tunnel was on the far side of the cauldron. They'd have to get past the dragon and the lava she was dripping everywhere if they wanted to run away, which was what he really, really wanted to do.

Hissssssssssssssssssssssssssssssssssssssssssssssssssssss.

The dragon in the lava leaned forward and glared at them. Buzzing white steam seemed to be rising from her scales. Her tongue flicked in and out as she studied the two dragonets, and Starflight realized there was a glint of icy blue in the depths of her dark eyes. When she opened her mouth, he spotted two teeth that were the same shade of blue, looking more like icicles than regular teeth.

"Who?" she rasped suddenly. Her voice was hard to hear – creaky and quiet and rough and eerie, like claws scraping on ice several caves away.

"N-n-n-no one," Starflight stammered.

"Please don't kill us," Fatespeaker squeaked.

"Don't make me," said the lava dragon. She hissed again, her claws flexing around the edge of the cauldron. "How?"

"How . . . did we find you?" Starflight filled in. "We were looking for the queen – Queen Battlewinner."

"I," said the dragon. Her eyes narrowed. "You?"

"We're – we're the dragonets of the prophecy," Fatespeaker said. "I'm Fatespeaker and this is Starflight."

"Ahhh." The queen sank lower in the lava. "Hmm. Unimpressive."

"How is this happening?" Starflight burst out. "Why aren't you *dead*? The temperature you're immersed in – the boiling point – the physical reaction of lava and scales – I saw what happened to Vengeance. You *can't* be swimming in lava. It just *isn't possible*. Even dragons born from blood-red eggs, like Clay, could probably only withstand that kind of heat for a minute or two, and as far as I know NightWings don't have eggs like that anyway, so – this *can't* be happening, scientifically speaking."

The queen let out a small, possibly amused snort, blowing bubbles across the surface of the lava. "Mastermind's son," she rasped. She studied him for a moment, then leaned forward, opening her jaws as wide as they would go.

For a moment, Starflight thought she was about to lunge out of the cauldron and bite their heads off. But then he realized from her odd position that she was actually holding herself so he could look inside her mouth. His fear slowly started to fade as curiosity took over, and he stepped closer.

"Starflight," Fatespeaker whispered anxiously. "This wasn't in any of my visions! I'm really not sure about this!"

"Three moons," he said, his eyes widening. "Fatespeaker, look! You can see right down her throat . . . and it's *blue*." The walls of Battlewinner's throat were lined with what looked like pale blue frost, small swirling patterns that were feathery or sharp and all glinted oddly.

"What is it?" Starflight met Battlewinner's eyes again.

She snapped her mouth shut. "Ice." The creak of her voice seemed to rattle her to her wingtips; she took a deep breath, dipped her whole head in the lava, and emerged again.

"Ice?" Starflight echoed. His mind whirled into gear, trying to solve this mystery. Was this connected to the NightWing bacteria that killed their prey? Or had she just swallowed a lot of ice to combat the lava? That made no sense. Where would the dragons even get ice out here on the island, where it was perpetually too warm?

Queen Battlewinner was watching him, as if this was

a test and she had decided to save her breath and see if he could figure it out.

Her breath. . .

"IceWings!" Starflight burst out. "Their weapon – the frostbreath!"

Battlewinner nodded, her heavy shoulders sliding up out of the lava and back down again. Her black tongue flicked in and out again, and this time he saw that it also had a layer of thin shimmering frost on it.

"You got blasted by an IceWing," he said slowly. "You must have been on the continent when you . . . ran into one, is that it? And you fought, and it hit you, but not on the outside . . . maybe your mouth was open and it went right in and down your throat to freeze your insides. Which means you should have been dead within a day."

The queen flicked her wings back, scattering sizzling orange droplets around. "Not so easy," she growled.

"To kill you," Starflight finished. "You made it back here. And the lava – the lava stops the effects of the freezing? Is that it?"

"Indeed." The queen hissed again. "A balance."

"But how—" Fatespeaker said. "I mean, how did you know the lava wouldn't just kill you right away?"

Starflight could imagine it clearly – Battlewinner on the continent, perhaps looking for a new home for the

NightWings, running into an IceWing and nearly dying in battle. But she staggered back through that long, awful flight to the island, feeling colder and colder and closer to death by the minute. The fire that burned inside fire-breathing dragons like NightWings and SkyWings would have been working against the ice to keep her alive for a while, but it wouldn't be enough to save her.

By the time she'd made it to the island, she would have been shivering violently and feeling terribly sick as her stomach and intestines began to freeze and fuse together, spreading the icy plague out from her organs towards her scales. At that point, he could imagine she felt so cold that diving into lava sounded better than anything. Even if it killed her – and maybe she expected it to – it couldn't be worse than what she was already feeling.

And instead it saved her life. Queen Battlewinner was alive now, but the frostbreath was still inside her. She could never leave the lava, or else it would finish its work.

The rest was details, although he was still curious about all of it – like who knew her secret besides Greatness, how this room had been built and the screens put in, how the cauldron had been filled with lava and prepared for her. He wondered if she could still eat, or if she existed in kind of a suspended state, right on the edge of death.

The queen was watching him closely, perhaps reading his mind as he put all the pieces together. He guessed that speaking was painful, scraping and cracking the ice in her throat and mouth, and that was why she did as little of it as she possibly could.

"I'm sorry," he said to her finally. "It seems like an awful thing, what's happened to you."

Battlewinner's head spikes flattened and her snout lifted. "No pity," she snarled. "Revenge. Soon."

That sounded ominous, but worrying about IceWings would have to wait. Starflight reached out and took one of Fatespeaker's talons in his.

"We wanted to talk to you about the prophecy," he said hesitantly. "We're afraid Morrowseer is being too cruel and interfering too much."

The queen cut him off with a barking laugh and then doubled over in pain, clutching her neck. After a moment, she recovered enough to glare at him.

"Do as he says," she hissed. "The prophecy is everything."

"But he sent Squid away to die today," Fatespeaker pleaded. "And he says he's going to kill me or Starflight. And the RainWing prisoners are being treated so terribly. Please, it doesn't have to be like this, does it?"

"Anything to . . . save the tribe," said the queen. She began to sink down into the lava. "Leave now."

"Wait, please," cried Fatespeaker.

But lava was already closing over the dark dragon's head. She was gone. They had failed.

CHAPTER 17

Fatespeaker and Starflight trudged back to the dormitory in weary silence. He hoped against hope that dawn was further away than Deathbringer had said, but he had a feeling Morrowseer would be breathing angry heat into his face within a horribly short span of time.

"Poor Squid," Fatespeaker said, pausing outside the dormitory entrance. "I guess now we'll have to work with your SeaWing instead." She sighed and headed back to her sleeping spot.

Chills rippled through Starflight's scales like the clouds billowing outside the skylight. *Tsunami. That* was who he had to warn. Morrowseer had said, "We have another SeaWing. We just have to retrieve her from the rainforest." Had they gone after her already? Had they tried? Was she all right?

I can warn her. If it's not too late. . .

He hurried to his bed and scrabbled among the rocks until he found the tiny hole where he'd stashed the dreamvisitor. This time he'd find someone in the rainforest who would listen to him. He had to.

He pulled the blanket over himself again and cupped

the jewel in his talons, then pressed it to his head. *Tsunami. Please be there. Tsunami.*

As always, his first thought was of Sunny, and then the others flashed through his head: Tsunami, Clay, Glory. . .

And then he was falling, suddenly, through a bright, cloudless blue sky. He snapped his wings open, catching a rising wind, and looked up.

Above him, glimmering in the sun, were five shapes. He recognized Sunny immediately: her golden scales couldn't be mistaken for anyone else's. She was playing a looping game of chase with Clay, her quick agility outmanoeuvring his giant wings, both of them laughing.

Tsunami and Glory circled them, calling out suggestions. Glory's wings were dark purple, and she wore a small woven crown of iridescent ruby-red flowers.

And there was Starflight himself, flying along with the others and smiling like nothing could ever be wrong. He looked different here – bigger, kinder, warmer somehow. In fact, they all did. Tsunami and Glory rarely smiled so much in real life; Clay was almost never this fast or graceful.

Whose dream is this? he wondered, but it wasn't hard to guess.

Sunny darted away from the others like a dragonfly and dropped towards him, beaming.

"Two of you in one dream!" she said happily. "How weird is that?" She flitted around him, brushed her wings against his, and then zipped back up to tug on Clay's tail.

He couldn't bring himself to speak. Being near her, it all came rushing back – how he'd loved her his whole life and how impossible the whole thing was, not least because they were from different tribes.

If he could make himself talk, if he could warn her about Tsunami, maybe she would listen. . .

But the blue sky was abruptly swallowed in darkness, and he was falling again, until he was surrounded by bubbles and cool green light.

Underwater. *This must be Tsunami's dream.*

He waved his wings and spun slowly in the water. Sure enough, there she was, with her claws wrapped around the neck of a skeletal green dragon.

Gill, Starflight remembered. *Her father. The one she killed in the arena, before she knew who he was.*

This was a nightmare. Her face was twisted in despair – she'd never hear him like this.

Her little sister, Anemone, came swimming up, and, seeing her, Tsunami suddenly released the older dragon. He fell back, his jaws opening and closing pitifully. Tsunami turned to Anemone with her talons outstretched, like she was apologizing.

But then Anemone's eyes narrowed, and she lunged towards Gill, seizing his throat herself. Her tail smacked Tsunami aside as her talons sank into his neck. Thick blood bubbled out, staining the water.

Tsunami grabbed Anemone and tried to pull her away, but it was too late.

Starflight closed his eyes. He understood what Tsunami was worrying about: that Anemone would turn evil if she used her animus powers, and that there was nothing Tsunami could do to save her.

Just one more reason why we have to stop this war. If there was no war, there would be no one trying to force Anemone into using her powers. She'd be safe.

Crunch. Crunch crunch crunch.

Starflight opened his eyes again.

He was sitting in a vast, dry cave with torches flickering along the walls. The floor was nearly covered with all kinds of prey – boar, chickens, a cow, several ducks, two deer and a hippo. Some of them were still alive, wandering around, bumping into walls, oblivious to the two dragons in the cave with them.

The other dragon was Clay, who sat with his tail curled around his back talons, happily munching on something charred.

"Oh, hey, Starflight," he said, as if it were perfectly natural for his friends to suddenly pop into his dreams.

"Clay!" Starflight cried. "You can see me!"

Clay blinked a few times. "Should I . . . not be able to see you?"

"This isn't just a dream," Starflight said quickly. "I'm really here. I mean, I'm really talking to you."

"Of course you're really talking to me," Clay said cheerfully. "Hungry? There's a great pheasant around here somewhere." He looked around, scratching his head. "Oh, uh, I think I already ate it. Sorry."

Starflight *was* hungry, but he knew dream food wouldn't do him any good. "Clay, listen to me. I'm using a dream-visitor. I'm talking to you from the NightWing kingdom."

"Very cool," Clay said in an agreeable voice. "How about a pig? No, wait. I ate that, too."

"I'm serious," Starflight said, lashing his tail. "Don't you remember learning about dreamvisitors? They're these ancient sapphires that were animus-touched generations ago. I found one and I'm using it to visit your dream and tell you something really important."

Clay's forehead was scrunched in a puzzled way. "Sure, Starflight. I have dreams about you lecturing me all the time."

That stopped Starflight for a moment. "You do?"

Clay drew himself up and adopted a stuffy, scolding voice. "Weren't you *listening*? Didn't you *read* the *scrolls*? That was *before* the Scalding. *Everyone* knows that."

201

"The Scorching," Starflight corrected automatically. "And I do not sound like that."

"Sure," Clay said. "Anyway. Hippo?"

Starflight stamped one foot. "Fine, but just listen. Tsunami is in danger. Morrowseer and the NightWings are coming after her. Will you tell her that?"

"Look!" Clay said delightedly. "My brothers and sisters!" He jumped up and hurried to the cave entrance, where a small band of MudWings were coming in. The smallest dragonet jumped up to hug Clay's big neck, and the largest one inclined his head with a friendly smile.

Starflight hadn't met Clay's siblings, but he'd heard about Clay's encounter with them in the MudWing village. They were all soldiers now in the great war, fighting under Queen Moorhen on Burn's side, even though they weren't full-grown yet. One of them had died in battle already.

More dragons we need to save, he thought, anxiety and fear turning his scales cold.

He wasn't sure Clay had really listened to him. He had to keep trying.

Glory, he thought, closing his eyes.

The sound of paper rustling let him know that he was somewhere new right before he opened them again. Glory sat at a low table in one of the treetop huts in the rainforest, studying a scroll. In her own dream, she wasn't wearing a crown, and she looked more tired than anything else. Her scales were dark green and dappled with light, matching the leaves around her. The furry shape of her sloth curled around her neck.

"Glory," Starflight said, his voice breaking. Would she listen to him? He remembered what he'd heard Sunny say the last time he'd used the dreamvisitor. If Glory thought he was a traitor, she wouldn't have any reason to believe anything he said.

The new queen of the RainWings slowly raised her head and met his eyes. They stared at each other for a long moment, her green eyes searching for something in his face.

"Wow," she said. "You found a dreamvisitor."

He exhaled, feeling relief flood through his scales. Of course she remembered learning about them. He'd always wished he could remember things as easily as she did, instead of having to study so hard all the time.

"I didn't run off," he said in a rush. "The NightWings took me. I swear, Glory. I would never have left you all. Morrowseer is – is testing me, to see if I'm worthy of the prophecy – he has these other dragonets that he wants to use instead, only he needs a SeaWing now so Tsunami's in danger and I had to warn you—"

"Stop, stop," Glory said, rolling up her scroll and leaning on the table. "Tell me everything."

So he did, from the moment he was abducted through the terrifying encounter with the NightWing queen. At first he had that sinking sensation in his stomach again, worrying that he was betraying someone – this time his tribe – but then he thought of Orchid clamped to the wall, the SkyWings burning, and Squid flying slowly away to his death, and he squashed any guilt he felt. He was sure now who deserved his loyalty.

"So," he finished. "I'm worried about Tsunami. Please tell her to be careful."

Glory laughed. "Oh, sure, and you tell Clay to stop being hungry."

Starflight felt a smile trying to struggle on to his face. "He really does dream about food, it turns out," he said. "Like, lots and *lots* of food."

"Oh, Clay," Glory said affectionately. "Well, apparently I dream about homework, even though there aren't any scrolls in the rainforest." She waved her talons at the dream table in front of her, and then her face turned serious again. "I'll talk to Tsunami and put some guards on her, but I'm more worried about you. We're not ready to attack yet. But if you're in danger. . ."

She carved a line in the table with one of her claws. "I mean, it sounds like Morrowseer might kill you at any moment." She looked out the window, where glimmers of rainbow wings were visible in the trees around them. "But my tribe . . . they're not ready. If I take them through today, they'll be slaughtered."

"I understand," Starflight said. Glory was a queen now. She had to think about protecting her tribe as much as taking care of her friends. Every single bit of him wanted to yell, "Forget the RainWings! Please rescue me! Come as soon as you can!" But it was too easy for him to imagine everything Glory was thinking, all the information she had to take into account, the pros and cons and best battle strategies and unacceptable losses and collateral damage – all the things they'd studied as distant theories but never had to deal with themselves.

So instead he said, "I'm all right. I'll take care of myself until you get here."

Glory looked back at him, tilting her head to the side. Warm pink suffused with purple spread along the edges of her wings. "Starflight, I think that might be the bravest thing you've ever said."

He ducked his head, looking down at his talons. "Well," he added. "You know. Don't take too long."

She laughed again, and he felt a fierce, awful longing to be back with his friends, where, even if everything wasn't easy, at least he felt like he meant something to somebody – something more than a line in a prophecy.

Her face went serious, and she toyed with the corner of one of the scrolls between her claws. "So Deathbringer's in trouble for helping me," she said.

"I'm sure he understood the risks when he decided to set you free," Starflight pointed out.

"Hmm," Glory said sceptically. "*I'm* sure he thought he could charm his way out of anything. Idiot."

"Well, he still might," Starflight said. "I don't think Greatness wants to execute him."

Glory shook herself. "Can you tell me anything else about the NightWings?" she asked. "Anything that might help us when we do attack? Like, do they have mind readers posted at the tunnel entrance? That's what I would do, so they could sense anyone coming through and maybe even read our battle plans before we got there. I want to send in a camouflaged scout just to see how many guards are in the cave now, but that's why I haven't yet – I don't dare."

"I don't know," Starflight said. "I'm sorry, I don't know anything useful about what the NightWings are doing."

"I bet you know more than you think," she said. "Can you tell me more about the fortress? Or the layout of the island? Or how we might get there if we flew from the continent instead of using the tunnel?"

His heart sank. "You'd have to get through MudWing and SkyWing territory first," he pointed out, "before you could fly across the ocean to the island, even if I could find a way to describe the route." *And that would take weeks,* he thought. *Weeks to travel the whole length of the continent. Can I survive for weeks on my own?*

"Yeah, it's probably not the safest plan," Glory said thoughtfully.

206

Starflight shifted his wings. He felt chilly air against his scales, and it wasn't coming from Glory's rainforest dream. "I think I have to go," he said in a panicked whisper. "It must almost be dawn."

"All right," she said, standing up. "But come back tomorrow night if you can. We can figure this out, Starflight. It's going to be all right." She stepped over the table and wrapped her wings around him, which didn't work very well since he wasn't really there, but somehow it was still comforting.

"See you soon," he said. "Remember to watch out for Tsunami."

Glory rolled her eyes. "At this point, I bet most of my tribe would invite the NightWings to abduct her. She's not the calmest general on Pyrrhia, I can tell you."

Starflight smiled and lifted the dreamvisitor to his forehead.

The rainforest disappeared.

He was back in the gloomy, dimly lit NightWing dormitory.

Had he heard a scrabble of claws right before he'd opened his eyes? Starflight glanced around and realized that his blankets had shifted so he wasn't as well hidden any more.

Or someone moved them.

His talons, with the glowing sapphire trapped between

them, were visible; he pulled them back close to his chest, then leaned over the side of the bed to tuck the jewel into its hiding spot.

Sleepy mutters indicated that the other dragonets were waking up. But when he looked around the room, he couldn't see anyone who looked awake yet.

Did someone see the dreamvisitor? Was someone spying on me?

Maybe I imagined it.

But he couldn't shake the uneasy feeling that his secret might not be entirely safe any more.

CHAPTER 18

Starflight lay curled on top of the blanket, trying to calm his pounding heart.

I've done what I had to do. I warned Glory. Now I just have to wait until they rescue me . . . survive until they get here. Surely I can do that.

"Up," snarled Morrowseer from the doorway.

All the dragonets in the dormitory scrambled to their feet, neck spikes bristling. But Morrowseer's gaze was fixed on the prophecy dragonets, who came forward to stand in front of him. Starflight noticed that Flame kept his head down so he didn't have to meet the NightWing's eyes.

"Yesterday was stupendously unimpressive," Morrowseer growled. Starflight glanced over his shoulder and saw Fierceteeth watching them with an alert expression.

"Next time you're in that kind of situation," the NightWing went on, "I want to be sure you can fight your way out of it, even without backup. So. Today, battle training."

Starflight's wings drooped. Battle training was always his least favourite thing.

"*Next* time?" Viper snapped. "I'm not stupid enough to go through that again."

Morrowseer hissed at her. "If you would like to take yourself back to the Talons of Peace, too, there's the door." He swept his wing towards the outside.

Viper hesitated, scowling, then ducked her head and stopped arguing.

"My throat hurts," Flame said to Morrowseer without looking at him.

"There's water in the trough down there." Morrowseer waved at the other end of the dormitory. "Catch up to us as fast as you can."

The others followed Morrowseer out through the archway; a few moments later, Flame caught up, coughing and scratching his throat. Morrowseer led them out to the prison-caves side of the mountain, where a few rivers of lava flowed as swiftly as if they'd just erupted yesterday. The biggest was the one that ran in front of the RainWing prison caves. They landed a few lengths away from it, and Starflight spotted guards in every cave mouth, bristling with armour and spears and alarm gongs.

I should remember to tell Glory that tonight, he noted. *Looks like two guards for every RainWing prisoner.*

He saw Morrowseer notice the direction of his gaze and hurriedly filled his mind with other thoughts. "Aren't we a little close to the lava?" Starflight asked, nodding at the golden-orange liquid fire that flowed from the top of the mountain.

"Everywhere on this island is close to lava," Morrowseer

growled. "Let's begin with you two." He flicked his tail at Ochre and Flame, to Starflight's relief. "Try to kill each other and I'll step in when I think it's necessary."

Ochre regarded Flame dubiously. "Try to kill each other?" he said. "With no breakfast?"

Flame flexed his claws. "Fine by me. Any rules?"

"There are no rules on the battlefield," Morrowseer pointed out.

Flame immediately leaped at Ochre. His claws slashed across the MudWing's nose, leaving a bleeding gash, and then he spun and kicked the MudWing in the chest.

"OW!" Ochre roared, lunging at the SkyWing.

They grappled on the dark, rocky ground, red and brown scales flashing and soon smeared with blood. With the lava river so close, there wasn't a lot of room to manoeuvre or get out of the way. At one point, a burst of fire from Flame nearly singed Starflight's wing, and Ochre stepped on Viper's foot, earning a ferocious *hiss*.

"Here." Fatespeaker grabbed Starflight and tugged him up on to a tall boulder. He sank his claws into gaps in the rocks, nervously eyeing the lava below. Even from up here, he could feel the heat blasting along his scales. His fear should have helped keep him awake, but he was a little dizzy with exhaustion, and the heat made him drowsier. He rubbed his eyes, wondering what would happen if he fell asleep. He guessed he'd either tumble right off the boulder into the lava, or he'd wake up in Morrowseer's talons, dangling over the volcano.

He tried to pay attention to the moves the two dragonets were using, but unlike Clay and Tsunami, he could never figure out what was going on in a fight like this. Everyone was moving too fast.

Ochre suddenly burst into the air, winging in a circle around Flame, yelling, "Stop it! I want to stop!"

Morrowseer snorted. "An opponent on the battlefield wouldn't stop just because you asked them to."

"He's bleeding pretty seriously," Fatespeaker pointed out. "Look at the cut on his wing."

"Hmm," Morrowseer said, studying Ochre. "All right, MudWing, you're out – and *you're* in." He seized Fatespeaker's shoulder and threw her towards Flame.

The SkyWing didn't wait to be told twice. He jumped forward and sank his teeth into her neck.

"Yow!" Fatespeaker shrieked. She beat his head with her wings until he let go and fell back, and then she clawed at the air in front of his face and darted away.

"Send me in, too!" Viper said to Morrowseer. "*I* want to bite her! I can definitely kill her, just give me a chance!"

"Go ahead and try," Morrowseer said, tilting his head at the small NightWing.

Viper hissed with delight and rushed forward with her tail raised, just like a scorpion attacking. Fatespeaker yelped with dismay and shot behind the boulder, appearing around the other side as Viper chased her.

"That's not fair!" Starflight cried. "Fatespeaker against both of them?"

"Battles are never fair in real life. If she doesn't survive, well, we have you."

Starflight clenched his talons, watching the writhing shapes below him anxiously. Viper and Flame were both so angry. They hated being here, and he wouldn't be surprised if they took it out on Fatespeaker.

Flame shot a burst of fire at Fatespeaker's snout. She ducked and rolled away, barely escaping before Viper's poisonous tail stabbed into the ground beside her.

"If she's even scratched by Viper's tail, she could die," Starflight said to Morrowseer. "Maybe not right away, but the infection—" He'd watched the wound Blister had given to Webs for days as it got worse and worse. Only a particular cactus from the Kingdom of Sand could reverse the effects, and there certainly wasn't any of it on this island.

"If you're so worried, jump in yourself," Morrowseer said. He was studying the fight intently. "SkyWing, has nobody ever taught you how to hold in your fire until it's at maximum temperature? Like this." He shot a bolt of flames over their heads. "By the moons, Fatespeaker, stop rolling around and use your claws."

"Starflight, help me!" Fatespeaker yelped.

He had no choice. It was beyond terrifying to think of facing Viper's tail and Flame's talons, but he *couldn't* leave her to fight alone. He knew what his friends would do, if they were here. He closed his eyes, braced his legs, and vaulted off the boulder on to Flame's back.

The SkyWing roared and twisted, sending Starflight tumbling across the black rocks. Sharp stone edges slashed his scales and the membranes of his wings. He struggled up, bleeding from several small cuts, and saw Viper knock Fatespeaker to the ground and loom over her with her tail raised. Morrowseer watched, his claws tapping thoughtfully.

"Stop!" Starflight cried, running at Viper. "Leave her alone!"

"This is your fault," Viper hissed at Fatespeaker. "I could be back at camp with my parents if it weren't for your stupid tribe."

Starflight smashed into Viper just as her tail jabbed down towards Fatespeaker's neck. A sharp smell of venom filled his nose and his head collided with one of her wings. As she staggered back, her tail flew out for balance and sliced neatly across Flame's face.

Flame roared with agony, clawed frantically at his snout, and slammed his body forward into Viper's side. The force of the blow sent her reeling away.

Starflight watched in horror as Viper teetered on the edge, and then fell with an ear-splitting shriek right into the lava river.

"No!" Morrowseer roared, leaping forward. But he wasn't reaching for Viper – he seized Flame's head between his talons and glared at the wound she had inflicted. "SkyWing! Don't move! Can you see?"

Flame's only response was a keening, guttural sound of agony.

"Viper!" Fatespeaker cried. Starflight followed her to the edge of the river, but the SandWing had vanished below the lava. "Viper!" Fatespeaker screamed.

Through his horror, Starflight's brain flashed him a message, and he whirled around. "Ochre, you can go get her," he yelled. "Maybe we can save her if you pull her out right away."

Ochre blinked slow, painfully dull eyes at him. "What in the three moons are you talking about?"

"Your scales." Starflight grabbed Ochre's forearm and tried to drag him towards the lava. The MudWing sat down firmly, as heavy as an entire fortress. "Ochre, please! You have fireproof scales – you can go into the lava without getting hurt! You can find her and drag her out. Please, please, just try!"

"Fireproof scales?" Fatespeaker said.

"Because he was born from a red egg," Starflight said,

"like it says in the prophecy, and that means fireproof scales *come on why aren't you moving*?"

"Let go of me," Ochre growled, planting all his limbs even more solidly on the ground. "I have no idea if my egg was red or whether my scales are fireproof and I am CERTAINLY NOT JUMPING INTO A PIT OF LAVA TO FIND OUT."

"But—" Starflight protested. "But if you're in the prophecy – if you could be the MudWing – then you must have been born from a blood-red egg, just like Clay." His heart wasn't in it any more. He turned to look back at the lava, knowing it was already too late. Viper hadn't even come up to the surface once. She was gone.

"Prophecy shmophecy," said Ochre. "I wasn't hatched on the brightest night either, so I'm not going to base any life-or-death decisions on some old words in a scroll."

Starflight pivoted slowly to stare at the MudWing.

"You *weren't* hatched on the brightest night?" he echoed.

Ochre shrugged. "Neither was he. We had the same hatching day, a few weeks before the brightest night." He nodded at Flame, who was curled on the ground now, still making that horrible sound of pain with his talons pressed to his face. Morrowseer stood over him, lashing his tail furiously.

"But—" Starflight's words failed him.

Suddenly everything seemed a lot clearer . . . and yet more confusing at the same time.

216

The alternate dragonets weren't real. They *couldn't* be the dragonets in the prophecy. They were entirely false, an illusion Morrowseer was trying to create.

The giant NightWing wasn't just tinkering with fate – he was trying to rewrite it entirely.

CHAPTER 19

Fatespeaker was crumpled in a ball by the lava river with her wings over her head, weeping.

Viper and Squid were horrible to her, from what I saw, Starflight thought. *Viper was trying to kill her just a moment ago. And yet she's still devastated by losing them.*

Because she's not a heartless monster, like some dragons.

"Get up," Morrowseer snarled at Flame. "You are not expendable."

The red dragonet's only response was a low moan.

Tsunami would yell at Morrowseer. Sunny . . . Sunny would probably try to reason with him.

Starflight's wings were shaking uncontrollably, but he made himself step in front of Morrowseer. *Pretend you're Tsunami. Or Clay. Or Glory or Sunny.*

"What are you doing?" Starflight blurted.

Morrowseer glared down at him. "Now is not a good time to annoy me."

"These dragonets *can't* be in the prophecy," Starflight said. "They don't even have the right hatching day. Is there anything about them that *does* fit? Was Viper's egg found on its own in the desert, like Sunny's? Was Flame's egg the largest in the Sky Palace? Why are you pretending they could fulfil the prophecy when there's no way they can be the right dragonets?"

"You don't know what you're talking about." Morrowseer bared his teeth.

"Maybe," said Starflight, "but I *want* to know. Everything I ever read – all the scrolls written by NightWings for generations – said 'Don't mess with fate. Things will happen the way they're foretold and nobody can change that.' Prophecies aren't like treasure hoards where you can mix and match which gems you like and trade out the ones you don't. I bet these dragonets are dying because you're trying to force them into a destiny that's not meant for them. You should leave us all alone and let fate unfold the way it's supposed to." He took a deep breath, astonished and terrified at his audacity in talking to Morrowseer this way. "That's – that's what I think anyway."

"You are an ignorant dragonet," said Morrowseer, "with no powers of your own, and no one will ever listen to you."

Starflight felt as if he'd been stabbed in the heart by a SandWing. He stared up at Morrowseer, unable to breathe.

"Did you think I wouldn't notice?" Morrowseer snarled. "It's obvious how useless you are. You'll never be a true NightWing. You don't belong anywhere, least of all here."

If he *had* read Starflight's mind – and maybe he had – he couldn't have found anything that would have hurt Starflight more. All his nightmares had centred around this moment: You are not a real NightWing, there is something wrong with you, and you are a failure in every way.

Starflight took a trembling step back and felt Fatespeaker's wings brush against his. He hadn't noticed her coming up behind him.

"Leave him alone," she said to Morrowseer. "He's only telling you the truth about the prophecy. I have the wrong hatching day, too, and you know that."

"I know a lot more about prophecies than either of you," Morrowseer snarled. He shoved them aside and seized Flame's forearm, yanking him up. "You're not allowed to die. We're going to the healers. The rest of you, stay out of my way or you'll be joining that SandWing." He glared at Flame's face, which the SkyWing was still keeping hidden. Starflight could see blood dripping between the red dragon's claws. Morrowseer shook his head and muttered, "Now we need that stunted SandWing, too. I'm going to—"

Starflight didn't hear the rest, as Morrowseer launched himself into the air, forcibly dragging Flame along behind him.

But he'd heard enough. *Sunny's in danger now, too.*

He had to use the dreamvisitor again, as soon as possible.

He turned and found Fatespeaker staring at the lava, her wings drooping. The red-gold light of the river reflected off her silver scales, making them glint like rubies.

"Well," said Ochre. "If no one cares what I'm doing, I'm

going to find some decent prey, if there is any on this stupid island." He backed away, as if waiting for one of them to argue with him, then stamped around and flew off.

Starflight gently put one of his wings around Fatespeaker. "Let's go back to the dormitory and rest," he said. "You haven't had any sleep, right?"

"How can I—" she started, then stopped herself. "Actually, sleeping sounds like the only thing I could do right now. Although I'm afraid it'll be nothing but nightmares."

Starflight knew what she meant. He helped her up, and they flew side by side back to the fortress. The dormitory was deserted – Starflight guessed the other NightWing dragonets were at class, presumably learning something more useful than *how to push your friend into some lava* or *your whole life is pointless.*

Fatespeaker collapsed on to one of the stone hollows and closed her eyes. "You're lucky," she said just as Starflight was about to move away.

He hesitated. "I am?"

"I mean, if what Morrowseer said is true." She opened her eyes again and looked at him. "If you have no powers. I've always been so excited about being a NightWing. I thought my powers must be the most amazing thing. But clearly they're totally useless, if they couldn't even warn me about what was going to happen to my friends." She curled her wings and tail in close. "All my visions were of walruses and welcome-home parties and parents who were happy to meet me. So much for that."

"Have you—" Starflight started. "I mean . . . do you know who your parents are? Do any of you?"

"Squid's dad is the leader of the Talons of Peace," she said. "All of their parents are in the Talons. That's why Morrowseer picked us . . . them. Because we were *convenient*." She frowned. "I guess you were the only NightWing dragonet who hatched on the brightest night. My egg hatched a couple of months later, here, actually. I have this really vague memory of fire and rough scales rubbing my back. I didn't remember that until I smelled this place." She paused for a moment, then sighed. "But Morrowseer took me to the Talons when I was still newly hatched."

"I bet that was when they'd decided they needed a backup plan," Starflight said. "Another set of dragonets who were close enough, just in case they didn't like how we turned out." He shifted his wings. "Which they sure don't."

"I like how you turned out," Fatespeaker said softly.

Starflight took her front talons in his and squeezed them. "You too," he said. "I like you much better than all the other NightWings I've met who were raised 'properly'. I think we're actually lucky, in a way, that we didn't have to grow up here."

She nodded, but she still looked sad.

And I'm even luckier, growing up with dragonets like my friends. The cruelty of their guardians had been far outweighed by Clay's protective caring, Tsunami's fierce loyalty, Glory's insight and humour, and Sunny's . . . everything about Sunny.

Feeling suddenly awkward and guilty, he let go of Fatespeaker's talons.

"You have the face you get when you're missing your friends," she said.

He nodded, surprised that he was that transparent. "Sometimes I think there might be no other dragons like them in all of Pyrrhia."

"You're probably right," she said with a sigh.

Well. There's Fatespeaker.

He touched her shoulder lightly. "Get some sleep."

She obediently closed her eyes, and he moved back to his own side of the dormitory, waiting until he was sure she was asleep. After a few moments, her breathing evened out, and he reached for the hole where he'd hidden the dreamvisitor.

"Starflight?"

Starflight was so startled he nearly hit the ceiling. He whirled around and saw Mastermind standing in the doorway, staring curiously around the room.

"I haven't been back here in a while," Mastermind

said with a chuckle. "Morrowseer said this was where I'd probably find you. I'm in a bit of a conundrum, and I was hoping you could help me."

Starflight edged towards the wall, trying not to look at his hiding spot. He didn't have time for a chat with his sociopathic father. He needed to contact Glory, or someone who could tell her to put a guard on Sunny.

But Mastermind held out one wing and Starflight realized that saying no wasn't an option – not without a lot of very convincing explanations.

"Walk with me," insisted the older NightWing. "Have you seen our marvellous library?"

Starflight reluctantly trailed after him, casting a longing glance back at his bed.

Soon, Sunny. I'll make sure you're safe, I promise.

CHAPTER 20

Mastermind took a deep breath as they stepped into the library.

"There's something about the smell of scrolls that always calms me," he said, waving one talon at the walls.

"Me too," Starflight admitted reluctantly. He didn't want to believe he had anything in common with his father.

It frightened him to think of how he might have turned out if he'd been raised on the NightWing island. Would Mastermind have taken him under his wing? Would Starflight be helping him torture RainWings without any guilt or remorse? Would he be inventing new horrible experiments to try on them, never thinking about how they were real dragons he was harming?

He'd be eating rotting animals and studying with the other NightWings and arguing with Fierceteeth, and he'd believe, like the rest of them did, that he was superior to all other dragons in the world.

Except that Starflight had no powers, so he'd have been an outcast eventually, even if he had grown up here. He never would have belonged.

Not that he wanted to . . . but he didn't want to be useless either.

"Let's see," Mastermind said, studying the large catalogue scroll on the main table. Each end of the scroll was rolled around a spindle with a handle that could be turned to navigate quickly through the entire thing. Mastermind spun the scroll rapidly through to the *M*'s and paused on MEDICINAL RECORDS.

"Hmm." He tapped his claws on the list, then turned to the niches in the wall. "Help me brainstorm, son. The queen is very angry about what's happened to the SkyWing dragonet. I'm afraid he'll be dead by morning if we don't find some way to combat the SandWing poison. Which is apparently my responsibility, for some reason, as if I'm not already swamped trying to construct venom-proof helmets for the entire NightWing tribe in two days, using only my regretfully flawed prototype, which the queen says will simply have to do for now." He paused for a breath, pulling scrolls out and tucking them under one wing.

"Did you say two days?" Starflight echoed, trying to sound casual.

"In case the council votes to attack," Mastermind answered with a snort. "I tried to tell them that my research is still incomplete and I cannot guarantee that any operation will go smoothly."

I'm pretty sure I can guarantee that it won't, Starflight thought, remembering the look on Glory's face.

Mastermind flicked his tail. "So if you have any ideas,

let's hear them. The problem is that naturally I've never studied SandWing venom – orders were to do nothing to antagonize our ally – but if it's anything like RainWing venom, there is nothing that counteracts its effects."

Starflight blinked with surprise. His father hadn't figured out that the antidote to a RainWing's venom was venom from a blood relative?

It was kind of impressive that none of the RainWing prisoners had revealed that information. Perhaps they were a little tougher and smarter than Starflight had given them credit for.

It was also interesting that the NightWings seemed to have so much knowledge – this entire library full of scrolls – and yet they didn't know something as essential as how to cure someone who'd been stabbed by a SandWing. Sunny had been able to get that information out of Blaze in a matter of minutes.

Perhaps that's one downside to staying isolated, Starflight thought. *They keep themselves separate to seem more powerful, and yet they're cut off from so much potential knowledge. If they didn't feel superior to all other dragons, maybe they'd be better at listening to them, and maybe they'd learn something new.*

Mastermind had his nose in a scroll and was muttering grimly. "Unlikely. Tried that on RainWing venom and it didn't work. None of that nearby. Doubtful."

Imagine how much we could *know if the NightWings*

studied the right things, like the medicinal properties of all the rainforest plants, instead of torturing dragons and obsessing over their secret plan.

Starflight realized that the section they were standing in was labelled FOR NIGHTWING EYES ONLY. He pulled out one of the scrolls at random, curious.

It turned out to be a treatise by two authors about the plan to take over the rainforest. One author argued in favour of killing all the RainWings right away, while the other author suggested that enslaving them would be more useful in the long term.

Feeling ill, Starflight shoved the scroll back into its slot with so much force that it wrinkled and nearly ripped in half.

His father looked up at him. "Well? Any thoughts?" He barrelled on without waiting for a response. "We may have to contact Blister, although I fear she'll want to trade information this valuable for something of equal worth to her – like the location of our island." Mastermind scratched his snout with a worried frown. "Personally, I'm not sure it's advisable to give her any power over us."

"Definitely not," Starflight said. "I don't trust her."

Mastermind nodded. "Well, alliances aren't always about trust, I'm afraid." He picked up another scroll and unrolled it.

Starflight shifted uncomfortably, flexing his claws.

He knew the antidote to SandWing venom. But should he share it with Mastermind? On the one talon, it seemed dangerous to hand the NightWings any more secrets than they already had. He could easily imagine them abusing that information – by attacking SandWings, for instance, with no more fear of what their venom might do. Or they might take all the cacti in the desert and hoard it for themselves so only NightWings would have the ability to heal from a SandWing attack.

Or, from what he'd seen of NightWings so far, they'd probably come up with something even more horrible that Starflight would never be able to imagine on his own.

But on the other talon, Flame was dying. Without the cactus remedy, there was no hope for him. If Starflight told Mastermind, there might still be time for someone to fly to the mainland and get what was needed to save the SkyWing.

Wasn't that the most important thing? Starflight couldn't let him die. His friends would choose to save Flame no matter the consequences – wouldn't they?

Sunny would. Clay would. Glory . . . I'm not sure. She might say to look at the bigger picture instead.

And Tsunami would say that this is classic Starflight – dithering indecisively instead of doing something.

So, fine. If I can't make my own decision, then do what Sunny would do.

Starflight opened his mouth to tell Mastermind about the cure, but before he could, three NightWings encased in armour came rushing into the library.

"Mastermind!" one of them shouted. "You're needed in the council chamber immediately."

Starflight's father sprang to his feet and started reshelving the scrolls with fast, neat movements, carefully checking their marks to make sure they went into the right niches. "Why?" he asked the guard at the same time. "What's happened?"

"The extraction was a failure," said one of the other NightWings. "They tried to jump through and snatch her while she was watching the tunnel, but there must have been about forty other dragons hidden nearby, like they were guarding her or something. You should see what they did to the three we sent through."

"You say 'they,'" said the third soldier, "but we all know most of the damage was done by the SeaWing herself."

Starflight tried to contain the joy bursting under his scales; he hoped none of these dragons could sense it in his mind. They had to be talking about Tsunami. She was safe, at least for now. His warning had helped.

The first guard shook his head. "I hope Her Majesty never sends *me* after that dragonet. I'd rather carve out my eyes than try to grab her."

"I heard she nearly bit Wisdom's ear off," said the second.

"The healers are there already, but the queen wants you, too," the third said to Mastermind. "Hurry up."

Mastermind shelved the last scroll and hurried after the guards. No one had told Starflight not to follow them, so he did, hoping he'd learn something before anyone noticed he was there.

The council chamber echoed with the roars of angry dragons. Slumped by the entrance were three dragons who certainly looked as if they'd run into the sharper side of Tsunami. Claw marks were slashed along their wings, their tails looked bitten and dented, and all of their snouts were bleeding. Two other NightWings were dabbing at their wounds with bandages, ointment and disgusted expressions.

"The longer we delay, the stronger they get!" shouted one of the council members. "They could attack at any moment!"

"We should block off the tunnel so they *can't* come through," cried another. "It's the only way to be safe."

"Safe for a few days, perhaps," Greatness interjected from her spot by the hidden queen. "But what about the plan? What about the future of this tribe? We need that tunnel."

"What we should do is attack *right now*," bellowed one of the old dragons on the ceiling.

"Without the SandWings?" Morrowseer's voice interjected.

Starflight realized that the giant NightWing was perched not far from Greatness, but he didn't look in Starflight's direction. Perhaps he hadn't noticed him yet. Starflight ducked behind Mastermind and the three guards, watching through the gaps between their wings.

"Our plan is proceeding as it's supposed to," Morrowseer insisted. "We've chosen our ally and we have – well, we have most of the dragonets of the prophecy. But we need time to get them ready and marshal our forces for the attack. The plan was supposed to give us two more years. . ."

"Look at those soldiers!" another NightWing shouted, gesturing at the wounded dragons by the door. "We don't have two years – we don't have two *days*. Your dragonets are out of control. They're making even the RainWings dangerous, and they're threatening the whole plan. We need to go in *now*, take out the RainWings, and contain the dragonets before they do any more damage."

"We're not ready," growled a dragon with a missing tooth. "Mastermind said we still don't know enough about the RainWings."

"We know how to kill them! That's all we need to know!"

"But where are our extra weapons? Where is our specially designed venom-proof armour? Where are our helmets? What has Mastermind been doing for the last three days?"

"It takes a bit more than three days to make four

hundred helmets," Mastermind called from the doorway, bristling.

Suddenly Greatness rose to her full height and spread her wings. Silence fell almost instantly around the whole chamber. Every dragon turned to face the screen, watching intently as she leaned in to listen to the queen's instructions. Starflight imagined the creaky rasp of Battlewinner's voice echoing through the hidden room.

Finally Greatness straightened up and fixed the cavern full of dragons with a black-eyed glare.

"Queen Battlewinner has made her decision," she said. "We cannot delay any longer." She looked around as if daring anyone to argue back, but no one did. "We must go through under cover of darkness, kill all the RainWings, and take the rainforest as planned."

Not a sound disturbed the terrifying stillness of the cavern. The NightWings were frozen, listening.

Greatness took a deep breath.

"Tonight at midnight . . . we attack."

PART THREE

THE TRUTH

CHAPTER 21

Starflight raced through the empty halls. All the NightWings in the fortress seemed to be clustered around the council chamber, trying to hear what was going on. Once he'd fought his way out through the crowd, the passages were clear all the way back to the dormitory.

I can warn them. For once I can really help – I just have to get through to my friends.

Fatespeaker was still asleep, her wings tented over her, her side rising and falling with deep breaths. No one else was in the dormitory; Starflight had seen most of the NightWing dragonets in the crowd outside the council chamber.

He bolted over to his bed and reached into the hole where he'd hidden the dreamvisitor.

Even in the middle of the day, someone will be asleep. Maybe Kinkajou again. Another RainWing, if I have to. Maybe Glory will be having her sun time. I can get a message through to someone. I have to, or they'll all be killed tonight.

His claws closed on empty space.

Starflight's chest constricted, and he crouched, scrabbling through all the holes around his bed. He flung the blanket aside and searched from one end of the hollow to the other. He checked the beds on either side, his heart pounding faster and faster.

But there was no doubt.

The dreamvisitor was gone.

"No," he whispered, scratching at the hiding spot again. How could it be *gone*? Someone must have seen him – someone *had* lifted the blanket last night and realized what he had in his talons. Someone had watched from the shadows and taken it while he was away.

But who? Could it be Morrowseer? Surely the large dragon would have punished Starflight severely if he'd caught him with the dreamvisitor . . . but maybe the punishment just hadn't landed yet.

More important, what do I do now?

"Starflight?" He whirled around and realized that Fatespeaker was awake, and right behind him, watching with a confused expression. She hopped up on the nearest bed and peered into his face. "Why are you flapping around like a scavenger with its head bitten off?"

"I lost something," Starflight said. "I mean, I left it right here, but it's gone, and I really, really need it. Did you see anyone over here today?"

She shook her head. "Why, what is it?"

"It's—" He hesitated. How much should he tell her? She seemed like the only dragon he could trust on this whole island, and he needed help. But would she be willing to betray her tribe?

"Do you want to help the RainWings?" he asked.

"The sad dragons," she said, blinking. "Of course I do."

"Not just the prisoners here," he said. "The whole tribe is in danger. The NightWings are planning to invade the rainforest through that tunnel I told you about. They're going to kill all the RainWings – and they're doing it tonight."

Fatespeaker's eyes widened. "Why?" she cried.

"To steal the territory for their own," he said. "That's the thing, Fatespeaker. If you help me help the RainWings, it means stopping the NightWing plan. It means leaving our own tribe stuck on this island. It's hard – I can see how miserable they are here. But I can't let them do this to the RainWings."

"Me neither," Fatespeaker said firmly. "Tell me what I can do."

"Well," Starflight said, "I have no idea."

She smacked him with one of her wings. "You can't get me all riled up and tell me there's no plan! We're going to warn the RainWings, right?"

He turned back to his bed. "That's what I was trying to do, but the dreamvisitor is missing, and—" He turned back around and found her halfway to the door. "Wait.

239

Fatespeaker!" He leaped after her, caught her tail, and dragged her back towards him. "Where are you going?"

She looked at him as if he were crazy. "To warn the RainWings. Like we just decided."

"You mean – go to the rainforest?" he said. His heart was hammering and his legs felt as though they could barely hold him up, but something in his head was also shouting *YES YES THIS IS WHAT YOU HAVE TO DO! GO DO IT!*

He started pacing. "We can't fly there – it'll take too long. We have to go through the tunnel, but that's impossible. There will be a million dragons guarding it. I'm not Clay or Tsunami; I can't even fight one dragonet, let alone a whole squadron of full-grown NightWings."

"But we have to try," Fatespeaker said. "So let's do it." She pressed her front talons to her head and smiled. "My vision says we shall succeed! Let's charge the tunnel and see how far we get!"

Starflight winced. "Not to argue with your visions, but I can tell you exactly how far we'll get: into the cell next to Deathbringer's if we're lucky, or tossed into the volcano if we're not."

She dropped her arms and looked thoughtful for a minute. "So – what if I distract the guards and you sneak through? I have a vision that says *that* will totally work!"

He shook his head. "That's how Deathbringer got Clay here; I doubt they'll fall for that again. We have to do this the smart way. Maybe there's a way to trick them. Who *would* be allowed through the tunnel?" He tapped his claws on the floor. "The soldiers who tried to grab Tsunami were allowed through. Perhaps we could say the queen sent us to kidnap Sunny."

Fatespeaker looked down at herself dubiously.

"Right, two dragonets . . . they won't believe that at all." Starflight picked up a scroll from Mindreader's bed and turned it nervously between his talons. "So who else, or why else. . ."

It was like a thunderbolt hitting him.

"Oooo, you have an idea," Fatespeaker said.

"I do," Starflight said. "It's worth a try – but we need one more dragon to make it work."

In her nighttime wanderings, Fatespeaker had found the healers' hall, and she was able to lead the way back there without hesitation.

Starflight glanced in first. As he'd hoped, the healers were still in the council chamber with the soldiers who'd fought Tsunami. The large room was mostly deserted; a few dragons slept restlessly on the narrow stone beds, most of them with lava-related injuries, from the looks of it. Two of the NightWings bore recent RainWing venom scars, and he realized those must have been the ones Glory attacked during her escape. They smelled slightly of poppies and anise, and he guessed they were in some kind of medicine-induced stupor.

A fire blazed in a rough fireplace in the centre of the wall, and in the bed closest to it was Flame, fast asleep.

There was a strip of cloth tied around his head, but now Starflight could see a little more of what Viper had accidentally done to the SkyWing. A vicious slash ran from one corner of his mouth sideways and up across his face, straight through the opposite eye. It oozed blood and something darker.

"Oh, Flame," Fatespeaker whispered, her voice breaking.

"It's not as bad as I thought," Starflight whispered to her, trying to be reassuring. "Viper only hit one of his eyes – that means, hopefully, he'll still be able to see out of the other one, so he won't be completely blind."

"*If* we can save him," Fatespeaker said.

"Right." He took a deep breath.

"I wish we didn't have to wake him," she whispered.

"I'll do it." He touched Flame's shoulder with one wing. "Flame. Flame, wake up. It's important."

The SkyWing blearily opened his good eye. He moaned at the sight of them and closed it again.

"You have to come with us," Fatespeaker said.

"We know how to save you," Starflight added. "But it'll only work if we go *now*."

Flame mumbled something that sounded like, "Why would you save me?"

"Because you're my friend and it's the right thing to do," Fatespeaker said.

"Hrrmph," muttered Flame.

Starflight poked him in the side. "Because we can use your tragic face to get us off this island."

There was a pause. Flame lifted his head and squinted at Starflight. "That sounds like a real reason," he said in a stronger voice, although it still had a blurry sound to it, and his head wobbled like his brain was wrapped in sheep's wool.

Starflight held out his wing, and the red dragonet slowly slid off the bed, resting his weight on Starflight's shoulder. Fatespeaker hurried ahead to the door, waved an all clear, and led the way to the nearest balcony overlooking the prison caves.

Starflight paused on the edge of the balcony, looking out. Down there was the black-sand beach; down there was the tunnel to the rainforest. Down there was the gateway back to his friends. And down there were an unknown number of NightWing soldiers who might take one look at Starflight, Flame, and Fatespeaker and send them to the dungeon for life – or until the volcano erupted and killed them anyway.

There's no time to be afraid, Starflight told himself. *This is the only thing you can do. And you* must *do it.*

Supporting Flame between them, Starflight and Fatespeaker launched themselves into the sky and flew towards the tunnel.

CHAPTER 22

It wasn't hard to guess where the tunnel to the rainforest was. Once they reached the black-sand beach, the cluster of armed NightWings gathered in the entrance of a certain cave was a fairly strong clue.

"Be confident," Starflight said to Fatespeaker, thinking of Tsunami bluffing the SeaWing soldiers. "Act like we're doing exactly what we're supposed to be doing."

"Not a problem," Fatespeaker said. "I mean, we are."

Starflight guessed that she rarely had trouble with her confidence. Now he just had to follow his own advice. And he had to hope that the news hadn't got here from the council chamber yet – that these guards wouldn't know about the planned attack tonight.

They landed just inside the cave mouth, staggering forward under Flame's weight. The red dragonet slid slowly to the ground. He looked groggy and close to fainting.

"Stay with us," Starflight said to him, squeezing one of Flame's talons.

"What is the meaning of this?" growled the biggest NightWing guard. He paced forward to loom over them, glaring at Flame in particular.

Here we go, Starflight thought. *Maybe all those games*

of pretend we used to play will turn out to be useful after all.

"Didn't you get the message? I knew that would happen," he said. He wanted to sound bold and authoritative, like Tsunami, but his voice sounded higher and more anxious than he'd hoped. *So work with that. It makes sense that I'd be anxious about this plan. If I can't be Tsunami, then try to convince them as Starflight – the nervous know-it-all.* He pointed at Flame. "This is one of the dragonets of the prophecy. As you can see, he was slashed by a SandWing tail today."

Starflight peeled up the bandage a little so the guards could see the oozing wound underneath. All of them let out a collective gasp of horror and stepped back.

Starflight straightened and folded his wings. "The venom is extremely deadly. The queen has ordered us to take him through to the rainforest and from there to the Kingdom of Sand to find a cure."

"You?" said the head guard sceptically.

"I know, I was nervous about the whole idea, too," Starflight said, hoping they'd believe that was why his talons were shaking. "But she said I'm the only NightWing who won't be attacked or chased away by the dragonets in the rainforest. They know me. They'll think I'm on their side. Can you imagine – a NightWing being friends with a SeaWing or a MudWing? Or a *RainWing*, of all creatures?"

A few of the guards were nodding, but the biggest one didn't look convinced.

"I'll have to verify this order," the big guard said, signalling one of the other dragons forward.

"Of course you do," Starflight said, letting his panic spill into his voice a little. "I said this would happen! She's going to be so angry," he said to Fatespeaker, then turned back to the guard. "I told them you'd delay us by sending someone back to the fortress. I told them this SkyWing would be dead before we got through! But nobody listens to me. Her Majesty said you'd take one look at him and understand the urgency, and that I shouldn't worry." He wrung his claws together. "But of course I was right to worry. I'm *always* right about worrying."

"Um," said the guard. He was starting to look almost as nervous as Starflight felt. "He's really that close to dead?"

"It's all right," Starflight said, rubbing his head anxiously. "I'd do exactly the same thing in your place. She'll probably kill all of us, but what else could you do?" He nodded at the messenger. "Go ahead. You can tell her it doesn't really matter, since he'll be dead by the time you return." He nudged Flame with one toe. The SkyWing obligingly looked even more like a dying fish.

"But he *can't* die," Fatespeaker jumped in, as if she'd been having this argument with Starflight the whole way here. "He's the only SkyWing we've got. Without him, no prophecy, no plan, no rainforest home for our tribe."

The guards behind the leader were starting to mutter and crane their necks to peer at Flame.

"But he has to check the order," Starflight argued back. "What's he going to do, just let two NightWing dragonets wander through the tunnel with a SkyWing? Why, we might – we might—" He paused, then looked at the guard. "What are you worried we'll do?"

"Well, I don't know," he said, shifting his spear from talon to talon. "I'm just following protocol."

"See?" Starflight said to Fatespeaker. *Protocol.*

Flame wheezed in a dying-gasp kind of way.

"We gotta let them through, chief," said one of the guards. "The queen is right – this dragonet is the only one who can get into the rainforest. That's where we grabbed him from. He can get that SkyWing to the cure. No one else can."

Starflight gave her a grateful look that was entirely heartfelt.

The head guard flexed his claws with an uneasy expression. "No funny business," he said to Starflight. "You fix that SkyWing and come back."

"We'll be back by nightfall," Fatespeaker promised. "Maybe we'll even learn something about what they're planning over there. They'll probably tell this one everything." She jerked her head at Starflight. "He's got them wrapped around his tail, from what I hear."

"Makes sense," said another guard.

"Let 'em through," chorused two more.

Their leader glanced towards the fortress again, and then finally, warily, stepped back out of their way.

Starflight heaved Flame up, flopping the dragonet's red wing over one of his own shoulders, and then he and Fatespeaker dragged him down the long corridor to the back cave, where a dark hole in the wall radiated the *wrongness* that Starflight remembered from the tunnels in the rainforest.

The NightWing guards stared at them as they went past. Starflight kept expecting one of them to yell, "It's a trick! They're lying!" He forced himself to concentrate on their story. *Flame needs the cure for SandWing venom. We have to take him through to save him.* It had the advantage of being true, which helped.

As they reached the hole, one of the guards stepped forward suddenly, and Starflight just barely managed to stop himself from flinching away. It turned out she was reaching to help them lift Flame into the hole. Starflight nodded to her, and then hopped up to join the SkyWing.

We did it.

But we're not safe yet.

In the tunnel, there was just enough space to fly. Fatespeaker went first, then Flame at a wobbly flap that felt excruciatingly slow to Starflight, and they began the winding trek back towards the rainforest.

The air grew warmer and wetter and the sounds of insects and monkeys chittering began to reverberate off the walls. Fatespeaker twisted to glance back at Starflight with a grin. But he couldn't force his mouth into a smile, not yet – not until he felt the jungle earth crumbling between his claws.

Green sunlight shone up ahead of them. Fatespeaker twitched in a happy way and sped up without seeming to realize it. She shot out into the rainforest several lengths before Flame.

Starflight heard her scream . . . and then the scream abruptly cut off.

He shoved Flame forcefully out of the hole and burst out into a glorious warm day. Magenta-pink flowers dripped from the trees and a number of silvery sloths poked their heads through the leaves to examine the newcomers. A bird with long blue tail feathers strutted by, eyeing him beadily.

"Stop right there!" a voice yelled. "Don't move and put your talons on your head and surrender and claws where I can see them!"

Starflight wasn't sure which conflicting order to follow. He twisted rapidly in a circle and spotted Fatespeaker lying next to the stream with an orange-gold

RainWing sitting cheerfully on top of her, wrapping vines around her snout.

Another RainWing materialized slowly in front of him, her scales changing colour so she no longer blended into the background. "You're my prisoner!" she cried. "Run for your life!"

"Mango, you can't just yell things at random," said a familiar voice. Tsunami dropped down from one of the branches, frowning. "Try to *think* about what comes out of your – Starflight!" She interrupted herself with a cry of joy.

At the same time, another dragon cannoned out of the foliage and crashed right into Starflight. Starflight found himself circled by strong brown wings as Clay nearly flung him into the treetops with delight.

"You escaped!" Tsunami yelped, elbowing Clay aside so she could wrap Starflight in her own blue wings. "That's unbelievable! How – how – how – how—"

"I'll tell you everything, but I have to see Glory right away," Starflight said. He glanced around, hoping Sunny was also concealed in the bushes, but she didn't appear. He turned to Flame, who had collapsed, unconscious. "And this SkyWing needs the cactus we got from the desert – he's been slashed with a SandWing tail."

"Oh, poor guy," Clay said, crouching beside Flame's inert form. The MudWing gently lifted Flame's snout and peered at the wound. He waved to the trees and six more RainWings popped into sight. In minutes, they had produced a kind of hammock net, which they tucked around Flame so they could carry him off towards the village. "To the healers, as fast as you can," Clay told them.

"Glory told us everything you said in her dream, which, by the way, is crazy, visiting a dragon's dreams," Tsunami said to Starflight, winding her tail around his. "Well, except she didn't tell me about the stealth RainWing bodyguards she put on me. That was pretty hilarious. Everyone should suddenly have the air turn into seven bright purple dragons yelling hysterically whenever she gets attacked."

"Yeah, I wouldn't have minded something like that," Starflight said. The sunlight felt as if it was melting through his scales, chasing away all the darkness that had started to gather around his soul. "You scared the moonshine out of those NightWings. It was amazing."

Tsunami beamed.

"Who's that?" Clay asked, nodding at Fatespeaker.

"She's my friend," Starflight said, realizing guiltily that she was still gagged. "You can trust her. Her name is Fatespeaker – she's the alternate NightWing I told Glory about."

Tsunami signalled to the RainWing to let her up, and Fatespeaker came bounding over to them, unwrapping the vines from her snout.

"Hi! Hi! This is the most beautiful place I've ever seen!"

she said as soon as she could talk. "I've never even had a vision of somewhere this pretty! No wonder the NightWings want to live here." She seized Clay's front talons and shook them vigorously. "What's edible? I haven't eaten in *days*; you wouldn't *believe* how hungry I am."

Starflight felt his own empty stomach twist as she chattered on, but it was much more than food that was worrying him. War was coming to this peaceful rainforest, no matter what anyone tried to do to stop it. After tonight, would it be so beautiful? He remembered some of the awful things he and his friends had seen since leaving the caves – the violence in the Sky Palace arena, the dead MudWings lying broken in the swamp, the panicked SeaWings crushing one another as they tried to escape the fire bombs when the Summer Palace was attacked.

It was hard to imagine any of that here – hard to imagine anyone burning these trees or hurting these harmless, happy-go-lucky dragons.

But Starflight had seen the cruelty of NightWings, and he knew how desperate they were for a new home. He believed they'd do anything, no matter how awful, to escape their volcanic island.

Fatespeaker was eating ravenously from the pile of fruit Clay had offered her, but Starflight didn't think he could possibly eat until he felt that his friends were safe. *Although that might be never,* he realized ruefully.

"I have to see Glory right now," he said to Tsunami. "The NightWings are planning to attack tonight."

She gasped, and the trees around her all gasped at the same time. Tsunami turned to frown at the apparently empty branches.

"I told you all you could go back to the village," she said. "I don't need a bodyguard. I can take care of myself."

Nobody answered. Tsunami sighed.

"You've never seen instant loyalty like these RainWings have for Queen Glory," she said to Starflight. "Don't even try to convince them to disobey her. Never going to happen."

"That's great," Starflight said, pleased. *At least one of us is fitting into her tribe.*

"For her war strategy, yes," Tsunami said. "For the size of her head, no." She waved over the RainWing who had been sitting on Fatespeaker. Fatespeaker eyed him warily, but his tangerine-orange face was cheerful and extremely non-threatening.

"Take these NightWings to the queen," Tsunami said. "Clay and I have to stay on guard here," she explained to Starflight. "Especially on a really sunny day like this, I'm afraid RainWings have a tendency to fall asleep all over the place."

"Sure," Starflight said.

"But if there's any battle planning, I want to be involved," Tsunami added fiercely.

"Of course," Starflight said, spreading his wings. How long did they have until dark? Would the NightWings even wait until midnight, once they realized that Starflight had come through? Surely Morrowseer would guess that Starflight would warn his friends. What if that spurred them to attack sooner? They might invade at any moment – they might even be on their way right now.

He cast a worried look back at the hole. "Be careful," he said to Tsunami.

"I'm ready for them," she said. "Don't worry." She curled her claws menacingly.

Starflight and Fatespeaker followed the orange-gold RainWing up into the treetops, where there was even more sunlight. Fatespeaker ducked as a flock of tiny purple birds exploded past her head. She kept twisting to watch the shimmering azure butterflies that flitted by, and once she startled a large, spotted jungle cat so he nearly fell off the branch where he was sleeping.

"I can't get over how amazing this place is," she said to Starflight.

"The RainWing village is really cool, too," he said.

"It makes me feel sad for the NightWings." Fatespeaker tilted her head to catch more sunlight on her snout. "I mean, what if they had grown up somewhere like this? Would they still be the way they are, or would they be happy and kind, like the RainWings? It's not their fault they hatched in such a miserable place. Maybe they could have been good – or, at least, better – if they'd lived somewhere else."

"Maybe," Starflight said. "In fact, probably – but I think being a good dragon is about the choices you make no matter where you are or who raised you or how. The NightWings chose to kidnap and torture RainWings. That makes it hard for me to feel sorry for them."

"True," Fatespeaker said, and lapsed into uncharacteristic silence for the rest of the flight.

The orange RainWing led them to a tree house that matched the one in the dream Starflight had stepped into. The walls were mostly open to the outside, letting sunshine and fresh air pour in, and Glory stood behind a wooden desk, although there were no scrolls in front of her in real life. Three small RainWings were lined up before her in varying shades of green, apparently relaying reports from around the forest.

Glory saw Starflight coming and flared her wings.

"Starflight!" she cried joyfully. She jabbed her own forearm with one of her claws. "I'm not dreaming. You're really here!"

He landed beside her. "We found a way out – Fatespeaker and I – this is Fatespeaker – because I had to come warn you," he said. His eyes drifted to the trees around them. "Where's Sunny?"

"Teaching a dragonet class how to read, or helping the

healers with Webs, I think," Glory said, waving her claws. "Warn me about what?"

"The NightWings are planning to attack you tonight at midnight," Starflight said. "Maybe sooner, if they figure out where I've gone and why."

"*Tonight?*" Glory rubbed her front talons over her head. "Go get me Mangrove," she said to one of the small RainWings. "And you, find Grandeur." The two of them nodded and flew off in a hurry.

"I have some ideas for defence," Starflight started.

"I hope one of those ideas is 'attack them first,'" Glory said. "Because that's my plan." She glanced out the window at the position of the sun in the sky. "I can get my army ready to fly in an hour. Sure. Organizing RainWings, no problem. It's only roughly as hard as getting a hundred butterflies to fly in a straight line."

"Starflight?"

A glimmer of gold scales flashed in the corner of his eye, and Starflight felt his whole body fill with light as he turned around and came face-to-face with Sunny.

CHAPTER 23

Sunny spread her warm golden wings and Starflight fitted his own wings around hers for a hug. It always felt like exactly where he should be, even if just for a moment.

"I'm so glad you're all right!" she said, stepping back and examining him for injuries. "I was checking on Webs and then this SkyWing came in, of all things, and I was showing the healers how to get the cactus milk into his wound when someone said two NightWings brought him in and I knew it must be you. You know, *I* wanted to go through and find you, but Glory said no." She wrinkled her snout at the new queen.

"Glory was right. It's too dangerous there," Starflight said.

"Oh, please. Where have we been lately that *isn't* dangerous?" Sunny said. "All the more reason we should go rescue you. Although I wasn't really worried, because of course you had to be fine so we could fulfil the prophecy, right? And look, you rescued yourself, which is so impressive."

Starflight guessed that the grin on his own face was probably a little goofy, but he couldn't seem to squelch it.

"And you are?" Fatespeaker interjected, clearing her

throat and sidling so close to Starflight that she bumped one of his wings.

"I'm Sunny," said the little SandWing. She tilted her head at Fatespeaker. "Wow, your silver scales are so cool. That one looks like a bracelet – like you were born with your own treasure."

Fatespeaker's wings relaxed a little. She held out her talons to peer at the anklet of star-bright scales. "I never thought of it like that. I was about to say *your* scales are a great colour. All the SandWings I've met were sort of pale and dusty-looking."

"I know, I'm weird," Sunny said agreeably. "You're the alternate NightWing, right? Glory said Starflight had lots of nice things to say about you." Fatespeaker gave Starflight a delighted look that made him unaccountably nervous. "What was it like growing up in the Talons of Peace camp?"

"So bizarre," Fatespeaker said, folding her wings and leaning towards Sunny. "We were always moving so no one could find us. And everyone talked about peace, but it seemed like all we were doing was avoiding soldiers and waiting for the prophecy to come true."

"But it must have been amazing to live with so many dragons from different tribes," Sunny said, her eyes shining. "You'd get to see what really makes them different, and the ways they're all the same, too."

"I was thinking about that!" Fatespeaker said. "I was the

only NightWing, so I was always trying to figure out which other tribe I was most like. But—"

"—you could find something in common with all of them," Sunny guessed.

"Exactly!"

"All right," Glory interrupted. "As strangely adorable as you two are, I need you to either go away and discover your twin souls somewhere else, or focus on battle planning with me."

"Battle planning," Fatespeaker and Sunny said simultaneously.

Glory gave Starflight an odd, somewhat amused look, and he shifted uncomfortably, although he wasn't sure why. He liked that Fatespeaker and Sunny liked each other, but it also made him weirdly uneasy.

Luckily, at that moment, Mangrove arrived with the elegant older dragon Starflight had seen in Kinkajou's dream.

"Let's take this meeting to the tunnel," Glory said. "I need Tsunami's and Clay's input, too." She gathered her wings and soared off the balcony into the trees.

Fatespeaker and Sunny went next, talking to each other as they flew. Starflight followed, trying to keep his mind on the impending attack. Only a few minutes of sunshine and fresh air, and he was already finding it hard to believe what he'd gone through on the NightWing island – or that an army of angry dragons was preparing to destroy all of this before the next sunrise.

Once they were all gathered, within sight of the tunnel but out of hearing distance to be safe, Glory had Starflight explain everything he'd heard in the council chamber.

"So at least some of them are afraid of us," she said when he'd finished.

"I'd say most of them," Starflight said. "I mean, I think that's the whole reason they've been kidnapping RainWings and studying them, and why they haven't attacked before. They're terrified of your venom."

Glory showed her teeth and hissed. "They should be."

"Yours, maybe," Tsunami said. "But the rest of these dragons – I really can't guarantee that any of them will use it on another dragon, even in a life-or-death situation. They've been told their whole lives to never, ever use it as a weapon. I've done my best, but you try changing an entire tribal philosophy of life in three days."

"I know," Glory said, starting to pace.

"Which I'm not even sure we should," Sunny interjected. "I *like* their philosophy."

"I could do it," Grandeur said. "Attack another dragon with my venom, I mean, for the sake of my tribe. But I agree that the others would have trouble." She glanced at Mangrove.

"I'd try," he said. "For Orchid. She's really still alive?" he asked Starflight.

"And waiting for you," Fatespeaker said. "Starflight told her you were looking for her, and she said she'd survive until you came."

A faint wave of pink rippled across Mangrove's scales.

"I'm worried about attacking first," Clay said. "We'd have to come out the other end one at a time. If they're smart, they'll be waiting, and then they can pick us off one by one. But if we wait here and let them attack, we could do that to them instead – we'd be in the stronger position."

"I don't want them in my rainforest," Glory snapped. "If they think they're losing, they'll set the whole place on fire just to be horrible. Besides, we have to go *there* to rescue the RainWings. Even if we drive back their attack, we'd still have to go through at some point, and we'll have wasted resources on our defence. No, we go to them first. We just have to find a way to get everyone past the guards at the entrance."

"I have an idea," Sunny said.

"Changing your scales will help," Tsunami said at the same time. "They won't see the RainWings coming along the tunnel if you're all camouflaged. Then maybe we burst out and start attacking and hope we've surprised them."

"Doubtful," Starflight said. "Once Morrowseer figures out I went through, they'll be on high alert at the tunnel opening."

"I think it's a good idea," said Sunny. "The one I have, I mean."

"We need to choose the bravest RainWings for the first wave," Glory said. "Tsunami, I want you to make a list for me, based on what you've noticed during training."

Tsunami snorted. "A 'brave' list might be asking a lot. You can have a 'less sleepy than the others' list."

"One does not speak to a queen that way of her citizens," Glory said with mock haughtiness, then lapsed back into her regular voice. "Anyway, I think the RainWings will surprise you. I've been meeting them all, one by one, as fast as I can, and they're a lot more complicated than they seem."

"Doesn't anyone want to hear my idea?" Sunny asked.

"I do," said Starflight, but Glory was already speaking to Mangrove.

"We have to make sure that we pair up related RainWings in each squadron, so there's always someone to counteract the venom if there's an accident. I know Sunny's been taking notes on that, so make sure we use her chart when we form the squadrons."

With a stab of jealousy, Starflight saw Sunny lean towards Clay and whisper in his ear. Sometimes it seemed to him as though Sunny and Clay were always together, like the MudWing was the one she could trust more than any other dragon. He wished he could be that for her instead.

But he wasn't anything like Clay, and the truth was, if he had to choose someone to trust with his life, he'd pick Clay over himself as well.

"I don't know how to prepare them to fight NightWing fire," Tsunami said, a little hopelessly. "Most of these dragons have never even *seen* fire. They'll probably think it's shiny and pretty and try to touch it."

Glory coiled her tail and stared at the sky through the trees. Starflight guessed from her expression that she was thinking about how RainWings were going to die – there was no way to avoid it. Becoming queen of an entire tribe all of a sudden was hard enough. But leading dragons into battle, especially woefully underprepared dragons, was something none of the dragonets knew anything about or ever wanted to do.

We wanted to stop the war – not start a whole new one.

Do the RainWings have any chance against the armour-clad, fiercely desperate, violently unhappy NightWings? Are we all going to die today?

We're only dragonets. We shouldn't be leading anyone to their deaths.

But this is happening no matter what we do. We have no choice now.

"I tried to draw a map of what I could remember of the island," Glory said to Starflight. "I want you to fill in as many details as you can. I guess we should have several dragons go straight to the prison caves and try to free the trapped RainWings."

"Queen Splendor is inside the fortress," Starflight said. "In the same dungeon as Deathbringer."

"Oh," Glory said, and several colours shifted across her scales at once. "So another wing should go in there – maybe Tsunami can lead that group—"

"SLEEPING DARTS!" Clay suddenly yelled, making everyone jump.

Glory stared at him. "What?"

"Those sleeping darts the RainWings used to knock us out, when we first got to the rainforest," Clay said. He nudged Sunny forward. "Sunny says the healers have hundreds of them. The RainWings use them all the time – they play this game where they try to sneak up on each other before getting shot."

"That's true!" Mangrove said, lashing his tail. "And we take turns patrolling so we can shoot strange dragons who come into the forest, like you five, which is even more fun."

"Every RainWing already has a blowgun," Sunny said. "Arm them all with as many sleeping darts as they can carry, and use those instead of fighting."

"That's it!" Glory flared her wings, turning dark purple with lightning bolts of excited gold all along her scales. "That's exactly how RainWings should fight!"

"It was Sunny's idea," Clay said, nodding down at the SandWing.

"Maybe we can do this without casualties," Glory said animatedly. "Clay and Sunny, you're in charge of arming all the RainWings. Get all the sleeping darts you can find. Mangrove, Grandeur, it's time to tell the village. Everyone who's willing to fight, meet by the stream here in one hour. We're doing this before nightfall." She turned to Starflight as the others flew off. "Let's review the map. Tell me everything you know."

Tsunami unrolled a giant leaf with a sketchy map of the NightWing island marked out on it in some kind of dark fruit ink.

War is coming. There's no time to be scared, Starflight told himself as he leaned over the map. *You can't be the most cowardly dragon on Pyrrhia right now. Remember, you've read all the history scrolls you could find about famous battles. Now use that knowledge.*

It's time to prove that you really do belong in this prophecy.

CHAPTER 24

Two hours later, Queen Glory's army was on the move.

The sun was just starting to sink below the trees. It wasn't dark here yet, but it would be soon.

Starflight dug his claws into the mud by the stream, trying to beat down his terror. The clearing bustled with activity, but it was unsettling activity, because most of the gathered dragons were essentially invisible, carefully camouflaged against the background. Starflight kept being bumped and jostled by what appeared to be empty air.

Tsunami was trying to make all the RainWings face her and shut up so she could give them a rousing battle speech. The fact that this was proving difficult did not bode well for the overall attack, Starflight thought anxiously.

"Starflight," Glory said, materializing beside him. Her scales shimmered from dark green to a sort of worried-looking pale blue and back. "Are you all right?"

"I guess," Starflight said. He shifted from one foot to another. "You know. Nervous."

"Do you want to stay here?" she asked him quietly. "I'd understand if you do."

"No!" Starflight said. "I mean, I shouldn't. I can't." He glanced at Sunny, who was sorting piles of sleeping darts into little bags that could go over the RainWings' necks. She had none of the weapons other dragons had – no venom, no camouflage, no fireproof scales like Clay, not even the poisonous tail barb a SandWing should have. He'd never let her go off to a battle without him. Stay behind while his friends threw themselves into danger? How could she ever love him if he made that choice? "I promise I won't be scared."

"It's normal to be scared," Glory said. "*I'm* scared. You'd have to be crazy not to be – well, crazy or Tsunami, which is basically the same thing. You just have to push that aside and do what you have to anyway. But I meant, do you want to stay here because we're going to fight your tribe? If it's too much to ask, I understand if you want to sit this one out."

"They're not my tribe," Starflight said. "You are. You and Sunny and Tsunami and Clay."

"Aw, you big sap," she said, but her wingtips went all rose-coloured, and he knew Glory felt the same way even if she'd never say it out loud. "All right," she said, punching his shoulder, a rare gesture of physical affection from her. "Let's go change the world."

She bounded to the tunnel opening and summoned the first wave of RainWings with a flick of her tail. They huddled, listening to her orders.

Starflight looked around at Sunny again.

I might die today.

What if she never knows?

What if I die without ever telling her how I feel?

He lifted his face towards the setting sun. He'd bluffed the NightWing guards. He'd escaped from the NightWing island. Surely he could say three words to one dragon.

When he looked down again, Sunny was right in front of him. His heart seized as though someone had wrapped fierce talons around it.

"We're going to be all right," she told him, shaking out her wings. "Just think of the prophecy. We have to be alive to stop the war, right? So we *can't* die today. Isn't that comforting?"

"I wish I had your optimism," he said.

"It's not optimism," she objected. "It's faith. There's a reason we're here. What we do today is part of it, but there's more, too, and we have to survive to make it all happen." Her smile made him feel as if lightning were crackling under his scales.

"Sunny," he said hesitantly. "There's something – I mean . . . something I've wanted to tell you. For a long time."

"I'm listening," she said, tilting her head.

Across the clearing, Glory was flaring her wings and waiting for silence. It was now or possibly never, depending on what happened today.

"I love you," he blurted.

Sunny blinked, and then blinked a few more times. "I . . . I love you, too, Starflight."

"No," he said. "I mean – I mean you're all I think about, and I want to be near you and it hurts when I'm not, and everything I do, I think, what would Sunny want me to do? And I think you're the only dragon who sees me the whole way I am and likes me anyway. . ." He thought, uncomfortably, of Fatespeaker and spotted her at the same time, across the clearing near Glory, watching the RainWing queen with her eyes wide and her head upturned. But his feelings for her and his feelings for Sunny . . . well, they *couldn't* be the same.

"And I had to tell you," he hurried on, "in case something happens to either one of us today, although if anything happens to you I don't know how I'd be able to breathe or think or do anything ever again."

"Oh my gosh, Starflight, stop," Sunny said in a rush. "This – right now – how can I say anything, let alone the right thing, when we're – when everything—?" She spread her wings helplessly, indicating the mob of RainWings around them.

"It's all right," Starflight said, and realized that he meant it. "Don't say anything. You don't have to. I just wanted you to know, just in case."

She wrinkled her forehead, as if that didn't seem right to

her, but he twined his tail around hers and looked down at their talons sinking into the riverbank.

"Just promise me you'll be safe," he said.

"I hardly get to do anything in this battle," she said fiercely. "*You* promise *me* you'll be safe."

He opened and closed his mouth, wishing he could promise that and mean it.

"Exactly," she said. "So stop talking like a scroll and just tell me you'll see me soon, OK?"

"I'll see you soon," he said, and for a moment her certainty made him believe it, too.

"Good luck. Kick a NightWing for me," she said as Starflight stepped away, and then she pulled him back for a quick hug, and a moment later he found himself walking over to Glory, his mind a daze.

I did it. I told her. And the world didn't collapse.

The queen of the RainWings flared her wings one more time and the clearing finally fell silent.

"You know I don't like giving speeches," Glory said, "so I'll just say this. We're going to save our fellow RainWings, and we're going to make this rainforest safe, and we're going to do it like real RainWings. And by the three moons, try not to talk or sneeze or fall asleep in the tunnel on the way there, all right?"

She turned to the dragon standing next to her. It took Starflight a moment to recognize Glory's brother Jambu;

he wasn't his usual vibrant raspberry colour, but a rippling shadowy black that would blend in well with the tunnel walls. He was apparently one of the best shots with a blowgun, and he'd volunteered to be the first one through the hole. Starflight wasn't sure if that was bravery or just not knowing what he was getting himself into, but right now it amounted to the same thing.

Jambu hopped up to the hole and slid in; Glory followed immediately behind him, and then Mangrove, Liana, Grandeur and three other RainWings armed with blowguns.

According to the plan, Starflight and Fatespeaker were next, so that once the guards were knocked out, they could lead the RainWings to the prison caves and the fortress. He took a deep breath and looked back, hoping to catch Sunny's eye.

She was watching him, her scales glowing in the fading sunlight.

I can do this.

Starflight clambered into the hole and almost immediately, Fatespeaker followed, nearly stepping on his tail. Neither of them said anything, but he felt a little safer knowing she was at his back.

It was stifling in the tunnel, and eerily quiet; the RainWings ahead of him were stealthier than he'd have expected. He wasn't sure how far ahead they were, exactly;

even with his excellent night vision, Starflight couldn't make out the difference between shadows in here. The tunnel tilted down, and he crept along as fast as he dared, keeping his wings carefully folded to hide the silver scales.

Ahead of him, he heard a quiet *zzt*, and then another, and then seven more in rapid succession. Sleeping darts fired from blowguns, straight out of the shadows, hopefully knocking out all the guards by the hole before any of them noticed and sounded the alarm.

Next, Starflight heard a muffled *thump* as one RainWing after another jumped into the cave, and then he saw the flicker of firelight. A moment later, he climbed out of the tunnel and felt the warm rocks scraping below his scales.

Nine NightWing guards were lying around the cave, each looking as if he or she had just fallen asleep all of a sudden. Their chests rose and fell peacefully; their spears rested harmlessly on the ground nearby.

Glory turned to Mangrove and pointed at the spears. She made some kind of signal Starflight didn't follow, but Mangrove apparently did. He started gathering all the weapons in the cave and passed them to the dragons still coming through the tunnel. They were handed back talon over talon until they were safely stashed in the rainforest, far away from NightWing claws.

The NightWings are still dangerous. We can't take

away their talons or teeth or fire. But one less weapon in a
NightWing's claws can't hurt.

Jambu and Grandeur had already crept ahead; if he strained his ears, Starflight could hear the *zzt zzt* of the blowguns taking out the guards by the cave entrance.

How long was this going to work? How many NightWings could they send to sleep before somebody noticed? And once someone sounded the alarm, how soon before RainWings started dying?

"All clear." Grandeur's voice whispered along the tunnel like leaves rustling.

Glory's scales had shifted to grey and red and black to match the cave. Starflight couldn't see her, but he felt her wings lightly brush his. It was his turn to lead the way.

He glanced back at the hole that led to the rainforest. Tsunami and Clay and Sunny were supposed to stay out of sight during the first wave – if anyone spotted blue or brown or gold scales on this island, they'd know the tunnel had been breached and the NightWings would be on them all immediately. So they were to stay hidden until the stealth campaign turned into a real battle. On the one talon, Starflight was relieved that he didn't have to worry about Sunny, but on the other, he'd feel a lot better if Clay and Tsunami were leading the charge instead of him.

But this is the smart way to do it – the only way to do it.

He padded down the tunnel with Fatespeaker beside

him, stepping over the slumbering NightWing guards. He could hear the sound of the ocean waves crashing on the black sand below. Outside, the sky was even more grey and ominous than before, with grim lowering clouds that flickered with lightning, all lit by the red glow from the volcano.

After the bright warmth of the rainforest, the island air seemed even darker and smokier. As Starflight stepped out on to the cave ledge, he felt the ground tremble beneath his talons, then stop.

That's unsettling, he thought.

"What a nightmare," Grandeur's voice whispered behind him.

"It's worse than I expected," said Jambu. "How can anyone live here?"

"You carry this," Glory said, handing Starflight one of the guard's spears. "We might need it, and it'll look less weird in your claws – if I hold it, it'll look like it's just flying around through the air by itself."

Starflight nodded, although the weight of the spear felt extremely strange in his talons. It was more likely that he'd accidentally poke his own eye out than that he'd be able to use this to fight. He tried to hold it as far away from himself as possible as he lifted up into the sky.

"Take us to the prison caves first," Glory's voice said from the air beside him. "Once Mangrove and the others are set up to free the prisoners, you and I can head for the fortress."

"You?" Starflight said. It was really odd not being able to see her; he felt as if he were arguing with the air. "That's the most dangerous part. As the queen, shouldn't you keep yourself safe? You can send someone else for Splendor." He tilted his wings to soar towards the prison caves and the lava river.

He could feel air currents shifting around him as several invisible dragons flew alongside. He wasn't sure how many RainWings were following him, but he hoped none of the NightWings would hear the wingbeats and get suspicious. There were very few NightWings in sight – one or two on the balconies of the fortress plus the guards in the cave entrances below. Starflight guessed that the rest were assembling in preparation for their planned attack tonight.

"I'm not going to be the kind of queen who sends other dragons into danger that I'm not willing to face myself," Glory said. "And even if I could send someone for Splendor, I can't send anyone else to face Battlewinner."

Starflight sucked in a surprised breath. "Battlewinner?" he said. "Is that a good idea?"

"Weren't you the one who suggested diplomacy?" Glory said, and he could hear amusement in her voice.

Yes, but that was before I knew anything about the NightWings.

"Rescuing the prisoners is the top priority," she went on, "but if I can threaten her somehow – maybe if I tell her I'll expose her secret – perhaps I can get her to leave us and the rainforest alone from now on."

"I doubt it," Fatespeaker said. "The NightWings really want your rainforest."

"Well, too bad," Glory snapped.

"Shh," Starflight said. They were approaching the first prison cave. He dipped his head towards it and felt a *whoosh* of wind as one of the RainWings dived past him. A moment later, the two guards in the cave entrance both reached for their necks, looking confused, and then, in slow motion, they crumpled into slumbering heaps.

"We're lucky the caves line the river," Starflight said, circling around in the sky. "The guards at each entrance can't see any of the others get knocked out."

He saw the guards in the next cave collapse to the ground, and then the next, and the next. The RainWings were fanning out, following instructions Glory had given them before leaving the rainforest. He saw the shimmer of scales and teeth here and there as the RainWings landed in pairs, shifted colour, and darted into the prison caves.

"You said you saw Orchid in one of these caves," Glory said to Fatespeaker. "Do you remember which one?"

Fatespeaker nodded and twisted into a dive, aiming for

one of the caves closest to the fortress. As they approached, its two guards looked up. Although all they could see were two NightWing dragonets, one of them frowned a little as if he sensed something was amiss. Starflight's stomach lurched as the guard reached for the gong that would summon the rest of the tribe.

Then the air beside Starflight's ear went *zzt zzt*, and the two guards wobbled and went down.

"That was close," Starflight said, but after a moment he realized he really *was* talking to empty air. Below him, the two guards were dragged aside, and as he landed he heard the *thump* of talons hurrying to the back of the cave.

"I want to see this," Fatespeaker whispered, darting inside. Starflight followed just in time to see Mangrove appear in front of Orchid, his grey and black scales shifting all at once to a joyful pink shot through with worried green.

Orchid let out a cry of joy that was muffled by the iron muzzle around her jaws. She reached towards Mangrove and he leaped for her, wrapping his wings all the way around her and twining his tail with hers.

"I'm here," he said. "I wouldn't give up; I'd never give up on you."

She couldn't speak, but the rose colours of Orchid's scales said everything.

"Let's get her out of here as fast as we can," Glory said.

"If they're all chained to the wall like this, we have extra work to do. Starflight, give me the spear."

Starflight held the spear out and it was whisked away from him. A Glory-shaped shadow approached Orchid and carefully stuck the points of the spear into the lock on the mouth band.

"Liana, Grandeur, are you paying attention?" Glory asked.

"Yes," two voices said from the air. Starflight jumped. He hadn't realized the other two RainWings were with them.

"This is how you undo the locks," Glory said, twisting the spear. The muzzle fell off with a *clank*, and Glory set to work on the chains that bound Orchid to the wall.

"I was afraid you wouldn't care where I was," Orchid said to Mangrove. "I thought you'd move on and find someone else. . ."

"Never, never, never," Mangrove said fiercely.

"Do you feel the earth shaking?" Orchid asked.

"I think that's me," Mangrove said, holding out his trembling claws. "Like all the happiness inside us is trying to burst out."

Actually, I'm pretty sure that was a real earthquake, Starflight thought. He'd felt the tremor in the earth as well, rumbling up through his talons before it stopped.

"Done," Glory said, and the spear moved through the

air as she handed it to one of the other RainWings. Orchid shook off the loose chains and spread her wings, beaming and glowing like a ball of pink sunshine.

"Orchid, this is our new queen, Glory," said Mangrove. "She's the reason we found you, and she's the dragon who convinced everyone to come get you."

"It was really thanks to Mangrove," said Glory. "He's the one who knew you were missing and wouldn't shut up about it. If we hadn't brought an army to save you, he'd have come over here and done it himself."

"Thank you, Your Majesty," Orchid said with a half bow.

"That is *too weird*," Starflight whispered to Fatespeaker. "Hearing my friend called 'Your Majesty'."

"I bet watching her lead an invasion is fairly strange, too," Fatespeaker whispered back.

"Grandeur, Liana, disguise yourselves as NightWings, take the guards' spears, and go to the other caves," Glory ordered. "Show everyone how to free the prisoners. Move as quickly and quietly as you can. Then get everyone back to the tunnel. The most important thing is getting all fourteen prisoners home safe. Mangrove, you and Orchid take a moment to calm your scales down and then you can head back to the rainforest, too."

"I should come with you," Mangrove said. "If you're going into the fortress, you'll need backup."

"I'll have it," Glory said.

I hope she doesn't mean me, Starflight thought anxiously.

"But we went to a lot of trouble to reunite you and Orchid, so go be happy with her for a little while. We'll let you know if we need you."

Mangrove and Orchid both bowed.

Wings brushed against Starflight's shoulder and he started back for a moment before he realized it was Glory, heading up the tunnel to the lava river.

"Come on, Starflight," she said from the darkness. "Let's go have a talk with the NightWing queen."

CHAPTER 25

The fortress seemed eerily quiet as they flew towards it. The air felt thick with ashy smoke. Starflight's nose and throat hurt even worse than before, and occasionally he heard Glory and Fatespeaker coughing behind him.

He rubbed his stinging eyes and stared at the fortress ahead, wondering where an entire NightWing army would assemble. Queen Battlewinner wouldn't be able to lead it, since she couldn't leave the lava. Greatness would have to really make some queenly decisions if she was planning to lead their attack.

Had Starflight's absence been noticed yet? If not, surely at least Morrowseer would have gone to check on Flame and found him missing. How had he reacted?

Maybe he'll think Flame tried to fly home to the continent, Starflight thought. *We'd be in luck if Morrowseer tried to follow him.* He really did not want to encounter Morrowseer in the halls of the fortress.

"Please tell me there's an invisible army with us," Starflight said.

"I'm your invisible army," Glory said cheerfully.

"I'm serious," Starflight said. "We shouldn't go in there alone, just the three of us."

"Tell me something," Glory said. "The dungeons you saw – how do we get them open? Will those spears work on the doors, or do we need keys?"

Starflight closed his eyes for a moment, picturing the dungeon. "We need keys, I think," he said.

"So let's start with the queen," Glory said. "We'll make her tell us where to find the keys."

Starflight could not imagine making Battlewinner do anything at all, but then, Glory was a lot more persuasive than he was – and even more so now that she had a queen's authority. He swerved down towards the entrance closest to the council chamber.

The three of them padded silently through the hallways. Loud voices rang out from a few of the rooms. Starflight caught snippets of an argument about who would get to wear some shared armour, a monologue about another battle the storyteller had been in, and a conversation about how killing RainWings would have to be easier than killing MudWings.

He'd forgotten all about the dead MudWings on the rainforest border. *Why would the NightWings kill them?* he asked himself, and almost immediately a possible answer came to him: *to keep the MudWings out of the rainforest. If they believe there's a deadly monster lurking in there – that it's not safe to go anywhere near it – they won't be tempted to conquer the rainforest themselves.*

Leaving it untouched and ready for the NightWings to move in anytime.

That explains the howler monkeys, too. He remembered Jambu saying that the monkeys used to make a normal monkey sound, but then suddenly they started screaming like dying dragons instead. *I bet my dad is responsible for that. I bet he did something to the monkeys so their screams would scare the MudWings away.*

Everything the NightWings did was part of their grand plan of taking over the rainforest. Starflight sighed and glanced at the map as he led the way into the room with the secret entrance. If only there were somewhere else the NightWings could go . . . but they'd clearly been all over Pyrrhia, destroying scavenger dens, for whatever reason, and if there had been somewhere else for them to live, surely they would have found it.

"Someone's coming," Glory whispered a heartbeat before Starflight heard claws tapping on stone and smelled the rank odour of NightWing breath.

Fatespeaker shot across the room to the map, but before she could lift the corner and duck underneath, scales slithered in the doorway and they all whirled to see Greatness staring at them.

The ground rumbled under their feet.

"What are you doing in here?" the NightWing princess asked. Her glittering diamond necklace was askew, as if she'd slept in it and had forgotten it was on. Her eyes looked exhausted, red and raw from the smoke in the air. "Why aren't you with the others?"

"We . . . got lost?" Starflight tried.

Greatness squinted at them. "Oh, you're the two little prophecy dragonets. Morrowseer was looking for you in quite a towering rage earlier. Listen, like I told him, the prophecy is important, but it's even more important that we win this battle tonight. So the whole tribe is going, no exceptions. Everyone else is in the great hall – if you follow this tunnel down and take the fourth left, you'll be halfway there and someone can guide you."

"What about you?" Fatespeaker asked. "Why aren't you there?"

"I'm going to speak with the queen first," Greatness said. Her eyes darted involuntarily to the map.

"Actually," Glory's voice said from the air, "we're all going to speak with the queen." Greatness stiffened and pulled in her wings; Starflight saw a flash of scales changing colour as Glory's claws rested on the artery in the NightWing's throat.

"Don't call for help," Glory said. "I'm not an ordinary RainWing. My venom is aimed at your eyes right now and *I* am not afraid to use it."

"The dangerous one," Greatness whispered.

"That's right," Glory said. "Now we're all going up the

hidden tunnel to the queen, and you're leading the way, and you're going to keep in mind that my fangs are right behind you."

Greatness blinked and nodded several times, looking queasy. She hurried to the map and ducked into the tunnel. The rustle of wings indicated that Glory had followed her; Fatespeaker and Starflight were right behind them.

The rocky floor felt hot under Starflight's talons, hotter than it had before. Another rumble shook the mountain as they pressed forward.

"Um," Starflight said as a horrifying thought struck him. "There's no chance this volcano is about to erupt, is there?"

Up ahead in the shadows, the bulky figure of Greatness paused and looked back. "It shouldn't," she said. "Our scientists predicted that we have at least two more years before another major eruption."

"How can they be sure?" Fatespeaker asked. "Did someone have a vision?"

Greatness turned around and kept walking without answering.

Starflight braced himself against another tremble in the ground. "I don't like the feeling in the air," he whispered to Fatespeaker. "I don't know much about volcanoes . . . but I'm pretty sure it's a bad sign when they start doing this."

"Poor NightWings," Fatespeaker said softly.

"Hmm," said Starflight. "More like, poor *us*, if we don't get out of here soon."

They abruptly came around the bend into the queen's cave. Queen Battlewinner was sitting erect in her boiling lava cauldron, glaring at them with fierce eyes that reflected the red light around them.

Starflight inhaled sharply as he spotted another dragon in the back corner of the cave: his father, Mastermind. The scientist was fussing over several hunks of metal on the floor, and after a moment, Starflight remembered seeing them in the lab. All put together, they looked like a suit of armour that would fit over an entire dragon, with room to pour something in between the dragon's scales and the metal.

Lava, he realized. *This is how Battlewinner plans to get to the rainforest. Mastermind has been building her a portable lava device.* His brain immediately started taking apart the science of the idea. *But how would it stay hot, away from the volcano? Can any metal really contain it?* He also realized, tangentially, that his father had lied about not seeing the queen – he must be one of the few dragons who knew her secret, and was working to help her keep it.

Mastermind looked up as they came in and locked eyes with Starflight. His expression was startled, but in a distracted way, as if he was dealing with something far more important, and after a moment he bent back to the armour without saying anything to his son.

"Fool," Battlewinner snarled at Greatness.

Greatness hung her head, looking less like a queen than ever.

"Preparations?" the NightWing queen hissed.

"Everyone is gathering," Greatness said. "But, Mother, I can't lead them into battle by myself. Can't we postpone the attack? Mastermind says your armour isn't ready. . ."

"It will be," Battlewinner hissed. "Tonight."

"I don't think so," Mastermind said anxiously from behind her. He dropped a curved tailplate with a loud clatter and winced. "Your Majesty, I don't understand why you have to go. I need more time to make sure this will work for you."

"Must do this right," Battlewinner snarled. "Can't trust *you* to invade properly." She cast a scornful look at Greatness.

"You shouldn't," Greatness said, fingering the diamonds around her neck. "I don't know what you want me to do. So I was coming to ask you and then—"

"And then she ran into me," Glory said.

Mastermind let out a yelp of fright as Glory's scales shimmered into sight, shifting from the camouflage of the shadows to a bold royal blue shot through with veins of gold. She looked regal and out of place in this smoky red and black cave. "Well," she added, "more accurately, she ran into my claws." She flexed her talons and narrowed her eyes at Queen Battlewinner.

"And you are?" growled the queen.

"Queen Glory of the RainWings. I have come to give you one chance to end this war before we destroy you."

The dragon in the lava made an involuntary scoffing sound that clearly hurt her throat. She paused for a long moment, clutching her neck, then dipped her whole body under the lava and emerged again.

"Funny," she said finally.

"Not very," Glory said. "If you think an IceWing attack is hard to live with, wait until you experience a little RainWing venom. I'm afraid your lava bath won't be able to help you with that."

Smoke hissed softly through Battlewinner's nostrils as she stared at Glory.

"Oh, three moons," Greatness said anxiously, wringing her talons. "What do you want?"

"We're taking our prisoners back," Glory said. "You will never set foot in the rainforest again. You will leave the RainWings alone for ever. We'll destroy the tunnel between our kingdoms, you'll call off the invasion, and we'll never even sniff another NightWing near our village for the next twelve generations."

Starflight cleared his throat a few times significantly and Glory glanced at him. "Also," she added, "you will stop meddling with the prophecy dragonets – both the real ones and the fake ones. You'll let them save the world and stop the war however they decide to."

"Never," hissed Queen Battlewinner. "Never."

"Never what?" Glory said. "Because you don't have a lot of options here."

"I see one," Battlewinner croaked. "You die."

Glory bared her teeth at the NightWing queen, but Greatness interrupted, her voice pleading.

"Please listen. You're dooming us to a horrible end," she cried. "The volcano is not only a future threat – it's killing us now. There's almost no prey left. We're all starving. Fewer dragonets are born each year. And we're barely NightWings any more. Don't you see? The tribe is dying. We *need* a new home."

"Well, you can't have *ours*, you murderous entitled worms," Glory flared.

"Why not?" Mastermind asked, sounding genuinely confused.

"Because a whole tribe already lives there." Glory's scales were flashing to red and orange in places – hints of her anger showing through, although she quelled them quickly. "And if you try to hurt my RainWings, I will make you regret it."

"Wait," Starflight said. His brain was suddenly spinning forward – a new idea unfolding across his mind like a scroll rolling open. "Wait – maybe – maybe there's a way to compromise. Glory, stop and think. There's lots of space in the rainforest; the RainWings say so all the time. What if we let the NightWings move in and build their own village somewhere in the rainforest – but *only* if they all swear to accept *you* as their new queen."

There was a shocked pause.

"WHAT?" Battlewinner roared.

Glory tilted her head at Starflight, looking sceptical but intrigued.

"Think about it," Starflight said. "A new home for the NightWings, safe and peaceful, and all they have to do is give up their cruelty and violence and obey you. You know you'd be as great at being NightWing queen as you are at ruling the RainWings."

"Hmm," Glory said. "There would be something poetic about being the boss of a tribe that's always called me lazy and useless."

"NEVER!" Battlewinner shouted, then had to stop and double over coughing for a long minute.

Uneasily, Starflight felt the ground shake again, much stronger this time.

"We'll never bow to RainWings," Battlewinner snarled finally.

"Actually, Mother," Greatness said nervously, "it sounds like a decent plan to me."

Battlewinner spat out a shard of ice that sizzled into steam when it hit the lava. "You never wanted to be queen," she rasped. "You're a pathetic heir."

"I know I am," Greatness said. "Being queen is awful."

Battlewinner hissed again, loud and long. Starflight realized that he was also hearing something else – a faraway rumbling that seemed to be getting louder and closer.

"What about our real queen?" Mastermind asked.

Starflight stared straight into the icy blue depths of Battlewinner's eyes. "I think she knows she's not making it to the rainforest. There's nothing you can build that will work to keep her alive there. She's going to die here, crushed by the volcano along with the NightWing home, and if she wants her tribe to survive, she needs to hand them over to Queen Glory."

Battlewinner's tail was thrashing hard enough to spill lava over the edges of the cauldron, splattering dangerously close to their talons. "I am their queen. *I* am," she spat.

"Wait, Starflight," Glory said. "I haven't agreed to this. How could we ever trust the NightWings in our rainforest? These are the same dragons who've been abducting and torturing my tribe. How can we just forgive them? I don't want them anywhere near us." She shook her head. "I don't think it'll work."

Mastermind looked sick at the words "abducting and torturing." He turned away from Starflight, staring down at the armour in his claws.

"It might work," Greatness said desperately. "Give us a chance, please! I promise we can be better."

"Shameful," Battlewinner snarled.

"It's not up to you," Starflight said to the NightWing queen, and realized his voice wasn't even shaking. He was right, he could feel it, and that helped him get past his fear. "You're stuck here. We're negotiating with Greatness now." He turned to the NightWing princess. "Come on, let's talk about this somewhere else."

"No!" roared Battlewinner. "You can't do this. *I won't let you.*" She gripped the sides of the cauldron with glistening claws, and then, to Starflight's horror, she heaved herself up and out of the lava. Her back talons crunched down on the edge of the cauldron. Her wings flared open, scattering molten orange droplets across the room. Her thick head swung back and forth, glaring at all of them. She was massive, as big as Morrowseer, and glowing horribly as lava dripped between her scales and claws and slithered off her tail.

"Mother, stop," Greatness cried.

"Your Majesty!" Mastermind shouted. "You can't come out! Wait – my experiment—" He scrabbled frantically at the armour around him.

"*I* will lead my tribe to safety," the queen hissed. She landed on the rocky ground with a *thud*, but the aftershocks went on too long to be caused by her. It was an earthquake, a serious one, Starflight realized as bits of the walls began to crumble.

"We have to get out of here," he said to Glory.

Queen Battlewinner took a step towards Glory and Starflight, then stopped, clutching her neck again. She hissed in a frightening, hoarse way and took another step. Her tongue flicked out and in and she started to shake. When she stared around at all of them, Starflight could see the icy blue spreading rapidly over her eyeballs.

"Mother!" Greatness yelped. "Get back in the lava!" She darted to her mother's side and tried tugging on Battlewinner's wing. Mastermind dashed up on the other side and started wrapping bits of metal around the queen's limbs. But Starflight could tell that even if the armour would work, it was already too late.

With a bone-rattling shriek, Battlewinner threw off her daughter and Mastermind and surged towards Glory. Glory took a step back, and the NightWing queen collapsed on the floor in front of her. Her limbs twitched violently; her wings spasmed; her tail thrashed back and forth. White frost was starting to march between the scales of her neck, spreading rapidly across her body.

Lava dripped off Battlewinner, faster and faster as the ice started to win the battle for her body. Greatness pressed herself against the wall, whimpering, as far away from the dying queen as possible. Starflight wanted to look away, but somehow he couldn't. He felt Fatespeaker bury her face in his shoulder.

The NightWing queen's neck froze solid first, then her

chest, her ears, her wings, her snout, all the way out to her claws and her tail. Within moments, the dragon's entire body was encased in jagged whorls of ice. Her eyes were blue pools of rage. Her mouth froze wide open, as if she'd wanted to end her life with a howl of fury, but it was too late; nothing could come out.

Greatness and Mastermind stared down at the queen, disbelief and horror warring on their faces.

Then the entire island shook as if a giant dragon had pounded his talons into it, and Starflight felt his stomach twist with terror.

The volcano was about to erupt.

CHAPTER 26

"We have to go *now*," Starflight said, grabbing Glory and shoving her towards the door. He bundled Fatespeaker ahead of him, too, and they fled down the tunnel.

"Wait!" He heard Greatness yell as they ran, but when Fatespeaker tried to stop he pushed her forward. There was no time for more diplomatic conversation. Feet thumped behind them; Greatness would have to talk to them somewhere else, such as *not* in the middle of an exploding volcano.

The map caught on Starflight's horns and ripped away from the wall as he threw himself out of the hole at the end. He rolled forward, wrestling the map off his head and bundling it in his talons. Without really thinking about it, he shoved it under one arm and carried it with him as he bolted for the door.

"Where are the dungeons?" Glory shouted.

"There's no time!" Starflight yelled. Couldn't she feel the volcano shaking? Ash was raining down all around them; cracks were zipping across the fortress walls like lightning.

"We are not leaving Deathbringer!" Glory grabbed Fatespeaker. "Point the way and I'll go by myself. Starflight, get out of here. Get everyone off the island."

Deathbringer? Starflight opened and closed his mouth. He hadn't realized that rescuing the NightWing assassin was even on Glory's agenda, let alone that it was important enough to risk an erupting volcano for.

But she's right. He risked everything for us – for her.

Fatespeaker pointed in the direction of the dungeons and Glory took off without waiting for any more arguments.

I can't let her go by herself! Starflight's heart was trying to pound its way out of his chest. He remembered the NightWing skeletons in the old treasure room; he thought of the lava flow that had consumed the old forest and the skulls sticking out of it. He could feel the heat of the volcano as if it were trying to batter its way through the walls towards him.

All he wanted to do was fly as fast as he could to the tunnel and escape to the cool safety of the rainforest.

But Glory didn't know where she was going, or what to do when she got there.

He whirled around and found Greatness behind them, wringing her talons again and looking utterly wrecked. "Where are the keys to the dungeon prisons?" he yelled at her.

"The – the – oh – there's a set hidden in a coal niche on the dungeon stairs," she said. "What are we going to do about the volcano? Is this it? The one that kills us all?"

Yes. "Not necessarily," Starflight said, trying to sound

far less panicked than he felt. "Take Fatespeaker to the great hall and tell all the NightWings our terms. If they'll swear loyalty to Queen Glory, we'll consider letting them live in the rainforest. Anyone who agrees, send them through the tunnel as fast as you can. Anyone who doesn't, tell them to fly for the continent immediately. They need to get far away from here before the eruption – the lava and smoke could reach for miles."

"But Glory didn't say yes," Fatespeaker pointed out.

"I'll talk her into it," he promised grimly. "Go, quickly." He wrapped his wings briefly around Fatespeaker, feeling her scales slide against his, and then let go and ran after Glory.

He found her at the next intersection, looking around in furious indecision.

"This way," he called. He ran past her, towards the stairs that led down to the dungeon.

There was no time to talk, and the rumbling of the volcano was now loud enough to drown out any attempt at conversation anyway. The heat increased as they went down, and the noise grew and the walls seemed to shake even more.

We're going to die down here, Starflight thought with absolute certainty.

He stopped at each niche on the stairs, feeling gingerly around the coals and singeing his talons more than once. Finally, in the last one, he felt something metal and heavy hanging from a hook inside the opening, and when he tugged on it, he found keys resting in his claws.

In the dungeon, Splendor was awake, shaking like a leaf in the middle of her cell, with her wings over her head.

"It's all right," Starflight called through the bars, trying keys in the lock one after another. "We're here; we're rescuing you. You're going home."

Splendor looked up, blinking. Her scales were bright acid-green and her expression was dazed with fear.

Starflight glanced around and realized that Glory had gone right past them. She was at Deathbringer's cage, grabbing the bars. As he watched, Deathbringer reached his talons through the bars and wrapped them around hers, and they exchanged a look that said "thank you" and a whole lot more.

The lock finally turned under his claws and the door swung open. Splendor stumbled towards him.

"Wait here," he told her, hurrying to Deathbringer's door.

"Why aren't we leaving?" Splendor wailed.

Glory grabbed the keys from him and started trying them. It was hard to tell whether her talons were shaking from nerves, too, or whether it just looked that way because the whole mountain was quaking now without stopping.

"You don't have to do this," Deathbringer said, his gaze fixed on Glory.

"Oh, I don't?" Glory said without looking up from the keys. "That'll save me some time; good luck with the volcano, then."

Starflight glanced up at the ominous cracks appearing in the ceiling. He spotted a symbol at the top of Deathbringer's cage – a symbol he'd seen on one of the keys.

"Try this one," he said, reaching over and taking the keys from Glory. He stuck the key with the symbol on it in the lock and turned it. The door swung open.

Deathbringer yanked on his chains as they hurried into the cell. Splendor ran in behind them, flapping her wings in a frantic whirl of green.

"Something is coming through the walls!" she shrieked. "We're all going to die!"

Starflight looked out at the dungeon hallway and saw lava glowing in the cracks of the walls.

"She's right," he said quietly to Glory.

"You two go ahead," she said, concentrating on the keys and Deathbringer's chains. "We'll be right behind you."

"Let's go, let's go!" Splendor cried.

"One more minute," Starflight told her. He held his breath as Glory tried key after key.

"We don't *have* any more minutes," Splendor sobbed. "We're going to be exploded and covered in lava and melted and dead!"

A ferocious rumble answered her, knocking them all off

their feet. Glory scrambled up and stuck the last key in the lock around Deathbringer's chains.

"That's it!" she cried as they fell off, clanking and clattering like living things on the quaking floor. "Come on!" She seized Deathbringer's forearm and yanked him up. They took off down the hallway with Starflight and Splendor right behind them.

The mountain was shaking so violently now that it was hard to run; Starflight kept getting thrown into walls or the other dragons. He concentrated on the stairs up ahead.

"Watch your feet," Deathbringer called. Hot coals were scattered across the steps where they had fallen from their niches. Glory swept several aside with her tail, wincing as even that brief contact burned her scales.

They raced up the steps, covering their heads with their wings as bits of rock plummeted from the ceiling. Starflight stepped on a coal and bit back a yowl of pain. The stairs felt endless, like they were staggering upward for days, but finally they burst out on to a level floor.

"This way!" Deathbringer hurtled down the hall in a direction Starflight hadn't been before.

A loud crash sounded from the direction of the council chamber, and Starflight thought he heard a dragon screaming. He shoved Splendor ahead of him. Even Glory was green now; neither RainWing could camouflage their scales while their fear was so strong. They all raced after

Deathbringer, twisting through the fortress labyrinth, until up ahead they saw the sky – or at least, the dense cloud of ash and smoke that now surrounded the volcano.

"Try not to breathe," Glory said to Splendor. "It's not far to the tunnel."

Starflight flung his wings open and leaped off the ledge, flapping furiously through the thick air. He could see the lava river glowing and churning below him, faster and wider than ever. He could also see a growing crowd of black dragons down on the beach, some of them fighting one another tooth and claw.

"We have to bring them to the rainforest," he called to Glory, coughing and gasping. "Or else the whole NightWing tribe could be wiped out today."

"Serves them right," she called, but he could see from her face that she couldn't let that happen either.

Chunks of fiery rocks were starting to shoot out of the volcano, blasting into the sky and slamming into the ground with explosive force. One came so close to Starflight's wing that he felt the heat of it crackle along his scales.

Glory twisted in the air, scanning the caves below her. "I hope all my RainWings made it back safely."

Starflight found himself making a decision that shocked him, but the words were out of his mouth before he could take them back. "You go ahead to the rainforest, make sure they're all right, and prepare them for what's coming," he said. "I'll gather the NightWings and bring them through."

She gave him a surprised look, but didn't argue. "We'll have our spears and fangs and sleeping darts ready," she said. "Come on, you two." She flicked her tail at Deathbringer and Splendor, who sped after her. Starflight watched them all dive for the cave entrance, where green scales flashed as two half-camouflaged RainWings reached to welcome them in.

Now Starflight could see a cluster of spears bristling in the air by the cave, and he realized with a sinking sensation that the RainWings probably weren't letting any NightWings through. He'd sent Fatespeaker and Greatness on that mission, but the RainWings didn't know them – they'd barely met Fatespeaker – and had no reason to trust them.

They would listen to him, though. If he could convince the NightWings to accept Glory as their queen . . . if he could lead them into the rainforest peacefully. . .

But if he couldn't. . .

There were a million things that could go wrong. The RainWings might panic and attack the NightWings as they came through, even with Glory standing over them. Or the NightWings might lie to get to safety and then attack the RainWings anyway.

Or the volcano might kill them all before they got anywhere.

Another blast from the volcano sent sharp rock shards zinging around him. Starflight felt a stabbing pain in his side as one of them grazed his scales.

No more time for worrying, he thought, tucking his wings and diving towards the beach. *We escape now, together . . . or we all die.*

CHAPTER 27

It looked as though the entire tribe might be gathered on the beach below him. Starflight flew in a wide circle, scanning the crowd, until he saw Greatness and Fatespeaker standing on a boulder, waving their wings and trying to get everyone's attention.

"They'll never let us through!" shrieked a NightWing with long scratches along his side. "We have to take the rainforest by force!"

"We can't fight them," yelled another. "They infiltrated the island, took out all our guards, and escaped with the prisoners, and we never even knew they were here. They'll kill us the moment we step into that tunnel."

The volcano shot another blast of fiery rocks into the air, and many of the black dragons flung themselves to the ground with cries of terror.

"Listen to me!" Starflight called, hovering above Greatness. "There is a way to escape safely. I promise you that the RainWings will show you mercy if you accept Glory as your queen."

"How can a RainWing lead our tribe?" shouted a voice that Starflight recognized as his sister's. Fierceteeth flared her wings and shook her talons at him.

305

"Better than Queen Battlewinner can," Starflight said. "Since she's dead."

Shocked silence fell over the tribe; all of them stared at him in disbelief. Starflight spotted Mastermind, hopping agitatedly from one foot to the other, with his arms full of scrolls. And finally Starflight saw Morrowseer at the back, glowering at him. The look on the giant dragon's face gave Starflight chills from his wings to the tip of his tail.

"But Greatness. . ." one of the NightWings said half-heartedly.

"I've already agreed to this plan," Greatness called. "It is the only way for our tribe to survive."

"Glory will take care of you," Starflight said firmly. "She will be a fair and just queen, and you'll be safe in the rainforest instead of trapped here."

The smoke had got so dense that it was getting hard to see the dragons in front of him. Fine grey ash coated all their scales and made the sand slick beneath their claws.

The volcano rumbled ominously.

"I'll do it," Mightyclaws said from the front of the crowd. "It has to be better than this."

"How do we know they won't kill us all?" asked another dragon.

"I trust her," said Greatness.

"And guess what really will kill you all," Fatespeaker

added, pointing. "That volcano. So, come on, let's get out of here! All hail Queen Glory!" She took to the sky, flying towards the tunnel.

"Queen Glory!" shouted Mightyclaws, leaping into the air.

"Queen Glory!" shouted another dragon, and then another and another.

Starflight hoped that Glory could hear them. This had to be the strangest thing that had ever happened to her: the tribe that was always supposed to be so superior, now bowing down to the most "useless" of the dragonets.

He darted ahead of them to the ledge and found that the RainWings were gone. In their place were Clay, Tsunami and Sunny, and he felt himself breathe a little deeper when he saw them.

"I hope you know what you're doing," Tsunami said to Starflight as he landed beside her. "This is a terrible plan. NightWings can't be trusted."

"I think it's brilliant," Sunny said warmly. "I think *you're* brilliant. I think it's the best idea in the world."

Starflight hadn't even thought about what Sunny would think of his idea – for once. He gave her a shy smile, pleased that he had accidentally done something she was so excited about.

"We'd better hurry," Clay said, glancing up at the mountain, which was spitting bright orange sparks into the sky. "Come on, quickly," he called to the approaching NightWings, holding out his talons.

Mightyclaws was the first to land on the ledge. "Queen Glory!" he cried, charging past them down the tunnel. Starflight followed far enough to see the dragonet leap into the hole and disappear.

Greatness was next, moving just as fast. She paused briefly beside Starflight, her wings filling the tunnel, her eyes darting anxiously back towards the smouldering volcano. "I'm so glad I won't ever have to be queen," she whispered to him, then hurried off.

Escaping ahead of the rest of her tribe, Starflight thought, *instead of waiting to make sure everyone else gets away safely. The NightWings should all be glad she won't ever be their queen.*

He stepped back as a flood of NightWings started coming through.

"To our new queen!" he heard a few of them cry.

"Queen Glory!"

"This is so wrong," somebody muttered.

"Think of all the food!" said someone else.

"And the smell of the rainforest – have you been there?" said another. "It's amazing, like the air itself is full of water and light."

"You'll finally get to try a coconut," one dragon said to another as they went by.

"Real trees," a few of the dragonets were whispering to each other. "Real sunshine! Mangoes every day!"

Starflight pushed back through the tide of black dragons until he reached his friends on the outer ledge. The sky was full of boiling dark clouds, and grey ash was raining down like snow. A new rivulet of lava had snaked out of the top of the volcano and was bubbling down one side. The earthquakes were coming in waves now and getting stronger, like a giant dragon stamping its way towards them across the ocean.

"We're making all of them say 'Queen Glory' on their way past," Tsunami said to Starflight, grabbing one NightWing's tail. "Hey, you, speak up."

"Queen Glory," he grumbled, and Starflight recognized Strongwings, his father's burly lab assistant.

"Once more, like you mean it," Tsunami prodded. "Or you can discuss it with the volcano up there."

The volcano obligingly growled.

"Queen Glory!" Strongwings blurted loudly.

"Better," Tsunami said, letting him go.

Starflight was startled to see one brown dragon approaching in the middle of all the black, and for a moment he thought it was Clay – but Clay was right next to him. Then, with a huge stab of guilt, he remembered Ochre, who had gone off to hunt earlier that morning, which felt like weeks and weeks ago. *I might have left him here. I didn't even think to look for him.*

"Uh, hey," Ochre said, flapping on to the ledge and bobbing his head at Starflight. "So – I'm not sure what's happening, but – it seems like everyone's leaving? In kind of a hurry? And someone said something about bananas this way?"

"Just follow the others into the tunnel," Starflight said. "We'll explain everything later."

"Sure, all right," Ochre said. In a moment, he'd disappeared in the direction of the rainforest as well.

"Starflight, this dragon wanted to talk to you," Clay said, tugging Starflight aside.

"Oh," Starflight said, meeting his father's eyes. "Clay, this is Mastermind. My – my father."

The thin black dragon still had several scrolls clutched to his chest, and he was fidgeting with his claws anxiously. He tried to reach for Starflight's talons, dropped a few scrolls, gathered them up again, and blurted, "It's occurred to me, at this rather inopportune juncture, that our new hosts may very well, er – hate me. What do you think? Should I be concerned? Will they really let me live there? After everything? I'm afraid they might . . . have some grievances."

Starflight sensed that his father wanted a reassuring lie, but he wasn't about to give him one. "They probably do hate you," he said. "I think they should, don't you?"

"But," Mastermind fretted, twisting a scroll between his claws. "But, but science – and my orders – and—"

"Don't make excuses," Starflight said. "When you get there, tell the queen you're sorry and accept whatever punishment she gives you. That's my advice."

"Or don't come at all," Tsunami chimed in from behind him. "Take your chances on the ocean instead." She nodded out to sea.

Mastermind flicked his tail with a worried expression, watching the NightWings pour past them into the cave, faster and faster as the volcano's rumbles grew ever more ominous and closer together.

"I'll apologize," he said with a deep breath. "To our new queen," he added.

"All right, go on," Tsunami said, stepping back.

"Take this with you," Starflight interjected, realizing he still had the map with all the scavenger dens on it. He tucked the folded paper in among the scrolls in his father's arms, and Mastermind hurried into the tunnel with them all pressed to his chest.

"Just like you when we had to escape the mountain," Sunny said, bumping Starflight's side. "Trying to take all the scrolls."

"I hope we don't have anything else in common," Starflight said with a flick of his tail.

"Don't give up on him yet," Sunny said. Starflight thought she must be the only dragon in the world who'd be willing to forgive what Mastermind had done.

311

"Guys," Tsunami said quietly. "Look who the last NightWing is."

Starflight turned, already knowing the answer.

The last few NightWings hurried by, blurting "The new queen! Queen Glory!" as they ducked into the tunnel. And then the four dragonets were left standing on the ledge, facing Morrowseer as he landed.

He loomed over them, terrifying and menacing and furious, looking exactly as he had when they first met him under the mountain, only a few weeks ago.

NightWings are superior to every other tribe, Starflight remembered him saying in their secret meeting. *You have to act like a leader to be treated like one. Don't let anyone see your weaknesses. Don't have any weaknesses.*

All his life, Starflight had often felt like he was nothing but weaknesses . . . but after everything he'd done today, he was starting to think maybe he wasn't so useless after all, powers or no powers.

"This will never work," Morrowseer growled down at them. "NightWings will never bow to a dragon from another tribe, least of all a RainWing. Once we're safe, we'll turn on you all."

"Then you'll end up back here," Tsunami spat, waving her talons at the ash-covered, blackened landscape behind him. "Or dead. Either would be fine with me."

"We made you," Morrowseer snarled. "You dragonets

are only important because of us, and we can destroy you just as easily."

"No, you can't," Sunny spoke up. "We have a prophecy to fulfil, and there's nothing you can do to stop it from happening."

Morrowseer barked a laugh. "Stop it?" he said. "I've been trying to make it happen for almost ten years."

"Prophecies don't work like that," Sunny insisted. "You can't make them happen the way you want. Whatever's going to happen will happen – that's the whole point of destiny."

The volcano shot a plume of lava into the air and the ground shook hard enough that all the dragonets had to clutch the rock walls to stay upright.

"On the contrary, I certainly *can* make my prophecy happen however I want," Morrowseer said silkily, "considering I'm the one who made it up in the first place."

CHAPTER 28

The earth began to shake without stopping, a continuous tremor that jarred Starflight's teeth in his head and made him feel as though the ledge was about to drop out from under him. The volcano growled again, and another fountain of lava shot over the side and started slithering down the craggy slope.

Morrowseer's face was lit by the orange glow of the volcano, cruelty etched into every line of his snout.

"You *what*?" Tsunami said.

The prophecy isn't real. The words didn't make sense in Starflight's head. He couldn't fit them into the way the world worked, the way his world had always worked. *The Dragonet Prophecy isn't real.*

"That's not true," Sunny cried. "You're just saying that to be awful."

The volcano let out a roar like twenty dragons having their tails stepped on at once.

"Oh, it's completely true," Morrowseer growled. "Queen Battlewinner and I wrote it together after the last eruption destroyed part of the fortress. We knew we'd need a new home soon, and the prophecy was our plan to get it."

"How?" Starflight asked, running the prophecy through

his mind. "What does the prophecy have to do with where the NightWings live?"

"The idea was that we would control the dragonets," Morrowseer said, "by including a NightWing, who, naturally, would be the leader of the group. Your abysmal failure in that department was our first problem. Then we'd choose a SandWing queen, and eventually the NightWings would join the war, with our strength in numbers tipping the balance so our ally would be sure to win."

"And then your ally, whoever you picked, would help you take over the rainforest," Starflight puzzled out. "It's all about you, but not in a way that anyone would notice. *Darkness will rise to bring the light* – that's the NightWings."

"Exactly. The only really important part of the prophecy; we couldn't be too obvious about it," said Morrowseer. Behind him, dark smoke was pouring out of the volcano at an alarming rate. "The rest of it? Smoke and mirrors."

"No!" Sunny almost shouted, making the rest of them jump. "The prophecy is real! We *were* born to end the fight – to end the war and save everyone!"

"Afraid not," Morrowseer said nastily. "You're just as ordinary as any other dragon."

"Wow," said Clay. "No wonder I've always *felt* ordinary."

"But you're not – you're *not* ordinary," Sunny said, her voice full of tears. Starflight had never seen her so upset. He took a step towards her, reaching out with his wings, but she shoved him away. "What about the red MudWing egg? What about *my* egg, all alone in the desert?"

"There are scientific patterns to things like the appearance of blood eggs," said Morrowseer. "We study them and use them in our prophecies to impress our less scientific inferiors. As for the SandWing egg, we planned to set that up, but as it happened, we got a tip that yours was there already. A coincidence."

"No, it wasn't, it – it was fate." Sunny hiccupped.

"On the one talon, you are the worst," Tsunami said to Morrowseer. "But on the other, Sunny, think about what this means. We can live our own lives. We don't have to follow some plan that the stars laid out for us. We're free."

"But I *want* to stop the war!" Sunny cried. "All those dragons out there – they believe in the prophecy. They believe in us! If we give up, who will save them?"

"No one," said Morrowseer. "Now there's no point – the NightWings are already in the rainforest, so we have no reason to join the war. It'll drag on endlessly, and more dragons will die every day, probably for generations. All of them wondering what happened to the amazing dragonets who were supposed to save them, but obviously failed."

Sunny let out a furious sob, then whirled, pushed past Starflight, and fled up the tunnel, disappearing through the hole to the rainforest.

Morrowseer took a step as if to follow her, and Starflight jumped into his way.

"You can't come to the rainforest with us," he said, his voice shaking as badly as the earth below his claws.

Clay and Tsunami closed rank on either side of him. "He's right," Tsunami said. "Even if you pretended to swear allegiance to Glory, we'd know you were lying. At this point we wouldn't trust you about anything."

"You should go," Clay said. "Fly across the sea, as fast as you can. Maybe you'll make it before the volcano really explodes."

"Not that we care," Tsunami added.

Morrowseer's expression was incredulous. "And who's going to stop me? The three of you?"

"Yes," Starflight said.

"And me," said Fatespeaker's voice from behind Starflight. He felt her tail brush against his as she slid up next to him.

The giant NightWing snorted, as if that only made things more amusing. "Here's all the dragonets I want dead anyway," he said. "In one convenient place."

He opened his mouth, hissing up a fiery breath.

And then the volcano exploded.

It was like nothing Starflight had ever seen or imagined. It was like the earth turned inside out, collapsing the top of the mountain and shooting a vast, billowing cloud of flaming smoke into the air, which rose to the height of a hundred dragons and then fell, sending all that fire and rock and ash and death charging down the slope towards them faster than any dragon could fly.

"Run!" Starflight yelled, turning and shoving Fatespeaker in front of him. They tore down the tunnel with Tsunami right on his tail and Clay behind her. The heavy footsteps of Morrowseer thumped after them, but there was no time left to confront him.

Fatespeaker dived into the hole first. Starflight found himself turning and grabbing Tsunami, shoving her in next.

And so he was facing the cave entrance, and he saw the fireball come barrelling at them, filling the tunnel wall to wall with bright orange flames. Morrowseer's dark figure was silhouetted against the fire for a brief, horribly bright moment, and then suddenly the huge NightWing was gone, swallowed by the volcanic explosion.

A second later, Starflight's scales were blasted with heat as if he'd fallen into lava. A stab of blazing agony went through both eyes, and he closed them with a howl of pain.

And then he felt wings wrap around him, and he realized it was Clay – Clay and his fireproof scales.

The MudWing lifted him, shielding him with his whole body, and shot into the tunnel.

Will the fire follow us? Starflight wondered dazedly. *How does the animus magic work – will we cross over to the rainforest side halfway through and be safe or can it reach all the way—*

Rain pattered down on his scales, sizzling softly, and he felt claws pull him from the tunnel and lie him down on wet moss. Cool wet leaves pressed against his face and he heard the murmur of hundreds of dragon voices against a background of rainforest night sounds, sloths chirruping, insects and frogs singing their night songs – and among the talons he was sure he felt Sunny's. He felt the warmth of her scales that he'd know anywhere, even with his eyes closed (*or . . . blind?*), and he felt her press close to him for a moment and whisper. . . But why did it sound like Fatespeaker's voice. . . ? "Starflight. You were so brave."

And then the warmth was gone, and he wondered if he'd imagined it, and then pain flared all along his body and he opened his mouth to scream but it hurt too much.

Something jabbed him in the neck and he had a moment to think, *sleeping dart, what a good idea*, and then everything, everything – the pain, the worry, Sunny and Fatespeaker, the truth about the prophecy, the fear of the volcano – everything faded away, and Starflight dropped into darkness as black as a NightWing's scales.

EPILOGUE

Snow was falling, thick and fast, and the snowflakes spun across the icy ground in the freezing wind.

A SandWing stood huddled by the walls outside her fort, wrapped in blankets and trying to breathe fire into the air around her.

"P-p-please can't we go inside?" she said to the tall white dragon beside her.

"No," said Queen Glacier. "No one can be trusted with this information until we make a decision." Her arctic-blue eyes regarded the IceWing guards who were positioned just out of hearing range, watching the skies for danger. Frost glittered along her wings and horns. The spikes at the end of her tail were as sharp and cold as icicles.

Blaze sighed. "You mean, until *you* make a decision."

"Your input is always welcome," Glacier said calmly. She knew there was no chance of the SandWing disagreeing with the IceWing queen.

"My neck hurts." Blaze stamped her feet and poked the bandage on her neck. "*Ow.* Do you think it's going to scar? I'll be so mad if it scars."

"You're sure about what you heard?" Glacier asked her. "The NightWings have chosen to side with Blister, and they're trying to force the dragonets to choose her as well?"

"That's what it sounded like," Blaze said. "But more important, that NightWing tried to kill me! You're going to kill him, right?"

"We're going to kill all of them, if we must," said Glacier. "I have no objection to the idea of wiping out the NightWings. But we should consider what to do about the dragonets of the prophecy."

"They seemed nice," Blaze said, rubbing her talons together to warm them up. "Some of them were a little funny-looking. And I still don't understand what that RainWing was doing with them. Besides, she was a little *too* pretty. I think it's better to be just the right amount of pretty, don't you? *Too* pretty is annoying."

"Indeed," said Glacier, barely listening. "We don't want them telling anyone they've chosen Blister. It would be very demoralizing for our dragons."

"But they can't possibly choose her now that they've met me!" Blaze cried. "Now they know I'm wonderful and would make a great queen! They'll definitely pick me."

"Hmm," Glacier said noncommittally. She didn't have quite the same faith in Blaze's persuasive abilities or dazzling charisma that Blaze did. Her own alliance with Blaze was based less on the SandWing's potential queenliness and more on certain promises of future new territory for the IceWings.

"Well," Glacier said, "just in case they're leaning in another direction, I think we should make an effort to find these dragonets. I'd like to have a chat with them myself."

"Fine, all right," Blaze said, shivering violently. "I'll tell you everything I know about what they looked like and what they said. But can we *please* do that inside?"

Glacier nodded thoughtfully and Blaze bolted for the door.

The IceWing queen was good at putting together clues and figuring things out. She would find those dragonets. And she really would start by talking to them – just to see which way they were inclined.

But of course, if it was the wrong way . . . well, a few dead dragonets here and there would hardly be noticed in a war like this.

A serpentine figure paced in the darkness, hissing softly.

Below her mountain ledge, in a hidden valley, hints of firelight flickered in windows, most of them covered with black curtains.

Blister narrowed her eyes at the scavenger den. Why did Morrowseer think she would care about a rat's nest full of crawling, squeaking, pale, two-legged creatures? She wasn't hungry. She didn't even feel like burning down their pathetic little huts. She was too angry.

A whisper of wings on the wind made her twist around, tail poised to attack.

But it wasn't an enemy, and it wasn't Morrowseer. It was that spineless leader of the Talons of Peace, the SeaWing. And he had someone with him. She squinted as they landed.

"Forgive my lateness, Queen Blister," Nautilus said with a bow.

"Where is Morrowseer?" she demanded.

"I – I don't know," he stammered. "I thought he would be here by now. I haven't seen him since he took the alternate dragonets from the Talons of Peace camp. But I knew he was supposed to be here to meet you tonight, and I had to speak with him." He squared his shoulders, obviously trying to look braver than he felt.

"Well, he's *not* here," Blister spat. "Who is that?"

Nautilus drew the dragonet forward, keeping one wing around him. It was another SeaWing, stunted and green and shivering.

"My son," Nautilus said quietly, touching the dragonet's head. "Squid. Morrowseer left him to die in the mountains, but, by a miracle, one of our spies found him first." His eyes were cold and glittering in the light of the two moons that were full overhead.

"I hate NightWings," Squid mumbled.

"I rather hate them, too," Blister agreed. She'd always

been irritated by this arrangement with Morrowseer – these meetings he called, at his choice of time and place, with no way for her to contact him in between. An alliance with the NightWings and control of the prophecy dragonets should make all this annoyance worthwhile . . . but so far she wasn't getting any of what she'd been promised.

Worse yet, it almost seemed as if she was losing allies. Her small band of SandWings, hidden away safely in the Bay of a Thousand Scales, were loyal, of course. She controlled them with careful precision, knowing every move they made and every thought they had. She tricked them all into spying on one another by making each one think he or she was in an exclusive elite who reported secretly to her. And any hint of insubordination or weakness was instantly punished with death.

But the alliance she'd formed years ago with the SeaWings had slipped through her claws like ice melting. After the destruction of the Summer Palace, Queen Coral had fled with her tribe to their secret underwater home, and no one had seen her or any other SeaWings since. Blister had gone to the wrecked Summer Palace almost every day since the attack, but there were no messages, no dragons waiting to tell her what was happening, no apologetic scrolls from the SeaWing queen.

And if Morrowseer didn't show up, then what would she do? She had no idea where the NightWing island was. No way to send him a message. In effect, no NightWing allies to speak of.

Maybe she did feel like setting a scavenger den on fire after all.

Nautilus sat with his wings wrapped around Squid, brooding. His glow-in-the-dark scales flashed dimly, as if he were telling his son something private, over and over again.

"If Morrowseer doesn't show up," Blister said, "I have a strong suspicion I know whose fault it is."

The SeaWings both looked up, surprised.

"The dragonets," she hissed. "Not this weakling. The originals. They've been nothing but trouble since they escaped their captors."

Nautilus winced. "We called them 'guardians'," he said. "But you're right. Everywhere the dragonets go, they seem to leave chaos behind."

"Well, they've caused trouble for the wrong dragon," Blister snarled. She glowered down at the slumbering scavenger den, her claws twitching with dreams of revenge. "Wherever they are, I will hunt them down. I will find them and then, prophecy or no prophecy . . . I'm going to kill them all."

The sun was hot and blistering, beating down on the sand around the stronghold as the squadron of SandWings landed in the courtyard. The smell of the decapitated heads on the walls was stronger than usual. Burn inhaled deeply. She enjoyed the decaying scent, but mostly she enjoyed the unnerved looks on her soldiers' faces every time she did that.

A dragon stepped out of the great hall, darting across the hot stones towards her. The black diamond patterns on his wings always reminded Burn of Blister, so it was difficult not to glare at her brother every time she saw him. But he was used to that.

"I wasn't expecting you until tomorrow," Smoulder said. His forked tongue flicked in and out.

She narrowed her eyes at him and waited.

After a moment, he remembered and added, "Your Majesty. I wasn't expecting you until tomorrow, *Your Majesty.*"

She didn't appreciate the hint of sarcasm in his voice, but she wouldn't point it out in front of her soldiers. She'd discuss it with him later, somewhere private, where she could dig her claws into his scales and get a truly sincere apology.

"How is our guest?" Burn asked, dismissing the soldiers with a flick of her tail.

"Still extraordinarily not pleased to be here," he said. "You may want to move her to a . . . more empty chamber. She's made a bit of a mess of what she could reach of your collection."

Burn hissed. "Ungrateful cow."

"Any word on the dragonets?" he asked, following her into the great hall.

"They've vanished again," she said. "Although there's a rumour going around the Sky Kingdom that they're responsible for torching the northernmost outpost and killing all those SkyWing soldiers – as some kind of revenge for what Queen Scarlet did to them."

Smoulder folded his wings back and looked up at her. "Do you think that's likely?"

"I don't know anything about them," she said. "In the arena, they didn't seem fierce enough to kill anything. But then they attacked Scarlet, so they're clearly more dangerous than they look." She stopped at the long table loaded with food that ran down the centre of the hall. "I do know I don't like them," she muttered. "And I wish I'd got my claws on *all* of their eggs before they hatched." She snatched up a dead hawk and ripped off its head with one bite, imagining doing the same to a certain SeaWing, or that insidious RainWing.

"It's not going well with Ruby?" Smoulder asked.

"The supposed new queen of the SkyWings is a bore and a nuisance," Burn snarled. "She wants to 'restore order in the Sky Kingdom' and 'establish the stability of her own throne' before engaging in any more battles at my side. She's even more difficult than her annoying mother, and she follows orders very poorly, if at all. We haven't had a satisfying battle in weeks. I'm considering getting rid of her."

"Sounds frustrating." Smoulder slid a platter of dates towards himself and popped two in his mouth.

"It is. I really need to kill something. It's been too long since I last ripped out a dragon's throat."

Her brother sidled a few steps away, perhaps thinking he was being surreptitious, but failing. "Well," he said. "There's always your prisoner."

"No, no," Burn corrected him. "Queen Scarlet is our *guest*. For now. I may change my mind once I decide how useful she can be." She glanced out at the blazing sun reflecting off the courtyard stones. "No, I have another victim in mind. Five of them, in fact."

"Of course," he said, ducking his head. "You just have to find them first."

"Oh, I will," she said. "Everyone will finally shut up about the wonderful 'dragonets of destiny' when I have their heads mounted on spikes on my walls." She bared her teeth at her brother, smoke rising from her nostrils. "Mark my words. Soon we'll put an end to this prophecy nonsense once and for all."

HAVE YOU READ?

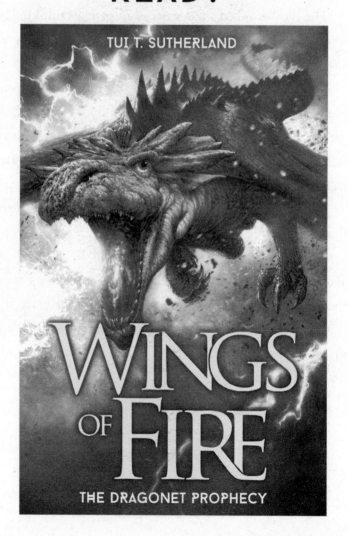

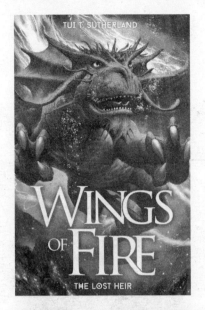

TUI T. SUTHERLAND

WINGS OF FIRE

THE LOST HEIR

TUI T. SUTHERLAND

WINGS OF FIRE

THE HIDDEN KINGDOM